JOY RIDE

BY LAUREN BLAKELY

Also By Lauren Blakely

The Caught Up in Love Series
Caught Up In Us
Pretending He's Mine
Trophy Husband
Stars in Their Eyes

Standalone books
BIG ROCK
Mister O
Well Hung
The Sexy One
Full Package
The Hot One
Joy Ride
The Wild One (July 2017)
Most Valuable Playboy (August 2017)
Hard Wood (November 2017)
CockTail (January 2018)
The Rich One (March 2018)
Far Too Tempting
21 Stolen Kisses
Playing With Her Heart
Out of Bounds
The Only One
Stud Finder (Sept 2017)

The No Regrets Series
The Thrill of It
The Start of Us
Every Second With You

The Seductive Nights Series
First Night (Julia and Clay, prequel novella)
Night After Night (Julia and Clay, book one)
After This Night (Julia and Clay, book two)
One More Night (Julia and Clay, book three)
A Wildly Seductive Night (Julia and Clay novella, book 3.5)
Nights With Him (A standalone novel about Michelle and Jack)
Forbidden Nights (A standalone novel about Nate and Casey)

The Sinful Nights Series
Sweet Sinful Nights
Sinful Desire
Sinful Longing
Sinful Love

The Fighting Fire Series
Burn For Me (Smith and Jamie)
Melt for Him (Megan and Becker)
Consumed By You (Travis and Cara)

The Jewel Series
A two-book sexy contemporary romance series
The Sapphire Affair
The Sapphire Heist

This book is dedicated to Rob Kinnan, who made me laugh with that hilarious email, who tirelessly checked car facts, who solved problems like a good mechanic, and who taught me about lime gold.

PROLOGUE

Here's something I want to know. Why the fuck does the term *guilty pleasure* even exist? If something brings you pleasure, don't feel guilty.

Case closed.

But let's be perfectly clear—I'm not talking about stuff a dude should feel ten tons of remorse about, like being a dick to your boss or cheating on your woman. If that kind of shit brings you pleasure, may all the guilt from the skies rain down on you, along with golf-ball-sized hail and toads, too.

What I don't get is why people feel bad about enjoying the good stuff in life. Buying that pool table just because it looks fucking awesome in your living room. Or drinking eighteen-year-old Scotch after a long day fixing an engine on a Mustang, instead of waiting for a special occasion to crack open the bottle.

Life is short. Savor it now.

Hell, if it floats your boat to sink into a steaming hot bubble bath every so often, turn the water up high and toss a bath bomb into the claw-foot tub.

Not that *I* do that. Hell, I barely even know what a bath bomb is. And I absolutely, positively did not use the zingy lemongrass-scented one the other night. The type that fizzes. I don't have a clue why it's missing from the cabinet.

In any case, I say *indulge.* Yeah, my pool table rocks, and so does the Scotch. But hands down, my favorite indulgence is the one-night stand.

What? Like that's such a crime? Nothing wrong with a night of round-the-clock fun of the X-rated variety. Besides, when I take a woman home for a one-and-done fiesta of five-star fucking, I'm honest about my intentions. I never promise more than I can deliver. But what I do serve up—in extra large quantities, thank you very much—is a fantastic time between the sheets with no strings attached when the sun comes up.

I've never felt guilty about this pleasure either, and that's because I maintain a few key guidelines when it comes to my favorite horizontal hobby.

Don't be an asshole.

Always be a gentleman.

And never sleep with the enemy.

Now, about that last rule . . . don't break it. Don't bend it. Don't even dip your toe on the other side.

Trust me on this.

I went on to shatter that last policy in spectacular fashion, leaving me wanting a helluva lot more than one time with a certain sexy brunette. That's how I wound up on the side of the road with a new tattoo, a wrecked electric-blue roadster, and a pet monkey to show for it.

Yes, I said pet monkey.

And that's a big fucking problem for the King of Pleasure.

CHAPTER 1

Cars are like ice cream.

There's a flavor for everyone.

Some auto enthusiasts opt for vanilla. For them, a basic sports car will do just fine.

Others want a sundae with everything on it, from the badass paint job to the jacked-up wheels to the sound system that registers on the Richter scale.

Then, you've got the car buffs who gravitate toward a dark chocolate gelato, forking over big bucks for a sleek Aston Martin outfitted with an engine that kills it on the autobahn.

Every now and then, though, you'll encounter the fellow who doesn't know what he likes so he goes for rainbow sprinkles, bananas, chopped nuts, and a cherry on top. Like this guy I'm talking to right now at a custom car show just outside Manhattan.

The bespectacled man strokes his chin then asks in a smooth, sophisticated voice, "Could you make an armored car?"

That's the latest question from this thirty-something guy in tailored slacks and a crisp, white button-down. Wire-rimmed glasses slide to the bridge of his nose as he gestures to an emerald-green, fully customized sports car that holds center stage.

"Armored cars are in my arsenal," I say, since I've made a few beasts designed to outlast a zombie apocalypse, courtesy of some survivalist clients.

He arches an eyebrow. "Could you add in some sleek tail fins?"

Ah, tail fins. I have a hunch where he's going now, and it's not to the land of the undead. "I can do that, too."

"And maybe it can even ride low and respond to commands?"

I stifle a laugh, since I have his number for sure now, and I fucking love the enthusiasm of the newbies. "Absolutely. I assume you'd want it in black?"

His blue eyes light up. "Yes. Black would be perfect."

For the Batmobile. Because that's what the dude just described. I'm not knocking him or the Batmobile. That vehicle is absolutely at the top of my bucket list, too. What self-respecting gearhead wouldn't want to tool around town in a superhero's tricked-out ride?

This guy's nowhere near done, though, as he peppers me with a new set of questions. "Would you be able to make a car that—just for the sake of argument—can jump incredibly far distances?"

I don't need precognition to know where he's going with this new scenario. "Would you want it to play a little song when you hit the horn?"

His eyes twinkle. "Oh, that's a nice feature indeed."

I wonder where I came up with that idea. Could it be my vast knowledge of the General Lee from *The Dukes of Hazzard?*

The guy is rolling through the greatest hits of cars on TV or film. And you know what? There's not a damn thing wrong with that. If he learns about cars from the tube or the screen, so be it. Maybe he'll ask me to make a VW Bug that talks. My sister has begged for that for years, and if I ever figure out how, I'm delivering it to her first.

"What about wings for doors?" he asks.

"Like a DeLorean?"

He nods in excitement. "I love that car so much."

"I haven't met a DeLorean I didn't want to marry, either. That's the reason I got into this business in the first place."

"Are you a *Back to the Future* fan, too?"

I hold up a fist for knocking. "You know it."

"Any chance you could put a flux capacitor in it for me?"

"Absolutely. And I promise it'll hit 1.21 gigawatts when you crank the gas," I say, and as we laugh, the *click clack* of many pairs of high heels against asphalt surrounds us. This show is swarming with women in heels, working the booths, posing seductively on hoods or beside doors. Can't say that bothers me. Nope, I definitely can't say I'm annoyed by the proliferation of female flesh one bit.

Cars and chicks—that's all I need for sustenance.

But now's not the time for checking out the scenery, because business always comes first. I extend a hand to the *Back to the Future* fan. "Max Summers of Summers Custom Autos."

He shakes with me. "David Winters. And I know this may shock you, but—*confession*—I know nothing about cars."

"Nothing wrong with that, since I know a ton."

He smiles and shrugs sheepishly. "Excellent. I'm looking for a builder who can make the best. Like this one, I presume?" he asks, pointing to the sleek green beauty I'm keeping watch over at the show. I'm here with a client. I customized this baby for Wagner Boost—an NFL lineman who's off signing autographs somewhere nearby. Wagner is a mammoth man. At six foot eight and 350 pounds—that's his morning weight, since he jokes that he shoots up to 360 after breakfast—he needed a car tailored to fit his frame. I made it for him, and he likes to show it off.

"Let me tell you something," I say, patting the hood of Wagner's prized possession. "If you can dream it, I can damn near make it. If you want aftermarket tires, a new engine, or custom upholstery, I'll take care of it. If you want to marry parts from a roadster you've seen in a gangster flick with a futuristic prototype, I'll find a way. I'll deliver on your vision because that's what I do."

The *tap tap* of stiletto heels sounds closer now, like someone is approaching, as David fires off another question. "Can you—?"

A woman's voice interrupts. "Can you paint a badass tiger on the door?"

No. Fucking. Way.

That voice. That sexy purr. Like honey, like whiskey. Like dirty dreams.

Everything in me goes still. I haven't heard that voice in years. I don't even have to turn around because one more click, then another, and here she is, standing in front of me. Looking hotter than she ever did before.

Long brown hair. Dark chocolate eyes. Legs that go on forever.

Henley Rose Marlowe.

Fuck me senseless.

It's her.

The woman who drove me crazy.

I'm momentarily speechless as I take her in, because she's not twenty-one anymore. She's five years older and twenty-five times hotter. Yes, her hotness has squared with the years.

But I'm not about to let a potential deal slide through my fingers. I never let women get in the way of work, especially not one who's inserting herself into the middle of a conversation with a fucking *tiger* comment.

I get around her interruption by going along with it.

"The tiger can even be roaring," I suggest, as if she's just some random car lover who's keen on chitchatting, not a girl who used to work under the hood in my shop.

"Maybe even breathing fire," Henley offers, like we've got this wordplay down pat, *Who's on first?* style.

David gets into the action, too, emitting a *rawr* as he holds up his hands as if they're claws.

Henley flashes him the sexiest smile I've ever seen, and in less than a second, the fire-breathing tiger inhabits me. Because I'm jealous as hell. For no good reason.

David smiles back at her.

Okay, maybe for *that* reason.

Which is not an acceptable reason at all. I shake off the useless emotion as David speaks again. "That's it. I've officially decided I want a tiger on the door of a DeLorean. Painted in green, like the color of money."

Yep, he's rainbow-sprinkles all the way, and I focus on the sprinkles, not the flirty grins exchanged between this guy and a woman who was never mine, not even for one night.

"You can have it in royal purple, in emerald green, in sapphire blue," I tell him. "You can have it with a flag on the hood, a pinstripe on the door, and the sweetest stick shift you've ever felt in your hands."

"Purple and a sweet stick? I'm sold." He clasps my hand in a good-bye shake. "I'll be in touch." He takes a step to go then stops. "Is purple too crazy a color? What do you think?" he asks the woman who'd make any red-blooded man gawk.

Perfect figure. Pouty lips. Tight waist. Gravity-defying tits. If God created an ideal woman to sell anything to any red-blooded man, he'd make her just like Henley.

Not sure he'd intend her to have such a smartass mouth, though.

She licks her lips. "Purple is hot as sin," she says to David, like the words are for his ears only. She presses her fingertip to her tongue then touches the hood of the car as if it burns her. She raises her hand, letting the imaginary flame fly high.

David eats up her show, laughing and grinning.

"That's an excellent selling point for purple. What about you, Max? Favorite color?" He holds up one hand as a stop sign. "Wait. Let me guess. Gold? Silver? Red? Blue?"

I shake my head. "Black."

Then David says good-bye and heads off, and I'm left with this vexing vixen who hates me. She stares at me like a cat that won't look away till you give her your hamburger. I don't break her showdown, nor do I offer her a bite.

"*Black*," she repeats, tapping the toe of her red suede pump as she glares with dark brown eyes full of fury. "Like your heart."

Have I mentioned the last time I saw her she marched out of my shop in a blaze of angry glory?

Might be because I fired her sexy ass five years ago.

Yeah, there's some bad blood between us.

CHAPTER 2

Henley Rose and a hot car go together like peaches and cream, like fine Scotch and a long, dirty night. Which means working with her was like walking into the Garden of Eden every single day. It was a test of willpower because the woman could craft a car as if it were an erotic dance.

Not a striptease.

Not an in-your-face pelvis thrust.

But a beautiful fucking ballet of a woman seducing a machine. Those hands, the way she wielded tools, the intensity in her focus—it was sensual, and it was sinful, and it was this man's fantasy made flesh.

Imagine what it was like working with her for one, hard-on year.

I mean, hard year.

I survived the challenge because she had talent to spare. And I never treated her differently because she was a woman, or because I thought about her naked an obscene amount of the time. I treated her like anyone else—specifically, all the people I work with who I never ever imagine in anything less than full-on Siberian winter garb, complete with the thermals and Michelin Man coat.

"Black heart still intact." I tap my sternum. "Same model as before."

"I'd have thought you'd get an upgrade by now. Faulty parts and all."

"No recall needed on the ticker. It works just fine in this *cruel bastard*," I say, reminding her of the words she'd uttered the day she stormed out.

She arches a brow. "Shame. You should have let me replace it. I'm good at making all sorts of clunkers run better."

Jesus Christ. She still takes no prisoners. "I've no doubt you have all the tools to fix anything, and if you couldn't find the right one, you'd use a blowtorch."

She adopts an expression of indignation. "There's nothing wrong with using a *blowtorch*," she says, taking extra time on the first syllable.

How the hell did I ever last with this woman? Before I can even fashion a comeback, she taps her toe against the tire on Wagner's car. "I see you still like to make your cars with *big, manly* wheels."

I roll my eyes then make a *give it to me now* motion with my hands. "All right, Henley. Deliver the punchline."

She bats her lashes. "What punchline?"

"*Big? Manly?* You're going to say it's some sort of compensation thing going on. That's what you always said about the guys who wanted the biggest cars with the biggest wheels."

She smirks. "Was I wrong in my assessment?"

I laugh. "I don't know. I didn't check to see how that added up for them."

"Nor did I. My focus was *always* on the work."

"As well it should have been."

"That's what you taught me."

"I'm glad you learned that lesson."

"I learned *so many* lessons from you."

I take a deep breath and change directions. "What was up with the badass tiger comment out of nowhere? Couldn't you just wait till I was done to say hello?"

She winks. "C'mon. I was just having fun."

"Fun? More like trying to get involved in everything."

She feigns shock and dances her fingertips along the hood of Wagner's car. "I was merely being helpful and trying to land you a client. Don't you remember? I was always trying to help you."

I park my hands on my hips. "Why do I feel like you're here more to taunt me than to deliver generous humanitarian aid?"

She clasps a hand to her chest. Her ample chest. "Taunt? Me? I was just excited to say hello to my former mentor. Forgive me for my exuberance," she says, in a too-sweet tone. "How are you these days?"

"I can't complain." I don't know what to make of her, and I don't know that I want to let her in. "What about you? It's been a while."

"Five years. Three weeks. And two days. But who's counting?"

"Sounds like you are."

She shrugs as if it's no big deal, then pops up on the hood and parks her sweet ass on Wagner's car. Wagner won't care. He likes pretty ladies, especially when they're on his prized ride. The problem is he'll probably want to bang Henley when he returns from signing autographs, and that's not going to fucking happen on my watch.

Not that I have any control over who she's banging. But I'll do everything I can to make sure it's not a client of mine who gets his hands on her.

"What brings you to this neck of the woods?" Last I heard from her she'd gone back home to Northern California to work with a rival builder there.

She points her thumb in the general direction of Clint Savage, a burly, bearded, foul-mouthed motherfucker who kills it with some of the hottest custom rides on the planet. "I'm just booth bitching at Savage Rides," Henley says.

"Yeah?" That surprises me, but I don't let on. Henley had never been just a pretty set of legs and tits at a show. She was under the hood, working on the engine, getting her hands dirty.

She nods and smiles. "He has me pose on top of the cars. We clean up like that." She snaps her fingers.

"Is that so?"

She runs her eyes up and down my body. Checks out the tribal bands on my biceps. Lingers on my chest. Well, my T-shirt. I'm not some ass who parades shirtless at a car show. I save that for when I drive with the top down. No, seriously. Do I look like a douche? I don't drive shirtless, either.

She straightens her spine and hops off the car. "*No.*" That's all she says, but that one word comes out exactly like "*No, you idiot.*"

I sigh. She still fucking hates me. "What are you doing here, then?"

She narrows her eyes. "You think you're the only game in town? I run a shop now in New York."

I didn't keep tabs on her when she walked away in a cloud of black smoke, and I figured it was best for me not to stalk her. I needed to stay away from the kind of temptation she brought to work every day. "Good for you."

She sets one hand on her hip and stares at me defiantly. "You really thought I was a booth babe?"

"You said you were here as one."

She huffs. "You never thought much of me, did you?"

You don't want to know the half of it. You don't want to know how much I thought of you and how much of it was vastly inappropriate.

"Henley," I say, keeping my tone measured, "you were the most talented apprentice I ever worked with. I thought the world of your skills, and you know it."

She sneers, and then she pokes me. She stabs her index finger against my chest, her red-polished nail scratching me and instantly stirring up not-safe-for-work fantasies of her nails down my chest then my back.

"Actions speak louder than words. And yours made it clear you never thought I was good enough," she says.

I let my gaze drift away from her eyes, down to her neck, then to her shoulder. She follows my path, then I say, "I see you haven't had that chip removed yet from your shoulder. I know a doctor who can take care of that for you."

Her eyebrows shoot into her hairline, but her voice is even. "Thanks for the tip. I'll be sure to think of you first when I'm ready to take it off, seeing as you're the reason I have one in the first place."

Let me revise my assessment. *A sexy chip on a fuck-hot shoulder.* "Glad to know you're finally giving me credit for something."

She rolls her eyes. "I gave you all the credit, and you gave me nada." She curls her thumb and forefinger into an *O*. "Zilch. Zero."

"Don't forget 'goose-egg.' Wouldn't want you to leave out another way to describe how I robbed you of all opportunity."

She purses her lips and shakes her head. "I don't know why I came over here to talk to you."

"That's a fascinating question. One I'd love to know the answer to."

"I don't know. Call me crazy. But I thought maybe we could have a civilized chat."

I laugh sharply. "You did? That's why you inserted yourself into a conversation with a potential client with your tiger comment?"

"It was supposed to be funny." For once, her tone sounds hurt, as if I've wounded her. "You used to tease me when I got all worked up about something. You called me 'tiger.'"

The memory smashes back into me—the first instance I called her that. She was pissed at herself over a struggle with a transmission tunnel that nicked her left hand, and I'd said, "Easy, tiger," before I moved in and helped her, showing her how to do it without slicing her finger off. She thanked me in the sweetest voice, and then I put a Band-Aid on the cut.

I say nothing, maybe because I'm still lingering on the way she whispered her *thank you* that day five years ago.

Right now, though? She shrugs in an I-give-up gesture. "See you later, Max."

This woman was the most fiery, spirited person I've ever worked with, but I can't let her get under my skin, or make me want to put Band-Aids on her when she can damn well do it herself. I need a new approach, especially if we're running in the same circles.

She turns to go, but I grab her arm. "Wait." My voice is gentler now. "Tell me what you're up to these days."

"Building cars."

"I figured that much from what you said. What's your specialty?"

The corner of her lips curves up in a smile as she moves closer—so damn close I can smell her sweet breath, and I'm half wondering how she smells so good at four in the afternoon, like cinnamon candy. But then, that was one of her many talents. Smelling good, looking good, working hard. "The kind of car I would have made with you if you'd have let me," she says and steps one inch closer. So close I could kiss her cinnamon lips. "They're called . . . *the best*."

She spins on a heel and walks away.

I should call out after her. I should try harder to smooth over the past. But I'm better off letting her go. She's far too dangerous, even though a part of me likes playing with fire.

That part of me needs to stay the fuck away from a woman like her.

CHAPTER 3

"Smell this."

My sister, Mia, slides a vial under my nose.

I'm transported from the kitchen counter in my penthouse apartment in Battery Park to a tropical island. "Pineapple with a hint of coconut."

"And what else?"

My eyes are closed. She wanted me to wear a blindfold, but that's not going to happen. Ever. I sniff one more time. "Mango."

The vial clinks as it hits the counter, and she claps. "You still officially have the best nose in the history of noses."

I open my eyes. "Do I get a gold star for my olfactory system?"

She smiles brightly, her straight, white teeth gleaming. "You win the prize for being one of the two most amazing brothers I have."

"Wow. That's quite an honor, seeing as you only have two brothers."

"And they're both adorable," she says with a glint in her hazel eyes.

I glare at her. "I'm not cute."

She winks. "You'll always be cute to me."

I growl. "You're lucky I don't put you in a chokehold like I'd do to Chase."

Mia leans her blond head back and laughs. "You couldn't keep me in a chokehold. I'd slip out because I'm fast and nimble. Besides, you like me too much."

She's right. How could I not? She's the baby of the family, and she's also literally the most adorable person on earth. She's the size of a gymnast, and she packs the same punch pound for pound. Probably because she was a gymnast growing up. She twisted her body into some serious pretzel shapes on the balance beam and floor when she was in grade school and junior high, earning medals in all sorts of competitions. Now she's twenty-seven and an entrepreneur. She's staying with me for the week while she's in town for meetings, trying to land some new distribution deals for her line of cruelty-free beauty supplies.

I tip my head to the vial on the counter. "What's the story with your newest concoction?"

"My chemists whipped it up. It's a face wash, and we want to market it to men. I need to work on just the right angle when it comes to the messaging, but do you think a guy would like it?"

"A guy who wants to smell like fruit." I head to the fridge to grab a beer.

She swats my arm before I open the door. "Seriously?"

"Seriously. And look, I've been known to fall in love with a pineapple and want to spend the night with a coconut, but no, I wouldn't use this."

"*Max.*"

"It smells great, and I'm sure your customers who have breasts will love it. But why are you even trying to market it to men? If you want a dude to use a face wash, just make it smell like the ocean or the woods or whatever we're supposed to like, according to the great commercial wisdom of the world." I wave a hand at the glass vial. "But we don't need to smell like a tropical Popsicle stand." I take a pause. "Though, for the record, I'd absolutely stop and get a Popsicle at such a stand."

"I'm trying to market to men because I want it all." She bangs a tiny fist on the counter. "I want to market face wash to the penis-owning population, too, the same way car makers want to sell autos to people with vaginas. Don't you have any clients with vaginas?"

"You will never *not* love saying that word to me or to any man, will you?"

She shakes her head as her eyes glint. "Vagina, vagina, vagina. Now answer the question."

"Do I have any clients with vaginas?"

She gives me an I'm-so-proud-of-you look. "Yes. Do you?"

As I grab a bottle of porter, I consider her question, and one of my favorite clients comes to mind. "A few. Like Livvy Sweetwater. I need to take her Rolls home to her later this week."

"And how do you market to the Livvy Sweetwaters of the world?"

I shrug. "I just market the cars."

She mimes slamming her hand on a buzzer. "Wrong. You sell the sleekness. You sell the safety. You focus on the luxury. Women love luxuries. So do men. And I know you like your little luxuries, Mr. Tough Guy. You used the bath bombs I sent you the other week. I saw some missing from the cabinet. The lemongrass. *And* the coconut."

"Hey!" I bring my finger to my lips and shush her.

"Oh, who's listening?"

"No one. Not when you tell such blatant lies."

"I never lie. And I never tell your secrets. For instance, if you ever finally fall in love, I'll never let on that you have a soft side," she says, then covers her mouth and laughs.

"One, I won't fall in love. And two, I don't have a soft side."

"Your heart is a soft pillow, and you will absolutely fall in love someday."

Shaking my head, I take a long swallow of my beer then ask Mia if I can do anything else to help her prep for her meetings.

She nods excitedly. "Will you come shopping with me? Pretty please? I want to look for a new sweater for tomorrow."

"Anything but that."

"Oh, come on."

I knock back more of the beer. "I'm allergic to shopping."

"I'll take you out for burgers after." She dangles that tempting offer in front of me.

My ears perk up.

She seizes the opening, nudging me and grabbing the beer bottle. She drops it in the sink, hands me my wallet and keys, and grabs her purse.

I've never been good at saying no to my sister, so thirty minutes later, I'm parked on a pink chair outside the dressing room in a West Village boutique as Mia tries on clothes, showing me a sweater, then a shirt, then a royal-blue top before she returns to the small room to change.

As I wait, I fiddle on my phone, and I swear this isn't what it looks like.

This isn't me stalking Henley Rose.

I'm not trying to find every detail on her.

It's not her photos I'm staring at in Google images. It's not her face I see as she fixes up a Ferrari, looking like a scientist about to split the atom. It's simply the photo of a focused woman who happens to detest a particular guy. A woman who claims I didn't give her a fair shot.

A woman who got up in my grill today.

I clench my teeth. A woman I won't see again, so why the fuck am I tooling around online for her? I can't even find the name of her shop. Hell, maybe she's not even working in New York. She might have been messing with me. That'd be her style.

"Is there anything I can get for you?" the saleswoman calls out to Mia, and I glance away from the screen to check her out. I like what I see. The saleswoman is tight and trim and has full lips and dark red hair that would look fantastic twisted around my fist.

"I'm good," Mia shouts from the dressing room. "I think I'll get the turquoise sweater with the strawberry design. My brother approved it."

The redhead turns to me even though she answers my sister. "That sweater is perfect for you, so he has excellent taste." Then she lowers her voice and meets my eyes fully. "Is there anything I can get for a guy with great taste?"

Her meaning is 100 percent clear. So's mine when I say, "Your name and number."

The saleswoman gives me her digits with a flirty smile and then heads off to take care of another customer.

I save her contact info—her name is Becca—and close out the browser windows from my search. As I tap the last one, Mia appears at my side, the sweater over her arm. "Why are you looking up Henley?"

Quickly, I stuff the phone into the back pocket of my jeans as if she didn't catch me red-handed. "I'm not."

She scoffs. "Of course you weren't. That's just some other gorgeous, young ex-employee."

"Can we get that burger?"

"Only if you tell me why you were looking up the woman who used to drive you crazy. Wait." Mia freezes. "Is she why you're cranky today?"

I shake my head. "I'm not cranky."

"You're so cranky."

"I'm a natural grouch. It has nothing to do with that woman."

Mia raises one eyebrow, her eyes blazing with skepticism. "I know you, Max. I know you as well as anyone. You think you're so tough, but that woman had your number."

"Burger. Now."

Mia pays for her sweater, and we head out of the store. On the way to the restaurant, my phone rings. It's David Winters.

"If it's business, just take the call," Mia says, and so I do, talking as we stroll through the Village to my favorite spot. When I'm done, I tell Mia we might be celebrating a potential new client tonight.

Over dinner, I give her the news from David. We toast to the possibilities.

Later that night at my home, I scroll past Becca's number. No doubt she'd be game for a one-night stand. But I don't call her. It's not just because Mia's still in town.

My mind is elsewhere.

I'm focused only on new business.

And on making sure I shut down all the browser tabs on my phone after I check out the image again of Henley working on the Ferrari. I stare at it for a few minutes.

In my defense, the car is smoking hot.

Chapter 4

The second the metal music cranks up, I groan. I know what's coming.

I shake out my hand, cramped from signing checks at the end of the day, and step out of my office in the back of the shop. When Sam and Mike point at me, gangster style, I roll my eyes.

Sam takes a step forward, fixing me with a mean stare, then Mike joins him, going full peacock as he waves his big arms at the gloriously gleaming white car behind them.

"Yo." Mike adopts his best street-style voice. "Today, we are going to show you what it takes to restore an old Rolls to sick-as-fuck new."

"Rolls. That's Royce to you," Sam adds, his dark eyes forming slits. Then they stalk and glower as the screech of the abominable music grows horrifically louder. I lean against the concrete wall and cross my arms, letting them perform their act for thirty seconds or so, until Mike stabs his thumb on his phone, which has been blasting the music. If you can call it music. Suffice to say, metal and I don't get along. Give me the

Stones, Frank Sinatra, or some kick-ass new indie band, and I'm good to go.

"How'd we do?" Mike strokes his auburn goatee. "Think we can audition for *Pimp My Big Ass Peacock Ride with Tricked Out Wheels* now?"

"Remind me who carries that show? So I will never watch it," I say.

Sam and Mike are my main builders. When we're close to finishing a car, they like to pretend they're on reality TV, especially since those shows have about as much in common with our daily work here in the shop as medical dramas do with life in the ER. I feel confident in that assessment, since my brother, Chase, tells me that the number of impalements, for instance, he's seen in his line of work as a doctor is about two, whereas those incidents seem to occur with astonishing regularity on the tube.

Real mechanics are problem solvers. They aren't preeners who like to carve up metal with big, dangerous shiny objects, wielding chainsaws over their heads as they cackle. I hired Mike straight out of college, and Sam is attending night school classes, trying to finish up his business degree. These guys know how to tackle trouble, and they solved a helluva problem on this old Rolls, restoring it to its former glory under my guidance.

Mike runs a hand over the hood, stroking the metal with reverence. "How does she look?"

"Like a fucking dream girl," I say, admiring the beauty that we've worked on the last few weeks.

"Girl?" Sam shoots me a skeptical stare, dragging his hand through dark floppy hair. "Why are cars always feminine?"

Mike answers with a thrust of his hips. "Because when they're this hot we want to fuck them."

Okay, maybe my guys aren't civilized all the time. Maybe not even most of the time, given the way Mike continues to practice his dry hump routine, as if he's going for a master's degree in thrusting.

Sam shakes his head. "Mike, I hate to break it to you, but this car is a dude."

Mike sneers. "No way. She's too pretty."

"Nope. This is a total man car. She had a sex change. Just check the lug nuts if you need to be sure."

As much as their antics amuse me, it's time to cut them off. I hold up a hand. "Let's not play with the lug nuts, the dipstick, or the connecting rod on Livvy Sweetwater's prized automobile, please. The woman trusted us with her baby over John Smith Rides. And I need to deliver this Rolls to her Connecticut estate on Thursday, in all its shining beauty," I say, since I can only imagine what that sweet, classy dame with her pearl necklace and pillbox hat would say if she heard that Mike wanted to get busy with her vehicle, and that Sam pretended her car was a dude.

"Don't look at me. I'm not the one trying to screw a car," Sam says in his most innocent voice. "Also, why don't you just put it in a trailer?"

I scoff. "You don't know Livvy."

"No. I don't, man. That's why I'm asking."

And it's my job to teach these guys what it takes to be the best. That's what my mentor, Bob Galloway, did for me. Not only did he teach me how to restore a Bentley and perform surgery on a Bugatti, but he also taught me how to take care of clients, and how to better train the guys who work for me.

"You're right to ask," I say. "Let me tell you. Livvy is a long-time client, as you know. And she's quite particular with her cars. She has a certain routine she follows every time I finish a car for her. She likes me to drive her cars to her. Then she invites me in for tea, and over tea I tell her everything about how it felt to drive the car."

Mike narrows his eyes. "That sounds weird. Like a fetish."

"Watch it. Don't talk about the clients like that. It's how Livvy likes to do things. She likes to know what to look for when she drives it." I flick a speck of dust off the hood then swing my gaze to Mike. "You want to move up in the business, right?"

Mike nods, looking contrite.

I fix him with an intense stare. "Then rule number one is this: build the best cars possible and never cut corners. Rule number two is respect the client's choices and wishes. Don't impose your own."

"Got it," Mike says, his tone earnest.

Sam points at my shirt. "Didn't know you owned a button-down."

"You know I don't meet with clients looking like anything but a businessman," I tell him, peering at myself in the window of Livvy's car. Damn, I look like a million bucks. Pressed gray slacks, a crisp navy-blue button-down, and a patterned tie that Mia bought for me last year. "For the rare occasions when you need to show off your business side," she'd said, but those occasions aren't entirely rare. As the owner of the shop, I'm both the guy who gets dirty under the hood, and the one who cleans up to seal the big, fat deals.

I have a potentially huge one in front of me this afternoon when I see David Winters of *Back to the Future* fanboy fame in about thirty minutes.

"Is Snow White going to be ready tomorrow?" I point to the fifty-year-old Rolls, using Livvy's name for her baby, which she bought at auction a few months ago, with my input.

"Absolutely," Sam says. "A few little details in the morning and we're good." He looks at his watch. "I'm outta here, too. No classes tonight, so I have a hot date with the new mechanic from John Smith's."

I scowl. "Seriously? You're seeing someone from our biggest rival?"

"It's just drinks, and I won't tell Karen trade secrets over a pale ale," Sam says.

"Drinks can loosen lips, so be careful," I say, and that's another lesson I learned from my mentor. Be careful and watch your back, Bob used to say.

I'm cautious as fuck when it comes to John Smith because we jockey for top billing in this city. Earlier this year, he won a hotly contested bid to build a custom car for a new late-night talk show host, one I was sure I had in the bag. That was a tough loss, but then I nabbed a new client in a banker who rolls the dice big time on upgrades to his fleet of sports cars. Win some, lose some. Even so, it's best to be cautious when tangoing with the competition.

"Give me some credit," Sam says indignantly. "I have far more interesting things to discuss on a date than tales from under the hood."

Mike jumps in. "What do you discuss? Wine? Politics? The state of the world?"

"That and whether cars are guys or girls."

"And on that note, I'm off to discuss things other than the gender of automobiles with a potential client. See you cats tomorrow. Have fun tonight, Sam." I clap Mike on the back as he yawns, something he's been doing a lot less of these days. "Don't let the baby keep you up too late. Sing him a lullaby."

Mike's got a newborn, and the kid just started sleeping through the night, which means Mike has started looking human again, and not like daddy death warmed over.

I head out of the garage and catch an Uber across town. Ironic, isn't it? But there's little I like less than driving to appointments in midtown Manhattan. Nothing can make a guy like me hate cars more than New York City gridlock.

As the tiny Honda takes me to my meeting, I catch up on business on my phone—answering emails from clients, returning notes from suppliers, and responding to a request from a scholarship fund I've been lucky enough to support in the last few years. Can I help with a little extra for a promising eighteen-year-old from Kentucky who wants to study engineering in college so he can restore cars? Hell yeah, I reply. Then I move on to some other notes, making sure the shop runs in tip-top shape. I didn't get to where I am by missing opportunities or slacking off.

And I fucking love where I am.

Especially considering that David Winters offers me one helluva golden opportunity thirty minutes later. Turns out the guy who wanted to know about making wings for doors is a producer for a TV network, and they need a new car for a show.

Just my luck.

* * *

"Picture this."

The stocky Creswell Saunders III loosens his bowtie and makes a square with his big hands, like a screenwriter in Los

Angeles ready to make his big pitch. He's parked next to David Winters on a plush, chocolate-brown couch in a corner office overlooking Times Square, the end-of-the-afternoon sun reflecting off Creswell's naked skull. The man is bald, and from the looks of it, he's bald by choice. "*Midnight Steel* will have a modern-day *Magnum PI*-type hero. A ladies' man. Tom Selleck, but without the 'stache and the too-short shorts."

"I always did wonder how those shorts were even remotely comfortable," I say from my spot in the chair.

Creswell drops his voice to a conspiratorial whisper. "Confession: they weren't. I was a huge fan of *Magnum PI* back in the day. I even begged my mom to buy me a pair of those shorts for Christmas one year."

I laugh. "Along with the Hawaiian shirt?"

"Absolutely."

David chimes in with a question. "Did she get you the Ferrari, too?"

Creswell frowns. "No. But she gave me something better." He taps his chest. "She gave me ambition. She gave me hunger. She gave me drive. And that's why I'm here," he says, stabbing his finger against the table. "Because we're going to reinvent the detective-in-a-hot-car show for the modern day. And this time, our hero is going to have a little competition."

"Competition is always a good thing. I've been known to thrive on it," I say, keeping my tone light and even, lest I let on how damn much I want this gig. But this gig—it's as plum as plum can be, and I'm damn near salivating for it.

"Our hero is going to have a sexy, tough-as-nails, take-no-prisoners, brainy and beautiful female PI to vie with," Creswell says. "They'll be fighting for cases, running into each other at unexpected times, forced to deal with each other."

David rubs his hands together. "It'll have a *Moonlighting* sort of energy. Cat and mouse. Enemies to lovers."

"Since we're making confessions, I'll have you know I had a huge crush on Cybill Shepherd in high school when I binge-watched that show on DVD," I admit.

"Crush? Ha. I once planned to marry her," Creswell says with a broad smile. "I wrote out a proposal and everything."

I laugh. "You weren't kidding about being ambitious."

"Always have been. Now, David, why don't you tell Mr. Summers what we have in mind for him?"

Turns out the man I met at the custom car show was so familiar with TV and movie cars because he works in the business. He's a producer for the TV network RBC, and Creswell is the creative force behind the new Magnumesque reboot.

David adjusts his wire-rimmed glasses. "We want you to build the car our hero on *Midnight Steel* drives."

And I grow ten feet tall. This is what I want. This is the motherfucking bomb. I love deal making and I love big splashy opportunities. The chance to build for a TV show is huge, and it's why I strive to make sure business comes first, like I did when I worked that Sunday at the show. Because when you put business first, it pays off like a loose slot machine. That means I can take care of myself, my employees, and my future. I can take care of others, too, and that's damn important to me.

I've known since I was three that I wanted to make cars. I was *that* kid. The one who played with Matchbox cars and trucks. The boy who built model airplanes and vehicles. I loved everything about autos, taking them apart and putting them back together. Growing up in Seattle, I had parents who encouraged me and found opportunities for me to learn from local mechanics and car restorers. There wasn't a problem under the hood that I couldn't tackle by the time I was eighteen, when I was ready to find a job. But my dad insisted I go to college, and I'm damn grateful for that. I decided to study business so I'd have the skills to make a custom car business the best it could be.

The best—that's what I want to be. Why? *Because.* Fucking because. Why does Michael Phelps compete in the Olympics for more gold medals? Because he can. My job is the love of my motherfucking life, and the chance to perform at the peak is all I've ever wanted. I crave it like oxygen, like chocolate, like life itself.

Opportunities like this are why I climbed the mountain, learned the skills, and worked for the best builders before starting my own shop. "You're ready, Max," Bob told me one day when we'd finished an Oldsmobile. "It's time for you to branch out on your own."

It takes a while to be ready, and my mind flicks back momentarily to Henley. That's something we fought over the last few weeks she worked as my apprentice. Headstrong and fiery, bright and creative, boasting a degree in engineering, she was sure she was ready to conquer the world.

But why the hell am I thinking of Henley? I drag a hand through my dark hair, re-centering my focus to the here and now.

The female PI will have a name-brand car for her ride, since the show has an automobile sponsor. But the hero's car, a Lamborghini Miura, will be customized with added features.

"What do you say?" Creswell asks.

"Sounds like a plan. Let's nail down the details."

David tells me he'll draw up paperwork. "One more thing," he adds. "This show is one of the priorities on our network for the new season. We have a huge marketing campaign behind *Midnight Steel*, and we expect the car to be part of it. Would you be able to do some promo videos as you customize it, showing you making the car and whatnot? They'll run on our website."

"As long as you don't need me to act like a douche on a re-ality car-building show I'm game."

David laughs. "We'd prefer, in fact, that you don't act like a douche. We want to capture the real vibe of what it takes to make a car like this."

Creswell checks the time on his wrist. "I need to go. Must get home to Roger. He surely misses me."

David points to the door. "Of course he misses you. Go, go, go."

Creswell scurries out, muttering Roger's name as he leaves. I'm not sure if Roger is his lover, partner, or dog, or maybe it's the name of his in-house thermostat system. It isn't my place to find out.

David and I make plans to meet again on Friday evening to talk about the next steps, and then I say good-bye.

When the elevator doors close, I'm all alone.

"Fucking A," I say quietly as I punch the air.

As the elevator chugs downward, I say it louder. This must be how a receiver feels in the end zone. This is motherfucking awesome.

When I reach the ground floor, I call my brother, Chase, to see if we can celebrate tonight now that it's damn near official.

"Meet at Joe's Sticks in thirty minutes," he tells me.

"Let's do it. I'll text Mia, and she can join us, too."

Joe's is walking distance, so I make my way up the avenue in a cloud-nine mood. I don't even get annoyed when a messenger on a bike hops up on the sidewalk, nearly slamming the front wheel into my leg. I sidestep him.

I can handle a near bike run-in.

The run-in the next morning, though, is a little more difficult to dodge.

CHAPTER 5

Henley's To-Do List

—Black-lace combat boots will look hot tomorrow.
Set them out tonight.

—Start all that frigging paperwork that won't stop staring
me in the face.

—Try not to hate paperwork. (That's asking too much!)

—Take that new hip-hop workout at gym. Maybe it'll help
my complete inability to follow the steps in salsa class. Why
is dancing so hard?

—Figure out why the freaking screen-lock on phone doesn't
work. What kind of self-respecting fix-it woman can restore
an engine on a Challenger and not repair a screen-lock? (I'm
looking at you, girl!)

—Don't check out hot guy at gym. The one with tattoos
that look like one Max has on his bicep.

—Especially since it's such a sexy tattoo.

CHAPTER 6

I'm nearly at the climax.

Of the story.

The one I'm telling Livvy about the Rolls.

"And then she purred when I turned the corner," I say from my spot in her parlor, sitting on the ornate couch with the carved wooden arms and upholstery that looks as if it comes from Versailles.

Livvy's slate-gray eyes sparkle. She sits on the other end of the couch. "And?"

This is the cherry on the ice cream sundae. For Livvy, the car isn't complete until I tell her how it feels to be behind the wheel. "The purr turned to a deep roar when I cranked up the speed for the final mile."

"And when you parked it?" Livvy is on the edge of her seat, her hands clasped together.

"Like a parachute landing softly on the grass. Perfect."

"It sounds incredible. I can't wait to take her for a spin."

"Don't wait, then. Go out right now and do it." In a low voice I chant, "Do it, do it, do it."

Livvy giggles then fingers the strand of pearls around her neck. "I will soon. I promise. I have another delivery shortly, but then I'll slide on my leather driving gloves, toss a silk scarf around my neck, and head out for a drive through the country."

"Don't forget the Jackie O sunglasses to complete the look."

"I never forget the shades." Livvy gestures to the white china teacup on the table. "Can I interest you in another white peony before I have Peter take you back to Manhattan?" she asks, mentioning her chauffeur. He drives a town car, not any of Livvy's specialized rides.

"I'm all good in the tea department."

"Don't leave, then, without taking some treats. Ariel made the most delicious brownies for a party later."

A petite blond maid in a gray uniform with a lace apron returns to the living room to collect our cups.

"Thank you so much, Ariel," Livvy says to the young woman. "Would you pack up some brownies for Mr. Summers for the road?"

"Of course, Mrs. Sweetwater. I will take care of that immediately."

Ariel turns to go, but as she reaches the doorway of the parlor, she casts her gaze back to me and offers a shy, sweet smile. Ariel nibbles on the corner of her lip, her eyes on mine.

The unspoken offer is tempting, especially since I can't deny I wouldn't mind playing a little French-maid-with-a-feather-duster game with her. But fucking the client's help is verboten. I look away from the cute little thing as she spins on her heel and heads off to the rest of the mansion.

"Now, what shall we work on next time? You've customized an Aston Martin for me. You've put a new engine in my husband's Mercedes, and now the Rolls."

I stroke my chin, thinking about what Livvy might crave. "Wouldn't you say it's about time we make a sports car for you?"

"Actually," she says slowly, as if she's confessing, "I ordered one for my niece for a birthday present."

"Funny, I didn't get the work order for that. I must have misplaced it."

Her shoulders sag. "I used someone else. Please forgive me."

I pretend to be offended, even though I'm a little bummed to have lost the job. "I'm devastated."

"I would have used you, but it was a last-minute thing. I wanted you to focus completely on Snow White, but I needed to get this one done, too."

The unmistakable rumble of a Corvette engine lands on my ears. I snap my head to glance at the living room window. A sporty red car cruises up the long driveway.

Livvy squeals. "It's here now. I'll be right back."

She pops up at the speed of light and race-walks to the car before the driver can even cut the engine.

I whistle under my breath. Damn. That sleek beauty looks better than any Corvette should have a right to look. I don't even like Corvettes, but this one makes me want to get my hands on it, under it, and inside it.

"I prepared a sandwich for you, too."

The voice is soft and eager. I tear my gaze away from the window and meet Ariel's eyes. She crosses the room and hands me a small brown shopping bag—the classy kind, like my sister buys when she gives gifts to her friends.

"Thanks. Appreciate that."

"It's turkey with avocado and artichoke. It's my specialty," she says, her lips curving into a smile. "I hope you like it. I have lots of specialties."

Yeah, and I might like to get to know them, but that can't happen.

"I'll dig in on the ride back to the city."

The snap of the hood popping open catches my attention, and I peer outside again. I can't help myself. No matter the make, no matter the model, when someone pops open the hood of a car, I have to look. I have to drop everything and check out the engine. It's an affliction all car guys suffer from, but it's one we never want to cure.

Must. Stare. At. Engine.

Livvy and the builder are obscured behind the hood, which gives me an even better view for ogling. Fifteen seconds later, I cross the driveway and walk up to the car.

"That's a gorgeous 16-valve V-8 if I ever—"

My blood goes cold. It turns to an arctic chill as a brunette in combat boots, a short jean skirt, and a black T-shirt steps out from behind the open hood.

Her.

Henley's deep brown eyes go wide as moons, and her red-lipsticked mouth parts. Then, she presses her lips together as if she's holding in all the insults she wants to fling my way.

Livvy jumps in. "Max Summers, this is Henley Rose. She specializes in hot sports cars."

"I bet," I bite out. Why the hell is she here? Did she find out I worked with Livvy and snag the last-minute gig away from me before Livvy even gave me a shot at it?

"Henley, this is Max. He's done my entire fleet."

My one-time apprentice, who wasn't fucking ready to leave on her own, arches an eyebrow. "Is that so? I bet he's great at *doing* a whole fleet."

I seethe inside from her off-hand comment. Look, when she worked for me, I never hit on her. But that doesn't mean I was a choirboy in general. And that doesn't mean I did a good job hiding my late-night activities. But I've learned over the years how to be discreet. Now no one but me needs to know how very much I enjoy variety in the ladies.

"He is great," Livvy adds. "He's simply been fantastic with all my automobiles."

"He sure does know his way under the engine, doesn't he?" Henley remarks. "I'm a huge fan of his work," she adds.

Livvy nods enthusiastically. "This man knows how to make a car sing. How to make her purr. How to make her roar."

Henley's jaw drops, as if Livvy has said the most salacious things, and she kind of has. "Purr? Roar? Wow. He must have some serious skills."

I can't have Henley twisting shit around again. "I should take off. It was lovely spending time with you, Livvy."

Livvy gestures from Henley to me. "I hope you don't mind, but since I have Peter driving you back to the city, I thought he could take you both together."

My shoulders tense. That is not going to happen. No how. No way.

"You know," I say, giving my best casual, unperturbed shrug of a no-big-deal shoulder, even though this situation is the definition of a big fucking obstacle I must avoid like a video game character jumping across lava pits, "I really don't mind taking the train. Let Henley have the car *all to herself.*"

"Oh, that's not necessary at all," Henley says in a far-too-chipper tone. If she's even one-quarter as annoyed as I am, she's excellent at hiding it. "I'm more than happy to take the train."

A soft voice pipes in from behind me. "I can drive you, Max."

I turn to see Ariel standing a few feet behind us. "My shift ends in thirty minutes, and I live in Queens."

Henley clasps her hands to her chest. "What a kind offer. That's so sweet, Max. Isn't that so sweet?"

I clench my teeth. I'm not sure which is the more dangerous lion's den right now.

But Livvy cuts in, shaking her head. "Ariel, you were going to stay later to help me prep for my niece's party. I need you for a few extra hours." Then she whispers to her maid, as if we can't hear her discussing the tawdry subject of pay for the help, "Overtime."

"Yes, of course, ma'am." Ariel steps closer, lowers her head, and speaks softly in my ear. "I like the Rolls better."

"Thanks," I say as she returns to the house.

And when I turn back to Henley, the look in her eyes says she heard every word and is going to make me pay for them. Time to get the fuck out of the alligator pen. I point my thumb in the direction of the road. "Love the offer, Livvy. But I'm good with the train."

Livvy shoots me an admonishing stare. "Don't be silly, young man. Peter has errands to tend to in the city, and I'm more than happy to have him drive you back."

"I'll just catch an Uber to the station. I'm good," I say, since I do not want to be stuck with that chick in a car for a two-hour drive.

Livvy wags a finger at me. "I insist. We have cheese, crackers, and champagne in the town car. Grapes, too. Have a snack. Relax and enjoy the drive. Now, let me ogle this Corvette, then you'll be free to go."

When a client like Livvy says how it's going to be, you don't tell her no. Already Livvy has booked business with the new competition. I need to make damn sure the door to Henley closes, and that I'm the one who wins the commission for Livvy's next sports car.

"Your generosity is greatly appreciated," I say.

She lowers her voice. "There's some Pappy Van Winkle in the town car."

"I'm going to need that," I say, but mine's not the only voice.

Henley says the same words at the same damn time.

And that's how, fifteen minutes later, I'm sliding after her into the backseat of a sleek, sexy town car.

CHAPTER 7

I grab the bottle and sink into the buttery leather seat as Peter swings out of the driveway. There's a partition window and it's rolled up. I fucking wish this was a limo and Henley and I had some goddamn space between us. She's right next to me, and I can smell her perfume. It's soft and floral, like spring apple flowers.

Why can't I have a stuffy nose today?

These damn nostrils work too well for my own good. She smells amazing.

I unscrew the cap.

"You're going to just drink that straight from the bottle?" Henley fires off.

"I'm so sorry. Will that offend you?" I bring the opening to my lips and take a swallow, savoring the delicious burn of the whiskey as the car picks up speed.

She rolls her eyes. Her pretty, soulful, chocolate-colored eyes. "I'm sure you think you just marked that bottle and I won't touch it now. But you're wrong."

She leans into me, stretches an arm over my chest, and snags the bottle from my hand. Nothing else registers for a few seconds, because her tits brush against my bicep.

Not fair.

Not fucking fair.

I might be a tough bastard, but this is not in the rulebook. This is foul play, and my dick likes it. What does he know? He's Benedict Arnold right now. Especially since he seems to be controlling my eyes, because I can't look away from this girl as she brings the bottle to her lips and knocks back a swallow.

I stare at the way her throat moves. She winces for a split-second while she pulls the bottle away.

She licks her lips. The little tip of her tongue runs along her top lip like she's starring in a slow-mo commercial. I can see the next frame perfectly. She's the beauty on the hood of a car. Sprawling sexily across it. Batting those come-hither eyes.

The universe must want to test me somehow.

But then, I wrap my hand around the neck of the Pappy Van Winkle, taking it from her. I remind myself this is not a test because I don't even fucking like her. I take a long, thirsty drink, and I can taste her lipstick.

Jesus Christ. I can taste her motherfucking lipstick.

This isn't a test. It's a goddamn pop quiz I'm thoroughly unprepared for. Because her lipstick is unexpectedly delicious. I set the bottle back in its holder as the car slows at a light.

"Is this how it's going to be for the next two hours?" she asks.

"You mean are we going to go to battle with a bottle of bourbon?"

"Yes. Because I will go toe-to-toe with you."

I scoff, giving her a doubtful look. "Sweetheart, you'd never last. I'm twice your weight."

"But I'm three times as tough."

"You're a fucking piece of work. Would you prefer to one-up me by showing up at a client's house at the same time?" I smack my forehead. "Oh wait. You already did that."

She crosses her arms. "You think you're the only game in town, don't you?"

"No. But I'd like to know what kind of game you're playing."

She jerks her body away, giving me a you-must-be-crazy look. "When did it happen, Max?"

"When did what happen, Henley?"

"When did you go certifiably insane? Was it right after I left you, or a few years later?"

I sigh heavily, wishing I hadn't walked right into that one. I turn to face her. "Look, I think it's bullshit and suspicious to see you at her house."

She twirls her finger in a circle by her ear. "And I think that's paranoid and cuckoo. I can't believe you think I'm playing a game because Livvy Sweetwater ordered a rush job on a custom car from me. I'm fast, I'm furious, and I'm awesome at souping up Corvettes. Deal with it, Summers."

I laugh as I rub my hand over the back of my neck. "Ah, that's the Henley I remember. Always quick with a fiery comeback."

"What did you expect but a *true* answer? You're ridiculous if you think having the same client means I'm out to steal your business."

She rolls her eyes and drags a hand through her chestnut brown hair. Stupidly, I follow her gesture, wondering for a moment what her hair feels like.

Like straw.

Her hair feels like straw.

Her lips taste like wilted lettuce.

Her breath smells like a dog's.

Shit, I like dogs.

But, I remind myself, I don't want to kiss dogs, and I definitely don't want to kiss Henley.

"I think it's fucking fishy," I say.

"Look, Summers. Here's the deal. You were the king of the car business when I worked under you."

Under you.

Don't plant those images in my head.

My dick flirts with treason once more.

"Still the king," I point out.

"And now there's a queen in town. You're going to have to deal with the fact that you have some serious competition. I make hotter sports cars than you do. You might be a god at restoring a Rolls, or making an Aston sing, and I'm sure your neon-blue souped-up Ferrari is the baddest ride ever."

I cock my head. "How'd you know I did that car in blue?"

"I looked you up. You think it's easy being a woman in this business? It's not. I need to stay ten steps ahead, and I do it by knowing the business cold. I researched you, studied you, and understood you when I came back to town. You do an amazing job on nearly everything." I can't help it—I straighten my shoulders a bit from the compliment, loving it, even from her. "But I happen to be amazing at making sports cars, and Livvy wanted one for her wild niece, so she called this wild girl." Henley punctuates her speech by tapping her chest.

"Wild," I say, deadpan. "That sounds right, considering how you got a little wild with a client's car the last time we worked together, doing things he didn't ask for."

The look on her face tells me she's taken aback. "I thought it was what he wanted," she says with less intensity and more . . . worry. "I told you that."

I shake my head. I won't give in to her. "You did what *you* wanted. Plain and simple. You nearly cost me business."

"You nearly cost me a career."

I fix her with a you've-got-to-be-kidding stare. "Your career seems just fine. Speaking of, what's the name of this shop you opened?"

"I don't have my own shop yet. I'm the lead builder at John Smith Rides."

I groan. That name again. First, Sam dates a mechanic there. Now, Henley is on the fucking payroll of my rival, too.

I grab the bottle, and once more I don't bother with a glass. Nope. I might as well drink the whole thing down. This woman is going to be a thorn in my side.

* * *

After fifteen minutes of uncomfortable silence while the car rolls along the highway, Henley turns to me. "How about we try to make this ride enjoyable?"

"Let bygones be bygones? Or did you want to play cards?"

"How about charades?"

I'm walking into something dangerous. But I do it anyway. "What kind of charades?"

"It's a question I'm asking."

"All right. Have at it."

She adopts a perky little smile then leans forward, popping her butt off the seat. I remind myself that it's not a perfect ass she possesses. Like her straw hair and rubbery lips, her butt is flat and boring, not a round, heart-shaped dream ass ripe for spanking. She waggles a pretend object in her hand, almost as if she's cleaning. Dusting, perhaps. Next, she clasps her hand to her mouth in a Betty Boop move. *"Oops,"* she mouths.

"You're allowed to do that in charades?"

She doesn't answer. She sits back down on the seat and grabs her phone from a small purse. She points to me and shrugs as if she's asking a question.

"Did I?" I suggest.

She nods then opens her palm a few times as if she's grabbing something.

"Grab?"

She shakes her head.

"Get?"

She taps her nose.

"Did I get . . .?"

Henley does the dusting again then points to her phone.

Yep. Walked into it and then some. I drag a hand over my face and shake my head. "No, I did not get the maid's number. I wouldn't do that to a client."

"But she was hot, right?"

I turn and stare at her. "Why are you asking?"

"She was a babe. It's a fact. I was just curious if you got her number since she sure seemed to like you, too."

I point to the guy behind the glass. "You want Peter's number?"

"I don't know. Do you think he likes piña coladas and making love in the rain?"

For a flash second, a burst of wildfire curls through my veins. It feels like white-hot jealousy. Which is ridiculous since she's not *making love* to Peter.

Or me, for that matter, obviously.

I fight off the envy with a full dose of sarcasm. "Have you ever noticed you never have a good pair of headphones when you need them?"

She huffs. "Message received. I'll just shut up and read a book." She reaches for her phone on the seat, but accidentally knocks it to the floor of the car. I lean down to pick it up, and when I hand it to her I see her playlist.

Nena's "99 Luftballons."

The Go-Go's "Vacation."

Madonna's "Like a Virgin."

I smirk. That's too fucking adorable. "You like bubblegum pop?"

Her cheeks go red. "There's nothing wrong with bubblegum pop," she says as she tries to grab her phone from my hand.

I. Can't. Resist.

I don't know what comes over me, but I'm pretty damn sure it's the way this girl needles me. It's her French maid routine. It's her pushing all my buttons. It's the way she detests me.

I hold her phone behind my head.

"Max," she says, in a perfect plea. God, it's hot. I can hear her saying it in bed.

I feign surprise. "Oh, did you want your phone back, tiger?"

Her eyes widen when I use that word. Frankly, I'm surprised I said it. But she is a tiger, especially right now as she leans across the seat, reaching for it.

Damn, I'm an asshole. And yet, I can't seem to stop playing keep-away with her phone, jamming it far behind me so that it hits the side of the car. She lunges for it, thrusting her arm out, but only hitting my forearm.

She swats me. "Give it to me."

My brain short-circuits. God, she would sound hot saying that bent over the bed.

Then in a flurry, she unbuckles her seat belt and lunges at me.

Foul play indeed.

She's on me. She's fucking on me. She climbs, stretching high, her tits near my motherfucking face, so help me God. They are saggy, drooping, ugly breasts.

Except they're not.

They're perfect. Lush, ripe.

Like her sweet perfume scent. Like her cinnamon breath that flutters across my cheek as she rises higher. As she reaches, her T-shirt rides up, revealing a sliver of her stomach.

I've never seen anything so sexy in my life.

I don't move. I don't breathe.

I simply try not to grow more aroused. But then she wraps one hand around my wrist and pries the phone with the other as her breasts smash against my eyes.

Man down.

A second later, she wrenches back, dropping down to her seat, clutching her phone. She smooths her hand over her shirt. She won't look at me. "Something secret on your phone?"

She jerks her head and gives me a look that could kill.

I should be pissed at her. I should torment her more. But I feel as if she's got a legit fear, and I don't want to be a dick. Nor do I want my dick to be in charge. He's an idiot.

I breathe a silent sigh of relief that Operation Deflation is underway.

"Sorry," I mutter.

She nods as she stares ahead.

I take my phone from my pocket, toggle over to my Google streaming music, and search for a song. I turn up the volume, close my eyes, and let Cyndi Lauper's "Girls Just Wanna Have Fun" fill the silence between us.

When the song nears its end, I open one eye. Henley's not looking at me. She's gazing straight ahead, but there's a smile on her face that says she likes the song.

And the sentiment.

CHAPTER 8

The white ball screams across the table, straight at the purple one that's mere inches from the corner pocket. But the cue ball misses, whacking the side of the table with a dull thud instead.

That's how my night has gone.

I curse under my breath. Usually, I kill it at pool. Tonight, I'm a doormat.

"Allow me to show you how it's done."

My buddy Patrick takes a swig of his beer, sets down the bottle on the wooden side of the table, and lines up the pool stick. Narrowing his eyes, he takes aim. With a light tap, he delivers the white ball with a textbook stop-shot that sends an orange-striped ball neatly into the pocket.

And gives him the game.

"And that's how you beat the resident pool shark," he says, thrusting his arms in the air.

I shake my head in defeat. "Man, I suck tonight."

Patrick laughs. "You do. But I'm also awesome. So maybe you want to give me some credit, too."

He's right. And I'm sucking at that, too—basic human understanding. I extend a hand and give him a shake. "Good game. Apparently, I'm an asshole in all sorts of ways today."

"Aww." He adopts an overdone frown. "Want to tell Uncle Patrick all about your rough day?" He racks up for another round, his brown hair flopping in his face when he leans over the table.

Patrick lives in my building. I call him the half-timer since, well, he lives here only half the time. The rest of his days he's on the other coast.

From the hiking boots to the REI pullover shirts, Patrick is outdoorsy to the core. After offering wilderness camping, backpacking, snowshoeing, and cross-country ski trips and tours in the region, he recently expanded his adventure tour company to Northern California.

I shake my head. "No, thanks. I'll pass on the impromptu therapy session."

What's there to say, anyway? That woman gets under my skin. Henley's not just a thorn. She's the thorniest thorn in the entire history of thorns. Two hours with her and I feel as if I've been cut all over. She's like a kitten that paws at you and ten seconds later your wrist is bleeding.

"Then I'll tell you about my rough day," Patrick offers, and that gets my attention. He doesn't have rough days, unless you count a lack of snow or an excess of muddy trails. Though, in all fairness, those do sound like tough conditions, but the point is he's one unruffled dude. He's precisely the type of guy someone would want to guide them over trails and through wilderness areas. "I had to let one of my guides go today."

I make my way around the table, lining up my next shot. "Yeah? What happened? Did he turn left at a trailhead instead of right?"

Patrick pretends to guffaw deeply. "Actually, he fucked a client on the job. A married client."

"Ouch," I say, wincing as I nail a draw shot on the green ball. Maybe I'm back on my game. Maybe Henley hasn't totally knocked me off-balance.

"Gave him the heave-ho," he says, miming slicing a finger across his throat. "I can't have those kinds of problems chasing me as I build up a business."

That's one of the reasons Patrick and I get along so well. The dude might be the definition of laid-back, but he's no slacker. He works hard, he's disciplined, and he doesn't let his people get away with shit.

"Right there with you, man. You need to run a tight ship." Then I take a beat. "Screwing a chick in the tents is for management only, right?"

"Hey, now," Patrick says. "I haven't done that in—"

The sound of the door opening loudly interrupts us.

"Honey, I'm home!"

It's Mia, and she stops in her tracks when she sees Patrick at the table. Patrick stops in his tracks, too. He blinks as he takes in my sister in her jeans, high-heeled boots, and pink sweater. Her arms are laden with grocery bags from Whole Foods.

"I'll just make my way out of here," Patrick says in a time-to-help-my-buddy-score-by-making-myself-scarce voice.

I laugh. "Dipshit. That's my sister."

"Ohhhhh," Patrick says, then he strides across the hardwood floor and extends a hand to Mia. "Nice to meet you. I'm Patrick. I live a few floors down."

Mia smiles brightly as she takes his hand. "Mia. I'm just in town for another day for meetings. Then I head back to the West Coast."

"West Coast, you say?" Patrick raises an eyebrow.

"Don't get any ideas," I chime in, joining them as I grab the bags Mia carries and peek inside to find fresh pasta, tomatoes, and a small bottle of vodka. "Penne with vodka cream sauce?"

"And a pine nut salad," she adds, then turns to Patrick. "Max and I were going to cook dinner. My eyes are always bigger than my stomach, and bigger than Max's stomach, too. Want to join us?"

My money is on Patrick saying yes. In fact, it seems to take a nanosecond for him to utter, "I'd love to."

As Mia heads to the kitchen, I clap him on the shoulder. "Like I said, don't get any ideas."

Patrick puts his hands on his head as if they're giant brain suckers. "There. All ideas have now disappeared from my head. I'm completely idea-less. Also, I have no idea what you're talking about."

I roll my eyes. "You do know what I mean, and don't go there."

My concern isn't over him. He's a great guy. He'd totally do right by my sister. I say it to protect her. She hasn't had the best luck when it comes to falling for my buddies.

"Go where?" he asks as he follows my sister.

* * *

"You did not do that." Mia adopts a stern stare, her forkful of pasta poised midair en route to her mouth.

"What's the big deal?" I ask with a shrug.

"Max," she admonishes me before she takes a bite of the pasta dish we whipped up.

"She was getting under my skin," I say, defending my actions in the town car as I spear a piece of penne with my fork.

"Some women can do that to a man," Patrick says, chiming in as if he's my attorney. I feel as if I need one right now. Once we sat at the table, Mia asked me about my day. After I mentioned the car ride with Henley, Mia broke me down, wheedling all the details out of me.

Not the sordid ones about my thought process. But the ones about how I played hide-and-seek with Henley's phone. Which was, evidently, a violation of some girl code I'm unaware of. You know, not being a girl and all.

"You took her phone," Mia says. "You held it above your head. There's only one woman you can do that to, and you shouldn't do that to her either."

Patrick furrows his brow. "I didn't think you could do that with any woman."

Mia looks at him and nods, as if she's approving his statement. "This guy is smart. Follow his lead. And what I mean is that's the kind of stuff a brother does to a sister."

"Trust me," I scoff. "I do not think of Henley like a sister."

"Trust me. I've never done that to my sister," Patrick says, puffing out his chest like he wants to win all the gold stars tonight.

I smack his shoulder. "Dude. You're supposed to be my friend."

Mia jumps right back in, womansplaining. "Women are private people. Henley might have photos on her phone she didn't want you to see."

My eyes widen. "Like dirty photos?"

She rolls her eyes as she takes another bite. "I just mean pictures of friends. Maybe a selfie from the gym. I've taken pictures of myself to chronicle my progress when I hired a personal trainer."

"You do have really nice arms," Patrick says in an admiring tone, reaching for a glass of water.

She flashes a smile as she glances briefly at her arms, since she took off her sweater as we cooked. She wears a light blue tank top now, and her arms are indeed toned. But those strong arms belong to my fucking sister, so I shoot Patrick another hands-off stare.

"You think Henley was annoyed because she didn't want me to see shots of her arms?"

"Shots of her arms, pictures of her friends, photos of her cat. Maybe work information. Maybe she has contracts or memos on her phone. All I'm saying is no matter how much she needles you, you shouldn't have pretended to abscond with her phone. Just apologize."

I groan as I drag a hand over my jaw. "Crap."

"I agree with Mia," Patrick says.

I sneer at him. "I'm shocked you concur with my sister." I meet Mia's eyes. "I sort of apologized to Henley in the car."

"You need to do it all the way, Max. Say it and mean it. It's a small world, as you're learning, and chances are you're going to run into her again." She sets her fork down and smirks. "I have to say, though, hats off to that girl. The feather-duster maid charade sounds hilarious."

"Yeah, it killed me," I say, deadpan.

When we're done with the pasta and salad, we clear the plates and Mia returns to the table with a pint of coconut ice cream. She serves it, sliding a bowl to Patrick.

He points at the scoop, adopting an inquisitive expression. "Coconuts have hair and produce milk. Ever wonder why they aren't mammals?"

Mia catches his conversational volley and lobs it right back to him with, "By that same token, why are sweetbreads anything but sweet? They're organ meats. Glands, of all things."

Patrick shudders.

"Shouldn't sweetbreads refer to something sweet, like monkey bread?" Mia adds, her tone intensely serious.

Patrick takes a spoonful of coconut ice cream. "I do love monkey bread. So much that I have a theory."

"Please tell us your monkey bread theory," I chime in, but Patrick and Mia ignore me.

"Hear me out." Patrick's eyes are on my sister. "My theory is this—it's impossible to dislike monkey bread. Just try not to like it."

"You can't dislike it," Mia seconds. "Honestly, it's fair to say monkey bread can bring about world peace."

I arch an eyebrow. "World peace?"

They nod in unison.

Maybe they're onto something, because that gives me an idea.

CHAPTER 9

The next day during my lunch break, I run a quick errand to the Sunshine Bakery uptown and return to the shop, working hard the rest of the afternoon on a restoration. Tonight is the meeting with David—drinks at Thalia's to discuss our next steps. I should be able to patch up the Henley situation before then and cruise into business.

Since we start early in the day, once the clock ticks past four, I say good-bye to the guys and take off.

But my feet feel heavy, and a vague sense of dread courses through me as I walk. When a cab with an ad for a hot new action flick cruises by on 11th Avenue, I contemplate hailing it and heading to the nearest movie theater. As a leathered old woman leaves a bodega with a steaming cup of coffee, I consider ditching my plan and grabbing a French roast at a cafe somewhere else . . . anywhere but where I'm going.

But cafes aren't my style, and avoidance isn't either. I pride myself on being upfront and facing problems. Most of all on *fixing* problems. Ironic, in a way, since I thought I was pretty damn direct with Henley five years ago when I explained the problem with the '69 Mustang Fastback she'd been working on while I was gone. I'd left the car in her capable hands, but the final work didn't exactly go as planned.

I told her so when I saw what she'd done—a full-on paint job in champagne gold, but the client didn't want that color.

The guy wanted lime gold. Subtle difference in shade, but to a Ford loyalist, it's everything.

Her brown eyes had welled up with tears, and I'd felt like an ogre because she said she'd done what I told her to do. "You said it was champagne. I wrote down the paint code." Those watery eyes had tugged at my heart, but I knew she didn't want to be treated any differently because she was a woman, so I couldn't let her tears sway me. Or her insistence. She grabbed her notebook and shoved it at me, trying to show me her notes for the build. But it didn't matter that she wrote it down—she wrote it down wrong, and it had threatened my reputation. The client didn't want his car in a different color, and he sure as hell didn't want me delivering it late.

"I said lime. This is the kind of stuff you need to get right, because this is going to require a complete redo and that costs time and money," I'd told her in my best stern voice. My job was to teach her, not take her into my fucking arms and comfort her.

She'd swatted away her tears, raised her chin, and implored me to give her another chance. I gave it to her, fixing the Mustang with her, side by side, stripping the paint and starting over from scratch. Maybe that was my problem—being so damn close to her. It messed with my head, and every day I told myself, "Don't treat her any differently just because she smells so goddamn sweet." Every day, I grew more stern with her. Tensions between us were already frayed thin, and they unraveled even further. A little later, when it was time for me to choose which apprentice to move up, I told her it wouldn't be her.

I stood by the decision at the time. I still stand by it today. She wasn't ready. Plain and simple. My decision had nothing to do with her talent—she had more raw ability than anyone I'd ever worked with. It was all natural, too. Henley didn't come from a family of mechanics, and she wasn't raised by a dad who built cars. She was like me—drawn to cars in a bone-deep way from a young age, and that was why she studied engineering in school, and that was why she sought me out post-graduation so she could learn the trade.

My issue was simply that she needed more discipline to balance her talent. After the lime gold fiasco, I told her she could stay on with her apprenticeship and keep learning. I promoted one of the guys instead. She didn't like being passed over one bit, and she parked those hands on her hips and stared at me like I was Hannibal Lecter.

"Maybe I should have gotten it right the first time, but I bet if I were one of the guys, you'd forgive the lime gold mistake a lot more easily, wouldn't you?"

I'd blinked in shock and held up my hands, as if I needed to fend her off. "Whoa. This has nothing to do with you being a woman."

She'd shot me a pointed stare. "Are you sure it doesn't?"

I didn't like the way she was making accusations. I narrowed my eyes. "No. It has to do with you giving me attitude. Like you're doing right now."

"I'm not giving you attitude. I'm giving you the truth. I've worked my butt off for you, and this is ridiculously unfair."

"And you're acting ridiculously out of line."

"Why can't you give me another chance to earn the promotion?" Her voice shook as she asked that question, her eyes threatening to fill with tears again. "I told you it was an honest mistake. I showed you that I wrote it down wrong. Are you that cruel that you can't let this go?"

"Are you *this* dramatic? I'm keeping you on. I'm just not moving you up yet. You're not ready. It's that simple."

"This *dramatic*? Would you call a man dramatic?"

"If he was making a scene like you are, you bet I would."

That was when she'd hurled her insult, like an angry goddess on a mountaintop flinging a ball of fire from her bare hands. "You're nothing but a cruel bastard."

That shit was not going to fly.

I drew a deep breath, sucking in all my anger. "Maybe I am. But this cruel bastard just fired you," I said as calmly as I possibly could.

Her jaw dropped, and her brown eyes flooded with hurt. I couldn't bear to look at her. I turned away, stalking back to the office. I slammed my door and that was when I fumed—at her, but mostly at myself for letting it get to the point where we both were driven by anger.

I'd dragged a hand roughly through my hair, my jaw clenched tight, a vein pulsing so hard in my neck I could feel it beat. What the fuck was wrong with me? I'd just fired the most talented person I'd ever worked with. How the hell did she get so far under my skin?

I reminded myself again and again that no matter how skilled she was, nobody talked to me that way. I was the boss, and that was how it was going to be. The woman came to me to learn, and she was going to learn an important lesson. She didn't get to say whatever she wanted, no matter how pissed she was.

I would walk back out there, calmly explain why I was letting her go, wish her well, and encourage her to get a handle on that mile-wide stubborn streak.

I turned the knob to return to the garage and found she was already gone.

CHAPTER 10

Whatever bad juju is between us, I need to set it aside. I was younger then and more hotheaded. I'd like to think I'm smarter now, though playing games with her phone in the backseat of the town car might suggest otherwise. That's all the more reason for me to man up and say I'm sorry.

I draw a deep breath as I turn the corner.

When I reach the garage of John Smith Rides, I half wish I'd snagged that cab to anyplace else, while the other half of me takes a mental snapshot of God's most perfect union—woman and car.

Wearing a little black skirt, Henley is inspecting the hood of a cherry-red Alfa Romeo Spider.

I'm not sure which sight makes me harder—her or the car. Both are giving off seriously sinful come-hither vibes. But when my eyes roam down Henley's body to her shoes, I decide girl trumps car, because she wears dark red heels.

Fucking heels.

Who does that? Who fucking does that?

Someone like her, that's who.

Mind control. That's what I need. The most intense mental trickery possible.

She smells like cat pee. Her breath reeks of rotten eggs. Her strands of hair form poisonous snakes.

She's a slithery, stinky Medusa.

I zero in on that image, letting it fuel me to enter Medusa's lair.

As I walk to her, I notice for the first time she's standing next to a guy, a younger dude, maybe in his early twenties. I didn't see him at first, but how could I be expected to, given the twin sights vying for ownership of my King of Pleasure soul? Another woman is here, too. A petite blonde with her hair in a ponytail. I bet that's Karen.

Henley sets down the rag and brushes one hand against the other. Her back is still to me. "Tomorrow we'll polish the interior, and we should be good to go," she says to the baby-faced guy.

"Sounds like a plan, Ms. Marlowe."

She cocks her head. "Mark," she chides gently, "for the twentieth time, call me Henley."

"Just say it, Mark. You can do it," Karen says with a smirk, ribbing him. "*Henley.*"

"Henley," he says, then shakes his head like the word feels awkward on his tongue.

The guy makes eye contact with me, raising his chin and nodding a hello. "Ms. Marlowe . . . I mean, Henley. Max Summers is here."

Henley's shoulders square, as if a dose of adrenaline surges through her, powering up her *Fight Club* instincts—the ones that tell her to pummel me.

She spins around. Her lips are a razor-thin line, and her brown eyes take aim at me. *Rat-a-tat-tat.* Gunfire's coming now.

"Well, well, well. If it isn't the king of Manhattan's custom car business."

Her expression morphs to a gregarious grin, as if we're old buddies. She closes the distance between us and extends her hand. I can tell she's being somewhat civilized for the sake of her mechanics, and it impresses me as a business owner. I have to give it to her that she can rein in her distaste.

I take her hand, and then she squeezes the ever-loving fuck out of my palm, crunching her fingers over mine. I wince instantly and nearly emit an *ouch*. But I've still got my man card on me, so I suck it up. *I will not say ouch. I will not say ouch. I will not say ouch. Ever.* Her evil eyes light up, twinkling with mischief as she reads me right. I had no idea she was so strong or could catch me off guard so quickly in a handshake squeeze-play.

"Girls just wanna have fun," she mouths to me. Then out loud, so her mechanics can hear I presume, she says, "How the hell are you, Mr. Summers?" She drops my hand. I want to shake it off. I don't.

"I'm well. How are you, Ms. Marlowe?" Two can play at the formal name game.

"I'm fantastic." She snaps her gaze to the young guy, as well as to the blonde. "Mark and Karen, I have to head to my meeting. Can you two close up?"

"Absolutely," Karen says with a quick nod, and heads to the tool sets at the far end of the garage.

"I'll be right back," Henley says, then steps closer and whispers, "I can't wait to hear you grovel."

How the fuck does she know I'm here to grovel? But when I look down at the bakery bag in my hand, I suppose my mission must be apparent. Damn, this woman can read clues like nobody's business. She heads into a small office.

"Hey man," Mark says, nodding at me. "Love your work. I'm a big fan."

"Appreciate that." I gesture to the red beauty. "You're doing a great job on this Spider."

His blue eyes light up, and he proceeds to rattle off a few high-level details of the build. No trade secrets, just the basics of the customization.

"Damn," I say with an appreciative whistle. "You do nice work, Mark."

He beams. "Thanks." He shuffles his feet then clears his throat. "I got my degree a couple years ago. I had a partial scholarship, thanks to you."

"Yeah? That's fucking awesome. You clearly deserved it."

I hold up a fist for knocking, and he reciprocates. He stares at his fist for a moment. "Thanks to you. It helped me so much. I want to run my own shop someday."

"Do it. You can absolutely do it."

A smile as wide as Central Park fills his face, a reminder of one of the things I love best—giving young guys and gals a chance to realize their dreams. So fucking worth it.

The clack of heels across the concrete halts the conversation. Our eyes turn to the woman again, and I almost want to say to Mark, "Good luck working with that kind of distraction all day."

But that would be sexist and douchey. Not to mention, weak as fuck.

Men should be able to deal with beautiful women at work. With *any* women. They need to handle the presence of the opposite sex without making lewd comments to the lady, or to each other when she's not around. If a man can't do that, he's not a man. Hell, when Henley worked for me, I learned to seal up every last ounce of lust I felt for her in a Ziploc bag and make sure I never let on to a soul.

No way will I reveal my hand now, either, even though she cleans up well. There's not a streak of grease on her, and her chestnut mane looks like she just stepped out of a salon. She's a pristine, confident businesswoman. With a twist. She's changed from a work shirt to a T-shirt—a dressy, quirky kind, with a V-neck. It says *Rainbows and Unicorns for the Win* under a cartoonish image of the mythical creature breathing a rainbow.

"Cute shirt," I say.

"Thanks," she says, glancing down. "It's ironic."

"Figured as much."

A big booming voice calls out my name. I turn on my heel to see the silver-haired and mustached John Smith. "How the hell are you, Max?" he calls as he strides across the garage.

"Excellent, as always," I say. Even though we're rivals, we're civil. You know, since we're not dickheads. Besides, every now and then you wind up working together somehow for a client, or sharing one, like Livvy. "Nice work on the Spider. I was just telling Mark."

When John reaches me, he holds out his hand to shake. "My team does great work. So does my top builder," he says, tipping his head proudly to Henley.

I glance at her. "She's fantastic."

She smiles at both of us. "Thank you."

"And I'm glad she came back to town to work with me rather than you," he says, punching my shoulder and giving me an *I won* look. Fair enough, I suppose, even though we weren't fighting for her.

"You're lucky to have her."

He pats Henley on the shoulder. "I absolutely am. She's a keeper. See you around," he says, then he turns back to chat with Mark while Henley and I leave the shop.

Once we're out on the sidewalk, I say, "He sure likes your work."

"He has good taste," Henley says.

I point at her shoes. "Do you actually work on cars in heels?"

She rolls her eyes as she slides her purse strap higher on her shoulder. "No. I just put them on. I'm heading to a meeting. We can walk and talk."

"Shouldn't that be walk and grovel?" I suggest as we head off.

She arches an eyebrow. "Yes. Feel free to begin."

I'm about to launch into my apology when I'm struck with a realization—we just exchanged several sentences without slinging invectives at each other. "Do you realize we didn't insult each other for the last fifteen seconds? Must be a new record for us."

"Hmm. It must be. Let's break it right now," she says as we walk in step along the side street.

But I don't take the bait. "I got you something."

"Ooh, wait." She stops in her tracks, grabs her phone from her purse, and pretends to click a button. "It's apology time. I need to record this moment for all posterity."

I roll my eyes. "Forget what I said about the record." I wave a hand dismissively. "We'll just smash through it again, especially since you make me want to take back the apology."

"Fine. Say you're sorry for being a dick in the car. I didn't mean to stop you. I simply wanted to preserve history in the making."

I ignore her comment and show her the bag from Josie's bakery. "It's monkey bread. My friend Josie runs a bakery and makes the best everything in the world, including monkey bread." Her brown eyes soften. They're a lighter shade now, and reveal a hint of vulnerability. "I'm sorry I was a dick with your phone. I shouldn't have done that. Phones are private."

"They are," she says, without any vinegar in her tone. Just honey. "And thank you for saying that."

"Take the bread. It's been known to bring about world peace."

She peeks into the bag and her eyes widen with delight. I swear, they fucking sparkle when she sees the gooey, caramel, cinnamony-sweet treat stuffed with all the goodness in the baking universe. "Is it poisoned?" she asks, but this time she sounds playful.

It's a welcome change from the vitriol I usually hear, and the vitriol I usually give her back. Keeping my tone light, too, I say, "With arsenic."

She lowers her nose to the bag and sniffs. "I don't smell any poison."

"Arsenic is odorless, sweetheart," I tell her. My phone buzzes in my pocket, but I grab it and hit ignore before I even see who's calling. I want to be in *this* moment.

When she raises her face, she hands me the bag. "You better eat it first, then."

I grab a hunk of the bread and stuff it in my mouth. I chew and swallow in the most exaggerated fashion possible. "See? Safe as can be."

"Such a valiant taste-tester," she says with a flirty purr. That sound thrums through my bones. "My turn."

I rip off a smaller bite and hand it to her. But she doesn't open her palm. She steps closer to me so she's inches away. Then, she opens her mouth, and she looks like heavenly sin.

Those red lips form the loveliest O, and just like I do with some cars, I experience a kind of insta-love. It's official—my cock is head over fucking heels in love with her gorgeous mouth and thinking all sorts of filthy thoughts about how to fit inside it, the dirty bastard.

Gently, I put the bread in her mouth, my fingertips brushing over her lips. That slight touch sends electricity straight to my dick, reaffirming his obsession. She chews seductively, murmuring in delight, then swallows. How does she fucking do it? She eats sexily. She walks sexily. She grabs her phone sexily. She probably puts ketchup on fries like it's a sensual experience. Suddenly, I want to watch her do mundane things—wash laundry, open a jar of mustard, unlock her door—and determine if every single thing she does is a turn-on.

I'd file my report with the Man Council, informing them that I've indeed discovered the holy grail of sex appeal—Henley Rose Marlowe. No matter how hard I try to pretend she has the face of a groundhog, she defies me simply by being . . . her.

"You were right," she says softly.

I blink, trying to remember what I was right about. "I was?"

The corners of her lips curve up. "Yes. I feel so peaceful." She steps closer to me. "All because of the monkey bread."

Those lips dust my cheek and she whispers, "Thank you," in my ear. Her voice is everywhere, sending a sizzling charge across each inch of my skin. As if I'm buzzed. I'm not really sure where I am right now. I don't know if I'm dreaming, or floating, or fantasizing. This might very well be a mirage, or the world has turned inside out, because Henley is not only being civilized, she's being intensely flirty. It's disarming.

That's when I snap to it.

Disarming. Exactly. She's the competition. That's her trick. She probably wants to snag Livvy's next sports car from under me. She's Delilah trying to cut off Samson's hair with her flirty ways. I can't forget we're rivals, and monkey bread isn't a peace treaty; it's a panacea.

The cold war hasn't ended.

I back away from her. "Glad you like it. I should go," I say, gesturing to the sidewalk. I'm meeting David a few blocks from here at a bar.

She points at the pavement, too, and blinks as if she's reconnecting to earth. I furrow my brow, wondering. Did she feel that spark that was more than a spark?

Then I decide it's high time to check myself into a sanatorium. Maybe even ask Chase to perform that lobotomy. I'm not the kind of guy who gets fireworks or butterflies or feels as if his feet don't touch the ground over a woman. *Any* woman. And especially not this dangerous woman who has the same damn clients I have, and who's hungry for more. I'm the King of Pleasure, the master of one-night stands.

Fine. I haven't had one in a few weeks, since well before before I ran into Henley at the car show. Who cares?

"I should go, too," she says softly.

That soft side she's showing me today is one more reason why I can't let myself be fooled. It has to be an act. I take a step in the direction I'm heading. She does the same. Then another. And one more. Soon, we're at the end of the block, waiting to cross the avenue. "Just heading to a meeting," I say to fill the awkward silence.

"Same here."

We cross the street together and walk along the next block.

By the time we arrive at Eighth Avenue, neither one of us utters a word. We both just stare at each other, our eyes saying the same thing—*you've got to be kidding me.*

"Ironic, isn't it? Heading in the same direction."

"The spitting definition of irony," she quips.

As a bus rumbles to a stop when the light turns red, we cross and then we both turn right.

She gives me a side-eyed stare. "You have permission to stop following me now."

I scoff. "How do I know you're not following me?"

"As if I'd follow you."

Then she turns into Thalia's.

No fucking way.

I groan in annoyance and follow her.

In the doorway, all that sweetness from the monkey bread has evaporated. "Seriously. Enough's enough," she says. "I truly appreciate the apology and the sentiment, but we're all good, and it's time to move on, Max. I need to focus on my meeting."

She points to a table in the corner.

"And I need to focus on mine," I say, gesturing to the same goddamn spot.

David Winters rises, walks over, flashes a big buoyant grin, and says to us, "Join me."

CHAPTER 11

There are enemies and there are enemies. Even though David set this meeting up, I can't wrap my head around him wearing the black robe of doom.

Ergo, Henley must be the bad guy.

She's the Joker to my Batman, the Tom to my Jerry, the Wile E. Coyote to my Road Runner.

I stare at her, fumes surely coming from my nostrils, red clouds billowing from my eyes. How the hell could she ambush me like this? This is worse than an anvil on the head or a tail caught in a mousetrap.

Though, in all fairness, those predicaments do sound quite unpleasant. But judging from the shock on her face, she didn't see this coming. And that makes no sense, either.

I follow David and Wile E. Coyote to a quiet corner of Thalia's. It's a lounge-type place, with lots of chichi appetizers and fancily named cocktails. The chairs here are low and plush, in a shade of burgundy that matches Henley's shoes. Hey, I know my colors. No self-respecting car guy can get away without knowing a range of shades—royal purple, emerald green, sapphire blue, midnight black. Or even *lime gold*.

Henley glances at me as we cross the wood floor, David in front of us. "Did you know about this?" she whispers out of the corner of her mouth.

"No way," I bite out.

We sit.

"Please accept my apologies that I didn't alert both of you earlier about the change in number at this meeting," David says to both of us. He turns to me, looking over the edge of his wire rims. "I tried calling you a few minutes ago but it went to voice-mail."

His must have been the call I ignored. David looks at Henley. "And so did yours."

"I had mine on silent," she says.

"Well, phones are the devil, but here we all are, and I'm thrilled." David clasps his hands together. "I would introduce you, but I have a hunch you already know each other from the car show. And, I've got to be honest, once I saw the two of you interact, I couldn't resist. You really have a sort of fiery chemistry."

Fiery chemistry? Is he insane? More like acid. That's what we have.

"It gave me a great idea for the show, but I needed to work out the details, and now I have. I started noodling on this concept after our phone conversation last night, Henley."

Phone call? Last night? What the hell? I scrunch my forehead. "You two came up with an idea for the show?"

"I've asked Henley to play a role on the show, building the car as well. And bear with me, Max. I know we already brought you on, and we plan to honor that commitment and pay you the same fee." He pauses, takes a breath, and squares his shoulder. "We want you two to build the hero's car together."

Shock ripples through me. My jaw clangs to the floor, but I snap it back in place before they can see. My gut twists, and I feel as if I've been fucking played. This was my gig. My job. And here she is again, sneaking into my business.

"That so?" I ask in the most casual voice I can muster. Never let them see you sweat.

"Together?" Henley croaks out. She points to me, then to her. "You want us to work on the car together?"

I jerk my head. She seems as perplexed as I am. But isn't she in on it?

David nods enthusiastically. "I know this might seem last minute and topsy-turvy. But bear with me. That's sometimes how the TV business goes." He laughs in a self-deprecating fashion as he mimes tugging a light switch on. "New ideas pop into your head and you need to move on them lickety-split." He centers his attention on Henley. "When I first called you last night, I thought we might have you spruce up our heroine's car on the show, but the automaker wants to do that one all by itself. Since they're a sponsor, we said yes. But I remembered how well the two of you got along, and I thought, not only would it be great for the web promos we want for the car, but that kind of connection"—he threads his fingers together—"can make for a great car."

My brain goes haywire. All gray matter short-circuits. Is he for real? I scratch my head. "You think so?"

"We love both your work. You're the top two builders in Manhattan, and you make beautiful cars. Max, you bring unparalleled expertise and experience, and Henley, you bring a certain energy that we honestly think will help us win a female audience for this show. Add in the way you two seemed to connect, and it's a match made in TV heaven." He sheepishly adds,

"I sometimes fancy myself a casting director. In any case, we think it'll attract even more viewers if we have you two working on our hero's Lamborghini together."

And that's when his pitch clicks. Instantly, I hate how much sense he makes. I despise that my business side wants to agree with him. Because the *trouble ahead* sign flashing in front of me indicates I should run the other way . . . from Henley. But that's not what I'm going to do.

"I'm flattered," Henley says with a bright smile, setting her hand on the tribal band on my arm. I flinch for a split-second because I wasn't expecting the contact. She squeezes my bicep. Well, she tries. She can barely get her hand one third of the way around it. "Especially since Max is so very talented."

"And so are you," I manage to say, since I can't let her look better than me to the client. Can't let her appear more complimentary.

She meets my eyes, tsk-tsking me. "I mean it. If you'd have asked me who I wanted to build a car with, my dream co-builder, there's no question. I'd say this guy. Right here."

"Aw shucks. That's so sweet. And you know," I say, patting her hand then squeezing it, too. The monkey bread détente has ended. No more peace. Just pretending we dig each other like crackers dig cheese. "I'd say the same about you, Henley."

The only thing missing from this suck-up moment is the *pookie* nickname.

David eats it up, grinning delightedly. "That's what I'm talking about," he says, utterly enchanted with his matchmaking skills. He leans across the table, clasps one hand on my outside shoulder, the other on hers, and simply marvels at this two-headed hellfire demon he's created. "That's what I want. That kind of magic. It's going to be beautiful."

He lets go and drops back in the plush chair. "Let me tell you more about the plan. We want you to work on the customization for the Lamborghini Miura from the ground up. Conceive it. Shape it. Blueprint it. You'll need to work together every step of the way to plot each detail and then make it happen."

I get a feeling in my chest. That fire. That desire, just like I felt in his office. Like Indiana Jones when he first spotted the golden idol in the temple in *Raiders of the Lost Ark*. I'm sure Harrison Ford's fingers itched to touch it. His brain whirred trying to devise a path to it. I *want* this gig even more than I did when David first offered it to me.

Do I want to build with her? Hell fucking no.

But I can't blow this chance just because she drives me crazy. I flash back to Mark and his compliments. To Mike and how far he's come. To all the guys and gals I've helped in this business. I might have half a mind to walk right out of here because this feels like a bait and switch, but the part of me that won't back down from a challenge keeps my ass in the seat.

Henley lifts a finger. "Can you excuse me for just one little second? I need to go to the little girls' room."

"Of course," David says, gesturing in the direction of the restrooms.

I glance at her furtively as she moves through the crowd. She dips a hand into her purse and grabs her phone. Who's she going to call in the ladies' room?

Out of nowhere, that red-hot jealousy that flicked in me at the car show roars again. It burns more brightly as I picture her calling her boyfriend.

Make that white-hot envy.

CHAPTER 12

Henley's To-Do List

—Thank Jay for that amazing advice on the fly.

—Rein in the holy effing you-know-what look on my face . . . even though this is such a what-the-flippety-flip situation.

—Get down on my knees and thank my lucky stars for this opportunity.

—Call Olivia later so we can plan a girls' night out to celebrate and dance.

—Side note: Find some sort of techniques (hypnosis, perhaps?) to stop thinking Max Summers is hot . . . How can someone be hot when he needles a gal so much?

—Ask lawyer to speed up paperwork because this could be *huge*.

—Keep mouth shut.

CHAPTER 13

She returns from the restroom, stuffing her phone into her purse as she weaves her way through the early evening patrons —throngs of women in skinny jeans and heels holding cosmos and packs of men in tailored slacks and button-downs with cuffs rolled up.

Who's the lucky guy, I want to ask her.

I mean, unlucky guy. *Who's the fucking unlucky bastard you just called?* I feel sorry for any dude who has to put up with this firebrand. She must be the world's worst girlfriend. I bet she wins awards for being a nag. For refusing to let her guy hang out with his buds. For getting on his case about everything.

She sits next to me, crossing her legs. My eyes drift to her thighs. I bet she shaved this morning.

Holy shit.

What is wrong with me?

Must stop thinking of how those legs would feel hitched around my hips as I take her against the wall.

I look away from them to see her expression is giddy. Her smile is so wide; her straight, white teeth are gleaming. Her brown eyes sparkle. Her cheeks are going to hurt if she keeps this up. I clench a fist under the table then grab my beer with my other hand. I bet her stupid boyfriend put her in this extra good mood. He probably praised her on the phone for pulling off this ruse behind my back then told her he'd congratulate her with the best sex of her life.

And I nearly crush the glass.

"I'm in," Henley says.

And naturally, so am I. "I absolutely am, too."

For the next half hour, I force all the anger and annoyance out of the way. We discuss details with David over cocktails. As he sets down his empty martini glass, he checks his watch and declares it's time to take off for the theater. He tosses a Ben jamin on the table and says good-bye.

I swallow and push back my chair. Might as well hit the road. Go to the gym. Ride my bike with Chase. Then start sketching out kickass Lambo features.

Henley slams her palm to my chest. "Do not even try to insinuate that I was aware of his plan, like you did about me getting Livvy as a client."

Guess I'm not leaving yet. "I wasn't going to, but you brought it up. Did you know before this meeting what he was planning? Did you know he hired me then brought you on to share the work? Competing is one thing, but being underhanded is entirely another."

"I know that, and I know the difference. David called me a few days after the car show where I first saw you. I was busy on Livvy's car and I needed to give it my full attention. I wanted it to be perfect for her. I didn't want any *distractions*." The way she says that gives me pause, like it's her watchword. "I wasn't able to see him until this meeting, but we had talked on the phone last night. I honestly didn't know you'd be here. Max," she adds, and her voice is stripped of the barbed wire it usually contains, "I had no clue he would play this kind of bizarre car-building matchmaker game."

I arch a skeptical brow. "No clue?"

She clasps her hands together, as if she's imploring me. "No idea at all. That's not how I do business. I wouldn't try to pull the rug out from under you. I know better because you taught me better."

A small burst of pride surges in me. I loved teaching her. Loved the chance to share what I knew about our world. I'm glad some of it stuck with her. "Thanks for saying that."

"This is a huge opportunity for both of us. Let's just focus on work and not on . . . whatever this is," she says gesturing from her to me and back.

But what is this between us exactly? Bad blood? Enemies? Something more? Hell if I know. But business—that I can do. I've dealt with unruly clients. I've handled suppliers who are late. I've juggled insane deadlines and parts that don't fit and a million other things. I'm not just a businessman, I'm not just the front man—I'm a goddamn fucking mechanic.

That's what I need to be right now. A guy who fixes a problem.

That's why I'm surprised as hell when the next question out of my mouth isn't "How should we start?" but "What did your boyfriend think of the opportunity?"

"What?" She crinkles her nose and cocks her head.

"You called someone when you went to the bathroom." And that came out more defensively than I'd intended.

She wiggles her eyebrows. "You think I have a boyfriend? And you're totes jelly, aren't you?"

"No," I scoff.

She pokes my side. "Then why did you ask if I called him?" She holds up her thumb and forefinger, showing a sliver of space. "A teeny bit jelly? C'mon. Admit it. I won't tell a soul."

That question was the dumbest one to ever come out of my mouth, and trust me, it's had lots of competitors. But I can't back down yet. "Because you were there so long."

"Max," she whispers, as if she's about to confess, "I have to tell you something. I have an addiction."

"To what?" I ask with a sigh.

"To Pinterest. To DIY mason jar vase decorations with all sorts of flora and fauna. I got an alert that a new pussy-willow-themed jar had posted, and I could not resist. I have no self-control. That's why I took my phone in there." She pretends to break down and sob. "Don't tell anyone."

Yeah. I deserved that punking. "Your secret is safe with me. But how were the pussy willows?"

She raises her face and laughs. "Soft and so pretty. Just like a—"

I cut her off. "Anyway."

"I called my brother, Jay. I turn to him for advice a lot. He's kind of like a mentor."

Ouch. That's the role I was supposed to play with her. I should have been the one she called for advice. But instead, our work relationship is like a telephone line, snapped apart in a storm.

"Also, I don't have a boyfriend," she adds, and I try not to let my stupid lips quirk in a grin, because I can't stand how happy I am that she doesn't have a boyfriend. She waves at me, as if I'm a presentation on a game show. "But you . . . you must have plenty of women. You always did."

Briefly I think of Becca, the saleswoman, and Ariel, the maid, and I'm glad I can give a truthful answer when I say, "There's no one."

Now she's the one who seems to be fighting off a twitch of her lips, and that makes me want to move in closer to her, slide her hair off her shoulder, nibble on her earlobe . . .

Hear her moan.

The sexy smirk is gone as quickly as it came. Maybe I imagined it. Hell if I know if left is right anymore, let alone what a woman like Henley is thinking. I reach for my glass and take a drink. When I set it down, I aim for monkey bread peace once more. "Look, let's just concentrate on the build. Doing the best work and kicking ass on the Lambo."

"Our car baby," she coos. "We need to start making it."

"We can't waste a second."

She smirks. "I'm ovulating tomorrow, so that might be a good time to get started on our little Lambo. Do you think the connecting rod will be well-lubricated enough?"

I laugh. How the hell did we get from sabotage to dirty jokes? "The rod is always ready," I say in a deep, rumbly voice.

She drums her fingers on the table, her eyes hooking into mine. Her shoulder inches closer; *she* moves closer. "Then lubrication won't be a problem at all."

I drag a hand through my dark hair, holding her gaze. Her eyes harbor a hint of naughty, and I like it. Who am I kidding? I fucking love her innuendos, even though I've no clue why she'd make them. The air between us is thick with our silence for a moment. I don't look away, nor does she.

"I bet you could get the engine to purr," she says, breaking the silence. Her voice is a little husky this time. A little dirty.

"I bet I could get the engine to purr so goddamn loudly," I counter.

She raises a dark eyebrow and runs her finger along the edge of her cocktail glass. "I have no doubt." She brings the glass to her lips and finishes off the dregs of her mojito. Then, she's all serious. "So where should we meet? We should start on neutral ground to hammer out the details. Not at one of our shops."

"Makes sense. So, you're thinking Yankee Stadium?"

"Ha. More like Bloomingdale's."

"In the dressing room?" I toss back.

"Hey, how many babies do you think were made in dressing rooms?"

"In Bloomingdale's? In New York City? Throughout the history of time?"

"All of the above."

"Countless, tiger, countless." And somehow we're flirting again. "And Bloomingdale's is a no-go."

She taps her finger against her chin. "Maybe the M&M store. All the candy will help us be nice to each other."

I laugh. "Or the New York Public Library then, since we won't be able to yell."

It's her turn to laugh.

Then, an idea strikes me, and I tell her my plan.

Her eyes sparkle. "I like that. I haven't been on a big boat before."

"Then we'll pop your cherry tomorrow."

"Like a virgin no more."

Yeah, we're still flirting. I almost have no idea why we keep doing this, except for the obvious — it feels really fucking good.

CHAPTER 14

Henley's To-Do List

—Meet with lawyer.

—Ask John if we can really pull this off.

—Research drivetrain on Lamborghini Miura. Love that car hard!

—Figure out why I hate Max so much.

—Then figure out why I also don't hate him.

—Blow-dry hair in that new way, with the wavy curls . . . because . . . I know why. :)

—No!!

—Just no!

—He probably won't even notice my hair.

—Stop flirting with him.

—Really. I mean it.

—Don't tell me it's tempting.

—Woman-up and stop.

—Tomorrow. Stop tomorrow.

—No more innuendos. No more double meanings. No more metaphors for sexy times.

—Discuss other things with him.

—Ideas: hedgehogs, should guys be allowed to wear tank tops, merits of crunchy vs. soft-shell tacos, where do all the mismatched socks go, and how does David Copperfield pull off that crazy guessing trick.

—GUYS SHOULDN'T BE ALLOWED TO WEAR TANK TOPS. PERIOD. EVER.

CHAPTER 15

When Henley and I board the Staten Island Ferry the next day, I decide this will be a good time to practice *not* checking her out, *not* staring, *not* wondering how she'd look if I peeled those sinfully tight jeans off her lush frame.

I think instead about the boat. How big it is. How many people it can hold. How hot the engine gets. Not how lovely she looks as she walks across the deck to the railing, her hair a little different today, with lush waves near the ends.

We grab a spot by the big yellow metal railing, parking our elbows on it. We have a round-trip to Staten Island and back to figure out where to start on the car. We chat for a few minutes about basic features of the Lambo as more passengers board. Soon, the boat pulls away, and the breeze lifts her hair. It's long and wavy, and I want to run my fingers through those curls. Right now, though, her hair smacks her mouth, so she grabs a hair-tie from her wrist, and pulls it back while we talk about options for wheels and hubcaps.

As the ferry chugs across the water, cutting a path in its wake by the Statue of Liberty, we stop talking and watch the water for a few minutes. It feels natural and easy. She stares into the distance, as if she's contemplating deep thoughts. It's a new side of her. I've seen her fiery side, I've seen her flirty side, I've even seen her vulnerable side in snippets, and now I'm seeing something calmer. It's fascinating because it's so not her. Like watching a cat walk on its hind legs.

"I like big boats so far," she announces.

"Good to hear."

She raises her chin in Lady Liberty's direction. Her hands wrap tightly around the railing. "Do you ever think about how David Copperfield made that disappear?"

I jerk back, surprised by her random question. "I can honestly say I've never thought about that."

"I have," she says in an almost wistful tone. "In this one special he made the statue completely disappear. Poof. I get that it's magic and illusion, but I want to know how he did it. Did you ever see his show live?"

"No, but I went to Penn and Teller in Vegas with my brother when he graduated from med school. Those guys rock. Chase and I were determined to figure out how they pulled off every single trick."

"That's what seeing Copperfield was like for me." She leans against the railing. We're surrounded by people—tourists and locals. Some snap photos, others stare at the sea, and still others *tap, tap, tap* away on their phones. A mom with a big blue shoulder bag holds her young son's hand as he gazes at the water. "We went to see his stage show when I was a teenager, and I was dying to know how he did this crazy trick where he selected random people in the audience and then had them reveal facts about themselves, like they're wearing green boxers, or their favorite number is forty-nine."

I haven't seen that show, but I get the concept. "And the answers are actually inside a locked box that's been on the stage the whole time?"

"Yes! Exactly. And I tried to work out if the audience members could be plants, and if not, then how and when did he or his crew get the information from them into the sealed boxes within the three minutes they were on stage, with the boxes hanging from the ceiling the whole time. Maybe it's the engineer in me, but I was dying to know how he did it."

"I'm the same. Chase is, too. After we saw Penn and Teller, we were determined to figure out this one trick where they put an audience member's cell phone inside a fish and somehow the phone rang from the fish."

"Ooh, I want to know how that's done. Did you find out?"

"We tried. It drove us insane. At the show, they put the phone in a bucket on stage, then twenty seconds later, the phone rang in a box on an empty seat in the audience, and in that box was a fish and in that fish was the phone. After the show, we got on YouTube and looked up all the videos we could find of the fish in the phone. Every single one, I swear," I say, recalling the plethora of search permutations we plied Google and YouTube with to find the answers. "Was it a real dead fish or a fake dead fish? Did they record the sound of the phone ringing and then play that back? We had to know. And we thought we could figure it out."

"The mechanic and the doctor, after all," she says, tucking a few windswept strands of hair behind her ear. "Please, please, please tell me how they made a cell phone ring from inside a fish. The answer has to be online somewhere. Did you find out?" She wobbles for a moment. I dart out a hand, curling it over her hip to steady her.

"Thank you. Darn sea legs."

Nice legs. Gorgeous legs. Strong legs, I want to say. But I don't. "You'd think the answer would be somewhere on the web. And we did unearth a few details here and there, but there was always some missing piece."

"That's how the Copperfield show was for me, too," she says, shutting her eyes briefly and drawing a deep breath. She opens them. "You can make these logical conclusions about how he did a trick, and you can make assumptions, but then . . ."

I pick up the thread. "But when you get to the heart of the illusion—how he pulled it off—there are always some parts that will never make sense."

"Maybe it's a sign that we're supposed to just enjoy magic shows more?"

"Or maybe *our* enjoyment comes in trying to figure it out."

"I do like that part." She smiles faintly, then she presses her fingertips against her temples. "I think I'm getting a headache."

I furrow my brow. "You need something for it?"

She winces and closes her eyes again. When she opens them, she tips her forehead away from the water. "Mind if we go inside? I just want to sit down for a minute."

"Let's go," I say. She walks ahead of me, slower than usual. Must be those sea legs.

When we reach the doorway to the interior of the ferry, she sways and shoots out an arm to grab the wall. I slide in instantly, wrapping my hands around her shoulders. "You okay?"

Her hand flutters to her forehead, but she doesn't answer. I guide her over to the seats, and she plops down with far less grace than I've ever seen in her. "My head," she moans as she drops her forehead into her hands and yanks out her hair-tie, letting the chocolate strands spill over her shoulders. "Everything is moving."

Oh shit. I think I know what's going on now. "Henley, do you get seasick?"

"I've never been on a ferry, remember?"

"Have you been on a cruise or a boat?"

"Not since I was a little kid. Remember? I like roads."

"Me, too. But even so, I think you're seasick."

She raises her face. There's a sheen of sweat on her forehead, and her skin is pale.

"Henley," I say, genuinely worried.

"I think you're right."

"We'll reach Staten Island soon. We'll have to get off there and re-board," I say, reminding her of the ferry rules. "But we'll get on the next ferry back to Manhattan like we planned. Won't be too long from now."

"Okay," she mumbles, then she leans closer to me, resting her head on my shoulder. She breathes softly, a sweet and mournful sound. I reach across and stroke her hair.

I tell myself I'm doing this for reasons other than sheer physical want.

I can say that because it's the truth.

I love her hair, but more than that, I want her to feel well. That's a strange little shift from the last few weeks when she's most decidedly been on my Least Favorite People list.

I'm not sure which list she's on now.

"Max," she says, her voice a whisper. "I don't think guys should wear tank tops."

I laugh as I stroke her hair. "I don't even own a tank top."

CHAPTER 16

"Sweetheart."

A blond woman, her hair in a low ponytail and crinkles in the corners of her eyes, taps my shoulder. She holds the hand of a young boy, who has light locks, too.

"Yes?"

"Would you like something for your girlfriend's seasickness?"

"Oh, she's not my—"

Henley lifts her face off my shoulder and blinks at the woman. "Do you have something?" Her voice is weak. She's been resting on me since we got back on the ferry after reboarding in Staten Island.

"Dramamine. My son gets motion sickness, too."

"I'd love one," she says, and holds out a palm to the woman.

"Take two," the mom instructs, as she reaches into her big blue shoulder bag and grabs a box. She taps it against her palm and a few pills spill out. She hands a pair to Henley. "They're chewable. They work best if you take them before you get on a boat, but they should help ease the symptoms some."

Henley sighs deeply. "You're a lifesaver." She pops them in her mouth and chews.

"They taste yummy, don't they?" the boy asks.

Henley nods with wide eyes. "Like I'm eating an orange."

"I love them."

His mom squeezes his shoulder. "Ben, they're not candy."

Then she turns back to Henley. "Seasickness is the pits. As soon as I saw your face out there on the deck, I had a feeling. The weird thing is you're actually better off staring at a fixed point in the distance than sitting down. The fact that you were looking at the statue might have helped prevent it from being worse. Vomiting is no fun."

A look of horror fills Henley's eyes. "Lady Liberty was watching over me."

"She was indeed. Feel better soon."

"Thanks so much for stopping to help," I say.

"Bye-bye," the boy says, and they return to the deck.

Henley waves to their backs and says, "Yes, my non-boyfriend appreciates you very much." She pats my thigh. "Good thing you clarified right away that I'm not your girl-friend."

I roll my eyes. "I see the motion sickness hasn't dampened your fire."

"Why, of all the things you could say, would you say that first?"

I sink back in the chair, dragging a hand through my hair in frustration. "You've recovered quickly, haven't you? You're all piss and vinegar again," I say, crossing my arms and wishing the Henley who'd rested her head on my shoulder was back. This is the Henley who hates me.

But wait—why the fuck do I want that sweet version of her to resurface? We're enemies. We're rivals, and whether she has motion sickness or not doesn't change a thing.

"I'm more honey and cinnamon. And I'll have you know I'm an excellent girlfriend." She nudges me. "Want to know why?"

"I have a feeling you're going to tell me."

"One. I won't ask my man to give up poker night with his friends. In fact, I'll make you some of my amazing sandwiches and then make myself scarce so you can hang with the guys. Two. I don't nag. Three. I'm super independent. Four. I believe in mutual respect, and five—" But there's no five, because she slams her palm to her forehead and moans. "Oh God."

I snap to attention, forgetting the current battle. "You okay, tiger?"

"My head hurts so much," she says in a whimper. "Everything is spinning."

I don't think. I act.

I take her in my arms, wrapping them around her slim shoulders. I don't know that this is a cure for a headache or her dizziness, but it's all I can do. I gather her close and brush my hand over her hair. "We'll get you home, tiger. You can tell me number five on the way."

She tucks her head against my chest. Her face is buried in my shirt, her cheek against my pecs. "Max," she says softly, "sometimes it's fun to give you a hard time."

"You definitely give me a hard time," I say, and the double meaning is not lost on me.

"Max?"

"Yeah?"

"You're tall."

"I am."

"Are you six-three?"

I nod against her hair. "Nailed it."

"Max?"

"Yeah?"

"Your chest is really firm."

"Thanks."

"Max?"

"Yes, Henley?"

"That's a nice feature in a non-boyfriend."

"Feel free to make full use of it."

And she does for the next ten minutes as the vessel slows near the tip of Manhattan Island. By the time it docks, I have a warm spot on my shirt from her cheek, and I don't want to get up.

"Can I just curl up and sleep on you all day, please?" she asks.

"That's number five in what makes a good boyfriend. Letting you sleep here all day."

A tiny laugh falls from her mouth as she sighs against me. "I like number five."

"Me, too," I say, bringing her closer, since she seems to need it right now.

We stay like that for a little longer as the other ferry-goers rise and shuffle off the big boat.

"How's your head? Still dizzy?"

She nods against me. "A little, yes. I'm sorry."

"Don't be."

When the tinny announcement sounds over the loudspeaker that it's time to exit, I help her up, keeping an arm around her the whole time. Her boots click loudly against the metal ramp as we join the crowds leaving the ferry, slowly making their way to shore.

She inches closer to me, her side pressed to mine. I wrap my arm tighter around her shoulder, protecting her from a businessman jostling his way down the ramp in a rush. She sighs then loops her arm across my lower back, her hand curling over my side.

This feels way better than it should.

When we reach the sidewalk, I tug her out of the way of the crowd. She looks up at me, opens her mouth, and yawns, the hugest yawn I've ever seen, and it comes with a soundtrack as she murmurs something that suggests sleep is imminent.

Then it hits me. Dramamine makes you drowsy as fuck. I need to get this chick to her apartment, stat. I hail the next cab I see, making sure to beat out the other guys trying to snag one. I've got a woman to take care of, whether she's my girlfriend or not.

CHAPTER 17

"What's your address, tiger?"

She snuggles into my shoulder and says something I can't make out. All I hear is SoHo.

"Where to?" the cabby asks again as he peers at me in the mirror.

"Henley, where do you want me to take you?" I buckle her in.

"Home," she says in the faintest voice as she slumps against me.

"Where's home?" I try again, more insistent this time.

The cabby taps his meter.

"It's fine, man. I've got this." Then to her, I ask once more, "Where's home?"

"So . . ."

"SoHo?" I try.

And I get nothing else. I let out a long stream of air and scrub my hand over my chin. There's only one place I can take her now.

I give the cabby my address in Battery Park City, not far from here. He revs the engine, knocking Henley forward, and I'm sure this is when she's going to wake up. She'll snap to it, blink open her eyes, and say, "Are you a crazy man, trying to take me into your lair? Take me to my house, now."

But the chick snoozes through it.

She stays deep in slumber as the cabbie brakes at a light, as he slaloms through lunch-hour traffic, and as he turns onto my block in a wild arc.

Even when he reaches the building and stops the car, she stays sound asleep. I glance down at her. Her long lashes flutter over her skin, and she looks as if she's dreaming. I wonder what's going on in the faraway land where she is.

I grab my wallet and flip it open, fishing out some bills.

"Keep the change," I say to the driver, then I open the door, unbuckle my former apprentice, and lift her out of the car.

She's still asleep.

My God, it's like when your drunk friend conks out at a house party in college. Only then, you leave him there, and someone draws a penis on his face. But that's his fault—the acknowledged consequence among dudes for the crime of crashing in public. Every guy knows the rules, and every guy should stay the fuck awake if he wants a cock-free face.

There will be no Sharpie dick on this woman's cheek.

I scoop her into my arms, since that seems kinder than a fireman's carry. Call me crazy, but I've got a feeling she'd rather be handled like a princess than a victim.

I shut the cab door with the bottom of my work boot and rope her arms around my neck. I cross the sidewalk and push the building door open with my elbow. I smile at the concierge at the desk, and Edgar shoots me a curious look.

"It's time for her afternoon nap," I say, deadpan.

He simply nods and scurries to the elevator to press the button for me to the penthouse.

Henley's head flops against my shoulder, but she snuggles in closer as we ride up. When I reach my floor, I hoist her a little higher, doing my best not to wake her as I dig my keys out of my pocket. I manage to grab them without jostling her, then I head down the hall and open the door to my apartment. Afternoon sunlight streaks through the floor-to-ceiling windows, and I wonder if that'll rouse her from the land of nod.

Nope. Those Dramamine makers are some seriously honest fucking marketers.

I lower her to my big, cushy L-shaped couch. She sinks into it and shifts to her side. I yank a beige throw blanket from the arm. It's made of chenille—Mia told me when she gave it to me —and I cover Henley with it. A few strands of hair flutter across her cheek as she breathes, slow and even. Gently, I brush the strands off her face. She moves, flopping to her back.

I brace, figuring this is when she wakes up and curses me out. Except Henley doesn't curse. She just gives me shit.

She keeps snoozing, and even though I should get up and make myself busy, I stare at her for a little longer. I guess that makes me a freak, but if so, I'll wave the flag. Because, damn, this girl is so pretty to look at that it's hard to tear my gaze away. With her zonked out under a blanket, the sun casting afternoon rays over her skin, she seems so angelic. No one who saw her this second would be able to tell that there's a tiger inside this woman.

It's fierce and fiery, with claws as sharp as she needs them to be. But today, those claws have retracted, and I've seen another side to her. A side I almost wish I didn't know existed, since I have no clue what to do about it.

I drag my fingers roughly through my hair, as if that will shake off these foreign feelings. Then I stop. I just fucking stop the weird staring at her.

Because . . . I'm not that creepy.

My stomach rumbles. I head to the kitchen, slap together a quick sandwich, and chow down. Then I hang out with my laptop, sketching plans for the car as the sun dips lower in the sky, then lower still, till the flaming peach rays of the sunset flare across the horizon.

Henley stirs and flips to her side, her arm dangling off the couch. But her eyes don't open. I bury myself in work for another hour until I hear her voice.

"Did you kidnap me?"

I look up from the screen to find her sitting up and stretching on the couch. "'Nap' being the operative word. Wait —it's more like a sleep coma you've been in."

She rubs her eyes. "What time is it?"

"Just past seven."

She blinks. "Seriously?"

I nod. "You've been out of it for five hours. I would have brought you to your place, but you were dead to the world, and I didn't know the address."

She exhales deeply as she looks around my pad, taking in the huge windows and the vast space. "This is like a palace."

I smile. "Thanks. I like it here. How are you feeling?"

She stretches her neck from side to side, inhales deeply, and nods. "Worlds better. Thank you."

"Can I get you anything?"

She yawns again, covering her mouth. Then she says, "Any chance you have an extra toothbrush? I need to brush my teeth."

"I do," I say, then show her the bathroom. I grab a toothbrush from a drawer, popping it out of the pack.

"Is that so you have extra for women?"

"No. It's so I have extra for me. I happen to be quite aggressive with toothbrushes. I go through one a week."

Her eyebrows rise. "You're a toothbrush abuser?"

I nod. "I am and I'm not afraid to admit it. The dentist says I need to tone it down, but I prefer to think of myself as a power user. I brush often and vigorously, and I've invested in toothbrush stock."

She bounces as if this makes her outrageously happy. "I love to go wild on toothbrushes, too." She checks out her reflection in the mirror, and her jaw drops. She spins around.

"Max," she whispers in awe as she stares at a particular bathroom fixture.

"What is it?"

She points then walks as if in a trance to the tub. She falls to her knees and hugs the rim. "You have a claw-foot tub. Marry me now."

I crack up. "How about tomorrow morning? City Hall is nearby, but it's closed for the night."

She frowns. "Do you have any idea how small my shower is?"

I shake my head. "No. Tell me how small it is."

"It's the size of a high school gym locker." She strokes the edge of the white marble tub. "This feels incredible. A claw-foot tub is pretty much the greatest thing in the world. And you want to know the worst part?" She stands and marches over to me, narrowing her eyes. "It's wasted on you."

I furrow my brow. "Why would you say that?"

She flings her arm out at the tub. "It's beautiful and perfect and pristine."

I laugh again. "I like to keep my home clean."

"You probably never even use it."

That's when I laugh the hardest. I raise an eyebrow. "Surprise. I use it plenty."

She cocks her head to the separate shower stall. It's much larger than a locker. It's the size of most bathrooms. "You have a ginormous shower and a claw-foot tub, and you use the tub?" Her eyes bug out.

"Not all the time. But yeah, I do use it."

She points at me, swiveling her finger. "*You*? You like to soak in the tub?"

I nod proudly. "Bubble bath. Bath bombs. The whole nine yards, tiger." I'm not the least bit embarrassed to admit this to her, maybe because she's slept on my chest, and my shoulder, and my couch.

She shakes her head like this doesn't compute. "I've never known a man to like baths."

I shrug. "Guess you don't know this man."

A smile tugs at the corner of her lips. "Guess I don't."

I reach into the medicine cabinet and hand her some minty Crest, then leave her alone.

When she emerges a few minutes later, she makes a declaration.

Chapter 18

Henley's To-Do List

—Tell him your fish theory.

—Say thank-you profusely because, holy moly, I was a mess on the ferry!

—Ask Olivia what the hell this means. My bestie always knows this stuff.

—Find a way to steal Max's tub.

—Idea: slip him some Dramamine and spend the night in the tub?

—Bad idea. Keep your eye on the ball. This is your big chance.

—Don't blow it.

CHAPTER 19

"Fish scent."

I arch a brow as she stands at the dining room table, an *aha* look on her face.

"Feel free to elaborate so that your random declaration makes sense."

"They use the scent of a fish. Penn and Teller." She paces around the table, a *eureka* sort of excitement radiating off her. "Think about it. Perfume makers can bottle any sort of scent, from roses to peach to lilies to disgusting scents like ash or smoke. Why not the scent of a fish? Maybe the magicians use a fake fish, but it seems totally real because—well, let's be honest, anything can be made to look real."

I nod. "Sure. Hollywood. CGI. I'm with you," I say, because of course I've considered the fake fish idea before.

"But fish has a very noticeable smell. If they want the fish to appear real, it has to smell real, too. That would seem to be the sticking point. But scents can be manufactured, too. What if they made a fishy smell?"

A grin spreads across my face. "That's kind of brilliant."

She winks. "I'm good at figuring things out." She grabs a chair next to me, sets her hands on the table, and clears her throat. "Max, thank you. Seriously. Thank you for taking care of me today. I had no idea I was going to be that out of it. And you were a true gentleman. It means the world to me. If I were you, I'd have mocked me all day. But you didn't, and I appreciate that so much."

"I wouldn't mock you for having an adverse reaction to a drug. Besides, it's not that adverse to be drowsy."

"Can I get you dinner or something? Wait," she says, slashing her hand through the air as if she's erasing the thought. "Want to order in and then, you know, try to do some work on the car? Since we didn't get to it earlier and you're about as much of a work junkie as I am." She shoots me a knowing smile.

"Which would mean I'm obsessed with it?"

She smiles. "Yes."

"Guilty as charged. Also, I love your plan, and I did some work today that I'd like to show you. Do you like Thai?"

"It's my favorite, and it will be my treat. I insist. You did let me get acquainted with your couch all day long, after all."

"Pretty sure the couch enjoyed its day, too," I say, and it sounds like I'm flirting with her. Maybe we're making progress.

* * *

We spend the next few hours diving into noodles and chicken satay as we debate some of the features of our hero's Lambo. We settle on a few, and I'm remarkably surprised at how well we work together. I expected a bloody battle. But then, up until the Mustang fiasco, we always did work well together.

When the clock ticks toward ten, she says, "I guess I should go."

There's a note of longing in her voice. I don't know what to make of it, and I'm not going to attempt to read the tea leaves of Henley, so I ask if she wants me to order an Uber.

She doesn't answer right away, and my heart stutters, wondering what she wants. She doesn't want to stay over, does she? *Oh shit.* Is she game for my favorite indulgence ever? A burst of red-hot excitement tears through my body over the possibilities, even though it would be so immensely stupid to screw her. I tell myself that over and over as I wait for her to speak again.

Please say you want to stay so I can bang you against the wall.

Shit. No. I work with this woman. I can't do that. Must extinguish all wall-banging urges immediately. I shut my eyes momentarily, snuffing them out.

"Unless . . ."

She nibbles on the corner of her lips and my dick hardens. Screw the wall. The dining room table works just fine. Lift her up, spread her legs, make her fucking soar in pleasure.

Except, she's not looking at me with sex eyes. She's staring at my bathroom.

She doesn't want me. She wants my fucking tub. Great. Just great.

"Just say it," I urge.

"Say what?"

"You're only being nice to me for access to the bath."

"That's so not true."

"Say it."

"It's not true," she says, but I hear the smirk in her voice.

"Henley," I say, adopting a tone as if I'm talking to a kid, "do you want to take a bath?"

"Oh God, I do, I do, I do." There's nothing childish about her reply. She sounds desperate, full of desire. Like that, with her big, brown eyes, her sweet, sexy smile, her brown hair spilling down her shoulders, she's irresistible. She's the lion, she's the tiger, and she's the kitten you can't not take home.

That's why I somehow decide it's perfectly suitable for this gorgeous creature to be naked in my apartment while I'm in another room. "Do it."

She claps with glee. "I remembered reason five why I make a good girlfriend."

"What's that?"

"I'm very neat in the bathroom, and I always put the towels and bubble bath away."

I nod in the direction of the tub. "Get your ass in the tub or I'll rescind my offer."

She does, snapping shut the door to the bathroom. A few seconds later, the sound of running water fills the air. The image of her stripping to nothing fills my brain.

"Idiot," I mutter to myself, as I pour a glass of Scotch to get me through this Herculean challenge. "Do you fucking like torture?"

Evidently, I do.

But I also like it when she calls my name twenty minutes later. I leave the living room and my empty Scotch glass, and stand at the door of the bathroom. My hand is on the doorknob. She can't possibly want me to come in, can she?

"Max," she shouts again, "I have an idea for the wheels."

"You want to just shout through the door, or do you think it can wait till you get out?" I ask drily.

"It can't wait! You have to come in."

No. No. Just no. Just no fucking way. This is a trick. A setup. A test. And if it's none of those, it's definitely a very bad idea.

"You're in the tub, Henley," I say, pointing out the obvious.

Water sloshes loudly from the tub, hitting the floor. "I know, and it's to die for. I'm also covered in bubbles, so don't worry. You won't see any of my girlfriend parts."

I laugh, a hearty chuckle from deep in my belly. She's killing me with the girlfriend or non-girlfriend routine. But even though my hand is wrapped tight around the doorknob, common sense has me in its grip. "I'll catch you when you're not naked."

"Max, I swear I'm decent. I used so many bubbles I'm going to need to replace your ocean bubble bath. By the way, it's super manly, so you won't have to worry about me smelling like a girl. I smell like a dude, and I want to talk about tires. Get in here. Think of me as one of the guys."

One of the guys. One of the guys. One of the guys. She could never be one of the guys, but I let myself believe my own line of bullshit.

It's my excuse for doing something I shouldn't do.

For turning the knob.

For pushing open the door.

For stepping into the warm, steamy bathroom that smells like the ocean. The *feminine* ocean.

For shutting the door.

Most of all, for looking at her. She's like a dark-haired mermaid, a Venus of the sea.

Her hair is twisted high on her head in a messy bun. Her knees poke out of the water. Her arms rest on the edge of the tub. Her body, as promised, is submerged under gobs and gobs of bubbles.

None of the cover-up matters.

I can imagine her nudity perfectly.

My throat dries. I try to swallow. It's like a desert in my mouth. I should look away. I should be cool with this. But I can't. I just fucking can't.

"So here's what I was thinking . . ." She launches into her idea for the wheels as I cross my arms and lean against the door. Everything she says sounds good, and everything she does drives me fucking crazy. I listen, and I try not to stare. Then, I listen and I stare unabashedly. She's so normal about this, as if it's acceptable to lounge naked in my tub at this hour and discuss a car.

It's not normal.

It's insanely arousing.

It's ridiculously hot.

And I'm so fucking turned on I can barely take it. Everything about this moment is wildly inappropriate, and yet she's chattering on about how the rubber meets the road.

She stares at me. "What do you think?"

"Sounds good," I mutter.

"Really?"

"Yeah. Great."

She narrows her eyes and shifts ever so slightly but just enough for the rosy peak of her right nipple to rise above the bubbles before it sinks back down.

There's no breath in my lungs. There's no blood in my brain. I can't think. I can only *want*. I want her so much. And I hate that I feel this way.

"You think so?"

I blink, and then I unravel. "Yeah. Look. I said it's great," I say roughly. Then I point at her, waving dismissively. "And you need to fucking wrap it up."

"What?" she asks, blinking.

"I'm tired." Anger colors my tone. "You should go."

"Oh. Okay." She sounds chastened, a dog with her tail between her legs, but I can't care. I leave, slamming the door shut.

I hear water splashing around, then the suction of the drain.

CHAPTER 20

Three minutes later, she stands at the door, hastily dressed, damp strands from her bun hitting her face. "Are you okay?"

I rub my hand across the back of my neck, not answering her question. "I ordered an Uber. I gave it an address I knew in SoI Io. You'll need to adjust it to yours. But it's on my account."

"Okay." To say she seems hurt would be a gross understatement. She looks precisely like what she is—a woman being kicked out of a man's pad. "Did I do something wrong?"

I grit my teeth, trying to rein in my annoyance. But it slithers up, fighting to break free. I clench my fists. "I can't talk to you while you're naked in the tub. Don't you get that? That's just fucking wrong. We work together. We can't be this chummy. This whole night was a huge mistake."

Her eyes widen, starting to fill with tears, but she draws a deep, shaky breath. "Message received."

"I'll walk you out," I say, because I can't be a total dick.

"That's not necessary." Her voice is hard again.

"I'm doing it anyway."

She narrows her eyes and looks away, then yanks open my door. She walks two paces ahead and stabs the down button at the elevator. When it arrives, we ride in silence. We reach the lobby, and she says, "I can take it from here."

I don't listen to her. I walk her out the door to the curb and make sure she's safely inside the white Honda.

She doesn't say good-bye. I don't either. I seethe as I head back upstairs.

I stalk down the hallway, so much fucking annoyance rolling off me that I swear I can smell it—the fumes of my own frustration.

I reach my place, and the second the door slams shut behind me, my belt is undone, my hand is in my briefs, and I grab my cock. My aching, throbbing, insistent cock.

I stroke hard, letting the back of my head hit the door, shutting my eyes. Roughly, with one desperate goal, I grip my shaft and I jack it.

I can't take this. I can't stand being this attracted to her.

Wanting to touch her.

Wanting to fuck her.

Wanting to kiss her

Wanting to fucking get to know her. Most of all, I can't stand *that*. How much I'm starting to like her, and I can't like her. I just fucking can't.

But I can't walk around this hard. This aroused. This immensely turned on by everything she does.

She's killing me, and she doesn't even know it.

I groan as I wrap my fist tighter. I shuttle my palm up and down, rocking into it. My jeans slide down my hips, and the belt buckle smacks the door with every tug.

"Fuck," I mutter as I jerk faster.

Tighter.

Rougher.

I'm fucking my fist, like the world is on fire. My body is on fire. Unholy pleasure sizzles under my skin as I fight for some goddamn relief.

Every muscle in me is tight. Tense. Wound the fuck up from her.

Her sweet hair in my nose.

Her face on my shoulder.

Her nudges, her looks, her smile, her tits. Her majestic, wonderful tits.

God, I want to tear off her clothes and slam her to the wall. I want to crush her lips with my mouth, taste her tongue, suck on her neck. Feast on those tits until I get down on my knees and bury my tongue in her pussy.

I burn. Everywhere. Lust rattles through my bones as I imagine that first taste. How wet she'd be. How sweet she'd taste. How dizzy it would make me to sink my face between her legs and eat her till she came all the fuck over my jaw.

I want to drive her to the brink of insanity, like she's done to me. I want her crazy with desire, grabbing my hair, and moaning my name until she can't stop.

I groan so loudly it's criminal. The noises I make could wake the neighbors. I don't give a shit. Lust surges down my spine, a warning shot. I'm close, so damn close, and I'm desperate.

I hate how I feel, but I fucking love how this feels, too. I have never needed a release more. Never.

My mind trips back to a few minutes ago. To the flash of that perfect nipple, tipped up, begging me to suck on it. That nipple called out to me. I wanted to bite it. Wanted to see how much of her breast fits in my mouth.

I want her to feel this same goddamn frustration.

With my other hand, I grip my balls hard, tugging as I jack my cock more roughly. Another drop of liquid beads at the head, and I spread it down my shaft, barely coating me. Who fucking cares. I don't need lube or lotion for this.

Smack goes my belt buckle against the door.

Slap goes my hand on my dick.

Henley, Henley, Henley goes my brain.

I grunt like an animal, a fucking desperate man.

If there's a God, Henley will be in her apartment any second, jamming her hand down her panties and fucking herself with her fingers.

And that's it.

The switch flips as I think of her sweet, hot pussy. There's no place I'd rather be than inside it. There's no one I want but her.

My quads tighten. My muscles burn, and a shock of pleasure surges down my spine.

Seconds later, I'm there.

I come hard in my hand. It feels fucking amazing, like silver sparks raining from the sky.

But the pleasure ends far too quickly. It subsides in mere seconds, and I'm left with this empty, terrible want as I stand against my door, my belt undone, and my hand coated in my orgasm.

The trouble is I'm not sure she's out of my system.

In fact, as I wash my hands, I peer behind me in the mirror's reflection. The towels she used are neatly hung. The bubble bath lines the shelf. The tub is pristine.

She did everything she said a good girlfriend would do. It's almost like she was never here at all. And as I brush my teeth, nearly chewing through a new brush, I can't stop thinking about her.

I leave the bathroom and strip down to nothing, and she's still in my head. When I get into bed, I wish she was stepping out of the bath, drying off, and wandering into my room.

With that in mind, I try again to get her out of my system. Lying on the white sheets, I picture her climbing over me, riding my face.

Then in the morning, as I shower, she's on her knees taking my cock in her mouth, letting me fuck her lips.

Maybe, just maybe, she's out of my system now.

CHAPTER 21

Henley's To-Do List

—Meet John to discuss strategy.

—Prep for appointment with lawyer.

—Find new smoothie mix that makes me not give a crap about Max, that jerk.

—Drink it up. It isn't getting any easier building this Lambo with him.

—Practice my game face.

—Don't let on the ice-age treatment bothers me.

CHAPTER 22

I ring the buzzer of the walk-up on 18th Street, craning my neck to get a glimpse of the third floor.

A flower planter hangs from the window as promised—a cheery green one, bursting with tiger lilies. Fall flowers, Josie told me.

I manage a smile, thinking of the woman my brother loves. Chase and Josie have re-moved in together. They found a new pad in Chelsea, and they're having a mini housewarming party with the gang.

Mia suggested I bring a bottle of wine and a kickass new Scrabble dictionary, so that's what I've got in hand. As I wait, I glance behind me at the tree-lined block. A twenty-something brunette in sunglasses walks a pug down the street, and for a brief second, I imagine Henley.

I jerk my head away.

Somehow, I've managed to work with her for the last week since Bubble-Bath-Nipplegate.

It hasn't been easy, but we've pulled it off, mostly by taking turns on the Lambo. It's been living in my shop since I have more room. In the last week of working on the car, the network

JOY RIDE · 123

shot a few promos, including one with the actor Brick Wilson, as well as Henley and me. The buffer of Brick made it easier to deal with her.

When the buzzer sounds, I let thoughts of the show go as I head into Chase's building. I walk up two flights of steps to a long hallway on the third floor. My little brother stands in the doorway. Growing up, he was the happiest fella in the world, and that's even truer now that he and Josie are officially an item. His hazel eyes shine.

"Glad you could make it. I thought I'd have to surgically remove you from a Ferrari or an Aston Martin to get you here," he says, then claps me on the back. "You've been working hard?"

"Is there any other kind of work?"

Chase pretends to stare at the ceiling. "Nope." He gestures me into his and Josie's new digs. I've seen his place once before, and it's perfect for them—a one-bedroom with exposed brick walls and lots of light. On the wall by the door is a framed cartoon drawing of a cat in an apron serving cupcakes to a small dog. It has Nick Hammer's style all over it. I suspect the cartoonist drew it for his sister, and the signature in the corner confirms that. Nick is parked on the couch with his wife, Harper, next to him. They wave hello, and I say hi. On the coffee table in the living room, a huge bouquet of daisies spills over the edge of a vase, and a Scrabble board sits next to it. I spot Wyatt and Natalie in the kitchen, leaning into the fridge.

"Max!" Josie rushes over and throws her arms around me. "So good to see you. How did the monkey bread go over?"

"Great," I say, then look around, eager to move to a new topic.

She narrows her eyes. "Are you sure?"

"Yeah, it's amazing. Who doesn't love monkey bread?"

Chase gives me a studious stare as he taps his head. "Monkey bread? Hmm. Wait, I've got it." He snaps his fingers. "You bought monkey bread for Henley."

I scoff. Josie laughs.

"Did he?" Chase asks Josie.

She shrugs. "He didn't tell me who he bought it for. He just said it was a gift for a girl, and I said if she liked the monkey bread, then next time he should get her cinnamon rolls."

"Ooh, get me cinnamon rolls, pretty please."

The comment comes from Spencer, who had bounded up the steps with his wife, Charlotte, to join us in the entryway. "I love cinnamon rolls. Please say they're for me."

"Are you a girl?" Nick tosses out from the couch to his best buddy.

Spencer's eyes drift downward. "Nope. But men can like cinnamon rolls."

Nick rolls his eyes from behind his glasses. "She said he was getting them for a girl, dickhead. That's why I said it."

"Who is Max buying cinnamon rolls for?" Harper calls out from her spot next to Nick.

"Yes, inquiring minds want to know," Charlotte chimes in.

I grit my teeth and shove past them into the kitchen, setting down the wine and the wrapped gift.

"Ooh, Maxi-boy likes someone," Wyatt says as he strides through the kitchen, holding a beer.

"How about we talk about Chase and Josie's new apartment, not who I bought fucking baked goods for," I say.

The women all laugh. "Max," Josie says softly, setting her hand on my back as the others wander into the living room, "if you ever need girl advice, just ask me. Don't worry about these wieners. I'll help you. I adore you."

"Thanks," I mutter.

She tugs me aside, pulling me near the fridge and as out of earshot as possible. "Seriously. Are you okay? You're grouchy, and I know you've got a natural grouch in you, but you seem grouchier than usual."

"He hasn't gotten laid in a while, probably," Chase says as he walks by.

Josie shoots him a *shut up now* stare.

"What? He alluded to it on the bike ride the other day," Chase says, and he's right. Not that I blabber about my sex life to him, but when we were riding one morning, he made a comment about a hot woman who rode past us, saying I should chase her, and I said it had been a while.

"Is it Henley?" Josie asks.

I don't say anything. My silence is my yes.

"You like her?"

"No, I don't," I say, shaking my head. "I don't like her at all. Not one bit."

Josie gives me a smile then brushes a strand of pink-tipped hair off her neck. "Got it. But if you *were* to like her, she probably likes you, too."

I snap my head to stare at her. "Why would you say that?"

"I saw one of the web promos for the car you're building for the detective show. The one with you, Brick, and Henley. I could see it in her eyes."

Henley's chocolate-brown eyes with flecks of gold. Her eyes that are like a color wheel for her emotions. They darken when she's angry; they lighten when she's vulnerable.

Josie moves to take a plate of appetizers to the living room, while Chase grips my shoulder. "Dude, she's right. You're like Captain Grouchy Pants."

I look away, glancing at the thermostat on the wall. I put my hand on it, sliding up the needle. "Hey Chase, since this a house-warming party, can I just turn up the heat and call it good?"

A slow clap sounds from the couch. Spencer applauds me with a proud shine in his eyes. "Well done. I doff my pun hat to you."

"Glad I could entertain you."

That's how I know I'm not really affected by Henley. If I were, I wouldn't be able to make jokes. I wouldn't enjoy the meal. I wouldn't have fun with my friends.

I do all of those things, thank you very much. There's not an ounce of grouch in me.

I can't say the same for Henley the next time I see her.

CHAPTER 23

Henley taps the toe of her combat boot against the sidewalk as if she's going to jackhammer a hole through the concrete. She takes an inhalation so deep it makes her shoulders rise. Breath seems to puff from her nostrils.

Let's play *Why Does Henley Hate Me Today?*

Might it still be because I kicked her out of my house? We haven't exactly played the *what makes a good girlfriend or boyfriend* game since that night. Or is there lingering animosity over the pink slip I gave her five years ago? Let's just be safe and assume it's both.

The coffee I picked up for her isn't likely to abate her disdain. I've got a steaming cup in each hand from the deli around the corner, the only place nearby open this early on a Sunday.

I walk the final distance to her, crossing the small lot in front of my garage and hand her a cup. "Good morning, sunshine."

She doesn't take the cup. "I don't like coffee."

"Who doesn't like coffee?"

"People who don't like coffee, that's who. I've never liked it," she adds with a defiant little lift of her chin.

"Never?" I arch an eyebrow skeptically. "When did you last try it?"

"Shortly after college. Didn't like it then, either."

Shortly after college is when she worked for me. "You should try it again."

"Does coffee change?"

"No. But *tastes* do. Maybe your tastes have changed."

She stares at me over the top of her sunglasses, pink with sparkles on the frame. They make me think of the unicorn shirt she wore to the meeting at Thalia's—they're that cute. They contrast with her eyes, so dark this morning they're nearly black. "I highly doubt my tastes have changed in five years."

Five years. The subtext of this conversation isn't lost on me.

I raise my hands, the two blue cups I'm holding like white flags. "What do you like to drink, then?"

She doesn't answer. Instead, she takes one of the cups, yanking it from my hand. "Do you have sugar?"

"In my pocket," I say, grabbing a few packs for her. "So you like it sweet?"

She adopts a too-big smile. "Sweetness helps. We'll see if this is enough."

She stuffs the sugars into her giant black purse. Something silky hangs over the edge of the purse, like she has a change of clothes in there. She jams the fabric back inside. In her other hand is a pad of paper. It looks like the kind you snag from a hotel. I check out the name. The Hudson over on 58th, not far from here. The wheels in my brain turn. The Hudson is the ultimate boutique hotel for the young and beautiful and horny. It's the kind of hotel you check into when you want to have hot hotel sex. Maybe that's why she arrived early. Maybe that's why she has extra clothes in her bag. Maybe she fucking spent the night in one of those no-sleeping-allowed-only-fucking-is-permitted beds.

I burn with jealousy. "Late night at the Hudson?"

"Seriously?" Her eyes try to laser off my face as she waggles the note pad in her hand, like it's a weapon she could fire off at me any second. "This is our to-do list. We have a lot to tackle today. I was hoping you would've been early."

I make a big production of looking at my watch. I tap the face. I show her the hands. "It's nine a.m. sharp. This is when we agreed to meet."

"I was here at eight forty-five," she says, straightening her shoulders.

"Would you like a gold star for punctuality?" I ask as I slide the key into the lock and open the door. The alarm sounds its warning, and I enter a series of numbers, then another set before it turns off.

"No, I don't care about whatever little rewards you do or don't feel like bestowing at your whim."

"You think I bestow stars at whim? There's a detailed system in place listing qualifications for gold, silver, and bronze. No whim involved, tiger," I say, then down some of the coffee. It's burn-your-tongue-off hot. Somehow, this suits me fine today.

She huffs. "My, my, aren't you a particular one."

"Says the woman who's giving me a hard time for showing up on the dot."

"I'm here early because I'm worried about the seat," she says, as she follows me into the small front office. I unlock the side door into the garage. It's like a bank vault in here some days, given what we store inside.

"What about the seat?" I survey the garage, confirming the vehicles that slept over are still here. The Lambo is safe and sound, as well as a canary-yellow 1971 Dodge Challenger that Sam has been taking the lead on restoring. He asked me the other day for a little help on the engine to make it sing, but otherwise he's doing a great job on his own, coming in after hours and on weekends to work on it. We've got a Chevelle here, too.

I inhale deeply. Ah, the scent of motor oil and leather. It's better than freshly ground coffee.

Henley sets her purse on a chair. She takes the lid off the coffee, tears open a few sugar packets, and pours them into the drink. "I did some research on Brick's height," Henley says, as she drops the empty packets into a nearby trash bin.

"Okay," I say, as I run a hand on the cherry-red hood of the Lambo. "Did you sleep well last night, girl?" I whisper to the car.

Laughter booms behind me. I swivel around. Henley cackles, her mouth wide open. "Did you just talk to the car?"

"Of course," I say, owning my affection for this beauty. I stroke the hood, as if she's a loyal dog and I'm petting her in the morning. "She likes a nice, tender touch when she wakes up."

"Don't we all," she mutters, and I snap up my head and meet her eyes. Her sunglasses are off now; she wears them like a headband.

"Do we all?" I ask, turning her words around on her.

She narrows her eyes. Bitter dark chocolate is their color. "The seat, Max. Let's talk about the seat."

"What's wrong with the seat?"

She grabs her phone from her back pocket, stands next to me, and shows me a browser window with Brick Wilson's IMDB info.

"He is six foot four, right?" I take another drink of the near-boiling beverage. I pretend it's a vitamin that fortifies me against her.

A small smile plays on her lips as she shakes her head. "I was researching him last night. Don't get me wrong. He's one tall man, but he's not six foot four."

"How do you know?"

"I watched the video of the three of us, then I studied the publicity shot."

"And?" I ask, intrigued to see where she's going.

"He's shorter than you," she says, a hint of excitement in her tone, as if she's uncovered a clue to buried treasure. "By about an inch."

I scrub a hand over my jaw. "You could tell in the pictures and videos that he's six foot two?"

She points with two fingers at her eyes. "These work. And women are always being lied to about how many inches something is, so I've learned that a girl has to be able to tell size on her own."

"*Tell size*? Is that like telling time?"

"Yes. But you can only do it *fully* at certain times . . . so it can be *harder*. Unless you're really, really good. Like me."

I rein in a grin. I want to tell her *well-played*. But we wound up back in this barbed-wire boat after too many dirty innuendos that went too far. "So we don't need to move the seat back as much as we planned?"

"Nope. The network must have given us his glamour height by mistake, not his real height. So we slice off two inches," she says, and I cringe, picturing her as a demon barber, ready to cut.

"You okay?" she asks.

"Just a little uncomfortable with the juxtaposition of the word *slice* next to *inches*."

She rolls her eyes. Their shade is lighter now, like a walnut. I need to develop a cheat sheet to read her emotions, but I think this color corresponds to amused. "You have to know I'm not a woman who likes *less* inches. It pains me, too."

My jaw nearly comes unhinged, but I resist the urge to tell her that with me, she'd get all the inches she wants and then some. I resist it with another scalding drink of coffee.

She takes a sip of hers. Her nose crinkles, and her lips curl in clear dislike.

"I take it your tastes haven't changed?"

She shakes her head and sets down the coffee on a work-bench. My heart sinks the littlest bit. I wanted her to like the coffee, or at least to have another sip. To give it a chance.

Maybe to give something else a chance. Some*one.*

I shake off that thought.

She's all business now. "We should call David and tell him about the discrepancy."

I flash back to the comments I made to Sam when he went out with Karen at John Smith Rides, then to my own concerns about getting too cozy with someone who works for my main rival. "All business" is how I should behave, too.

"Absolutely. And I'm impressed with your attention to detail," I say.

After all, lack of attention to detail on the Mustang is what got her into trouble with me years ago.

"I've had to learn from my mistake," she says, an emphasis on *mistake.*

And it's unmistakable that she's referring to my comment during the tub incident.

CHAPTER 24

Henley's To-Do List

—Give him a piece of my mind.

CHAPTER 25

Henley plays cameraperson as I work on the seat adjustments. During a quick call to update David on the inch issue—he apologized profusely for giving us the glamour height—he asked if we'd be willing to shoot a DIY-style video today on our work. "Though, please don't reveal his real height," he told us.

And so the girl I got off to a week ago thanks to Bubble-Bath-Nipplegate is capturing me on her cell phone for all posterity.

"Tell us about the seat, Mr. Summers."

I give an overview of the plans for it, keeping the details straightforward and the height close to the vest, per David's request. Even though there's no love lost between car-build reality shows and me, I don't mind these promos. The work is real, and we're not asked to crank the metal music or talk like streetwise presenters. As I finish the explanation, I add, "And these cars are made for drivers who are average height and build."

"But Brick is tall and broad. He's a big man, right?"

I nod. "That's why we need to customize the seat."

"Besides," Henley quips from next to her cell phone, "you know what they say about big men?"

I resist the urge to roll my eyes. "What do they say about big men?"

She pauses, wiggles an eyebrow, and then performs a pretend drumroll with one hand. "A big man needs a big seat."

"That he does."

She taps her phone, ending the video. She drops the device back into her jeans. "You thought I was going to say something inappropriate?"

"Gee, Queen of Inches, I wonder why I'd think that?"

She winks. "I thought the network would enjoy a little fun banter between us. But we can go back to hating each other now."

I sigh heavily as we work on the seat, crouching close to each other by the driver's side. "I don't hate you, Henley."

"Could have fooled me."

She's mostly quiet the rest of the day, and so am I. We become the living, breathing definition of *all business* as we tackle this car.

When it's time to wrap up in the early evening, she grabs her purse and heads to the restroom. When she returns, her hair is thicker and fuller than before, and her lips shine with red gloss. She takes a deep breath then speaks in an even tone. "I have a question for you."

"Have at it."

"Did it surprise you that I could solve a problem?"

"Huh?" I ask as I gather the tools and put them away.

"You acted surprised that I figured out the issue with the seat."

I shake my head as I sort the wrenches into their drawers. "No. I wasn't surprised you figured it out."

"You seemed shocked." Her pitch rises.

"Well, I wasn't." My voice tightens.

"Is it because you really never thought I would amount to anything?"

I blink. "Are you insane? I always thought you were crazy talented."

"You didn't promote me because of one mistake on the Mustang. But maybe it wasn't about one mistake. Maybe it was that you never thought I was good enough."

I shake my head, my jaw clenching. "You went out and proved me wrong then, so why do you care what I thought?"

"That's a good question, isn't it?" She taps her chin. "Why do I care?"

I park my hands on my hips. "You tell me."

She shakes her head and walks toward the rear of the Lambo, then swivels around and paces back. As I snap a tool drawer closed, she enters my line of sight. I straighten, and she's standing right in front of me, her eyes brimming with red-hot pissed-off-ness.

Fuck the color wheel. She's a forest fire right now, branches and tree trunks snapping to the ground in a blaze. She bites out the next words. "There's something I need to say to you."

I tense because this can't be good. I lean against the hood of the Challenger. "Say it."

"Can you stop making insinuations about what I do after hours?"

I furrow my brow. "What are you talking about?"

She levels a hard stare at me. "You made the boyfriend comment at Thalia's. You thought I was calling some guy when I was actually peeing and calling my brother. Earlier, you made some sort of insinuation about what I was doing at the Hudson because I have a notepad from the hotel. Are you obsessed with my nighttime activities?"

"No," I scoff, rolling my eyes for good measure. "I don't think of what you do at night. Or during the day either."

It's a bald-faced lie. I've surpassed my recommended daily allowance of thoughts about one woman ever since she returned to town.

"Good. Because you shouldn't be thinking of what I'm doing." She flicks her hair off her shoulder. My eyes follow her hand, watching every move she makes.

A waft of something that smells like spring apples floats by. Did she spray perfume on her neck when she was in the restroom? My mouth waters, and my pulse pounds in my ears. The woman looks and smells absolutely sexy at five in the evening after working on a car all day—from mechanic to sexpot in one quick restroom trip.

Reality smacks me in the gut. She probably has a date tonight. She's probably seeing whoever she screwed at the Hudson last night. My jaw tightens. My fists clench.

That's why she's laying down the law with me. So I can stay the fuck out of her personal life. And you know what? That's exactly where I need to be.

Out.

I shrug, like this conversation is pointless. "I'm not thinking at all about what you do."

"Good." She raises that stubborn little chin. "Because I'm not thinking about what you do."

But I am thinking of that little streak of grease on her chin that I just noticed. I picture her meeting her date with that dirt on her face. Even I'm not that much of an asshole. I step closer, bring my thumb to my tongue, and wet it. She watches me curiously.

"You have . . ." I point in the direction of the streak.

She lifts her hand to wipe it.

"Don't do that," I say, harshly. "You'll smudge it and look stupid."

I bring my thumb to her face. Her big brown eyes follow my hand. Those eyes sparkle, and up close like this they darken. But not in that angry way I've seen. It's different now, as if they're blazing as she watches every move I make. When the pad of my thumb presses against her cheek, her breath hitches.

As I rub my thumb over her skin, a small gasp of air follows, then she clamps her lips shut.

Back and forth I rub, removing the streak. She's inches from me now, so close I can tell she sprayed the spring apple perfume on her collarbone. So near I can smell her cinnamon breath.

My pulse thunders.

When I finish, I don't let go of her face. I cradle her jaw in my hand.

It's her move.

And she makes it.

CHAPTER 26

She leans into my hand, and her lips part the slightest bit.

I crack.

I slam my mouth to hers.

I don't take my time. I don't ease into it. My lips crush hers, and I kiss her as if it's all I've wanted to do since the first time I saw her slide out from under a car in my garage. Since she sauntered up to me at the show weeks ago. Since the night in my tub.

I kiss her as if I've suffered without kissing her. She kisses me back the same way.

We aren't gentle. We aren't slow. We touch with fire and anger. She opens her mouth, and I sweep my tongue across hers, groaning as I devour her taste.

She's fresh and cinnamony, and it strikes me that she brushed her teeth in the restroom. The fact that I don't know if she did it for me or wherever she's going next makes me crush her lips harder. I grab her face, clasping her cheeks roughly as I back her up to the Challenger and shove her against the hood.

Her hands slide up my chest, and lust licks my veins. She travels higher, roping her fingers in my hair then tugging on the strands to bring my mouth even closer to her—such a hungry little thing.

I consume her mouth, getting drunk on her cinnamon taste, craving more of it. Jamming my thigh against hers, I push her legs open.

Then I stop, my breath coming in harsh puffs. "I'm not thinking about what you're doing tonight," I hiss as I grip her hips and hike her up onto the hood.

"I'm not thinking about what you're doing either," she fires back with her smart mouth. Those lips are no longer glossy. They're bruised and swollen. Good. I want to mark her. I want her to smell like me. I want her to wear the evidence of this moment all over her body.

I drag my fingers through her hair, yanking it. She emits a needy gasp. "So fucking pretty," I growl as I bring my mouth down on that delicious neck. I kiss the column of her throat so hard I'm sure there will be a sandpaper trail from my stubble on her delicate skin. And she doesn't seem to mind at all. She moans as I bring my mouth down on the hollow of her throat. I lick her there. Frantically, she opens her legs wider, as if she's trying to draw me in to the V. Heeding her call, I shove my body against her, my hard-on rigid against her thigh. She draws a sharp breath as I press into her.

"I don't care what you were doing at the Hudson," I say, as I bring my teeth to her neck and bite.

A yelp rings out, but she wraps her legs tighter around me. I grind into her, letting her know how much I want to fuck her, letting her feel how hard she makes me. I bet she's so fucking wet. Whatever grasp I had on common sense unravels in each rough press of my mouth to her neck. I bite, and I suck, and I devour her neck, keeping her hair wrapped tightly in my fist.

I grab her chin roughly in my hand, and meet her eyes. They're dazed, glossy. She's panting. "You fucking drive me crazy," I mutter.

"And you're nothing but a cruel bastard," she says, narrowing her eyes as she scrapes at my hair again with her fingers. The lion in her is fierce tonight. She jerks my head back then pushes my face down, down, down and right between her tits. "So damn cruel."

I yank up her T-shirt and bury my face in the most wonderful place in the universe. Jesus Christ, her tits are heaven. I shove the cup of her black lace bra to the side—of course she wears black—and bring my teeth down on her nipple. She cries out again.

"This nipple drove me insane in the tub."

She freezes. "Is that why you kicked me out?"

I raise my face and lock eyes with her. She looks so fucking desperate right now. "I couldn't take it. You moved in the tub, and I saw it, and I had to fight off every instinct to bite it."

"Do it now," she urges. Before she even says the last word, my mouth is wrapped around her, and she is as fucking delicious as I imagined. I moan with her in my mouth, my dick growing impossibly harder as I draw that tight peak between my teeth. I suck as she curls her hands around my skull.

I come up for air. Her brown irises are wild now, and she looks like an animal.

"You were such a jerk that night." She drags her hands over my T-shirt, lingering on my pecs. "You need to take this off now for being such a complete ass."

I grip the back of my shirt, yanking it off.

Her mouth falls open in the sexiest expression I've ever seen. "You're so . . ."

She doesn't finish the thought. She runs her fingers over my bare skin, exploring my pecs, my abs, my arms. Her nails travel along my bicep, tracing the outline of the bands there, then the hawk on my shoulder. When she returns to my chest, she draws the Celtic tattoo on my right pec. My skin sizzles in the wake of her touch. Her fingertips light me up. They send electricity everywhere.

I tug at the waistband of her jeans. "These are really fucking inconvenient, Henley."

"Why?" Her voice is feathery.

I bring my mouth to her ear, nip the earlobe, and whisper, "Because I'm going to fuck you right now. I'm going to fuck you and make you come hard, and you need to take off these stupid jeans."

I back up and rustle around in my back pocket for my wallet. I flip it open and grab a condom. She gives me her yes in her busy hands—they unsnap the top button of her jeans. Then she unzips and shimmies them down her ass.

"Wait," I say, as I put the condom on the yellow hood.

"Why?"

I grab my shirt. "Sit on this."

I slide the cotton under her ass. Then I help her, jerking one jean leg down to her boot.

"Fucking combat boots," I mutter as I regard the long string of laces on her shoes.

"Idiot, they have a zipper." She reaches and pulls the zipper down one side. I tug off the boot, tossing it on the floor, then pull off that jean leg only. No patience for both. She slides her black panties down that leg, and I can't fucking breathe for a second.

"Holy . . ."

She's so fucking wet and beautiful. *Jesus Christ.* Her pussy is divine. Pink and slick and utterly, fucking enticing, like the most delicious dessert ever. I can't resist. I have to eat dessert first. I scoop my hands under her thighs, spreading them, and I bring my face between her legs.

"Oh God, Max," she moans as I slide my tongue down her wetness. Her hands grip my head. She digs her nails in, and I love it.

One more lick, up and up, and then I suck on that delicious rise of her clit. It's hard and soaked, and she jerks against me as I feast on it.

A long, low moan comes from her mouth. It's my name. Then she purrs, "Do it again."

I planned to fuck her. Hard and furiously. I swear I did. I had no intention to take a timeout to eat her. But her pussy is too fucking wonderful to deny. I flick my tongue against her clit, and she jerks against me again. She pulls my hair hard, yanking me even closer. "This is what you could have had that night in the tub," she tells me.

I break contact for a second and meet her hot gaze, processing the enormity of what she just said—she wanted me that night, too. "It's what I had when I jacked off after you left. Let's see if you taste as good as you did in my filthy imagination."

I return to her and drag my tongue down, lapping up all this decadent wetness as I go. A long, feral noise comes from her mouth. It sounds like *please.*

Ordinarily, I'd tease her. Make her beg. But, for all intents and purposes, she is already. Besides, just this second, I have no tolerance for games. Not hers, and not my own.

All I want now is to have her.

I lick my way back up her pussy to her clit, sucking on that little hard diamond of pleasure until she bucks against my mouth. She chants my name. She grips my hair. She rocks against me. Her fingers tighten against my skull. And then she fucks my face on the hood of the car until she comes like a rock star in under two minutes.

My name has never sounded so good as it does when Henley Rose Marlowe falls apart on my mouth. Her breathing is wild and her chest is heaving, and she's absolutely glowing from her orgasm.

"I was wrong when I imagined how good you'd taste." I am nothing but pride and desire as I straighten, unzip my jeans, and take out my cock. "You taste even better." I grab the condom and roll it on as she comes down from her high. "And you come fast, tiger. Guess you like what I do to you."

She opens her eyes only to narrow them at me. "It's been a while. That's all."

I wiggle my eyebrows as I pinch the tip of the condom. Her eyes drift down to my dick. They widen. "Oh God," she murmurs as she stares at my cock.

"Like what you see?"

"That's a lot of inches."

"How many?" I shake my head and put my finger against her lip. "Don't guess. I want you to *feel* how many. Then see how fucking long it takes you to come again."

"You ass," she says sharply, as she grabs my cock and draws me to that sweet Promised Land.

"I'm glad you hate me so much," I say as I rub the head against her slippery entrance.

"Why?"

"Because it'll be that much better when you say my name again when you come for the second time."

She sneers as I sink into her, and then there's no more sneering, from her or me. Because *holy fuck*.

I still myself when I'm all the way inside her. "Jesus," I mutter. "You feel so fucking good."

"So do you," she says softly.

She's out of this world. She's warm and tight and her pussy fucking welcomes me. She's so goddamn aroused already that I have no problem filling her all the way.

She grips my shoulders, holding on as she rocks her pelvis up on my cock. "I bet you come first," she says, in a challenging dare. "I already came."

I grab her chin as I ease back out. "And you fucking will again," I say through gritted teeth.

"I doubt it. The first was a fluke. It's been a long time, like I said."

I grab her thighs, yank her closer, and punch my hips into her.

"Oh God," she gasps.

"That's right, tiger. You're too fucking wet to only come once."

I drive into her again, and a sharp intake of air is her response.

"What made you so wet, tiger?" I ask, riling her up.

She shuts her eyes and bites her lip.

I slide back out, inch by inch, so just the tip is in her. "What got you so turned on?"

"Max," she moans, like a protest.

"Was it the way I ate you out and made you come in less than two minutes?"

I rock back into her, filling her to the hilt and letting a jolt of heat rocket over my skin. "Oh wait," I say, whispering roughly in her ear. "Was it how I kissed you before I even took your clothes off? Was that what made you so fucking turned on you came in seconds?"

Her eyelids flutter closed.

I grab her hips and angle her up more so my cock slides against her clit as I fuck her with long, deep strokes that seem to drive her wild. She can't answer me. She only moans and groans.

"Tell me, Henley. What made you so wet?" I drop my hand between her legs and rub her clit.

She lets out the longest, sexiest sound. "Oh God . . ."

I slide out so I'm barely in her at all, and she shakes. "Say it. Say it was the way I kissed you," I command as I rub circles over her clit. A tremble spreads over her body, and watching it overtake her from her chest down to her belly is breathtaking. She's beautiful and sexy, and trying so hard not to give in to everything she feels. I swivel my hips and pound into her.

"Your mouth," she shouts at last. "Oh God. It was your mouth. It's the way you kissed me. It's how I want to be kissed."

She throws her head back, exposing her beautiful neck. I smother her skin in kisses as I fuck her hard, rub her clit, and bring her to the brink.

Her eyelids squeeze. "Oh God, Max. Oh God, oh God, oh God."

She's close again. She's chasing pleasure. And I want her to catch it. I really fucking do. But I want her admission, too.

I freeze with my cock buried deep inside her. "Say how much you want me," I tell her, my voice rough and husky.

She whimpers.

"Say it and I'll make you come so fucking hard. I promise."

She cries out in frustration, her fists smacking my chest.

"Open your eyes," I tell her, and she does.

I stare into those brown irises. "Say you want me . . . because I fucking want you so much."

Something in her bursts free. She loops her hands around my neck. "I want you. I want you so much," she shouts, and then I give it to her, fucking her through her next orgasm as she cries out in bliss.

She's limp, fucked within an inch of her life, but I'm not done.

I tug her off the car, pull out, and spin her around. "Hands on the hood, tiger," I say, and she listens, flattening her back and spreading her palms across all that yellow metal. She lays her cheek on the Challenger and looks back at me with dazed, lust-filled eyes. I run a hand down her one bare cheek, then I shove into her hot, tight pussy once more.

And then we fuck it out.

All this anger.

All this frustration.

All this almost . . . hate.

I fuck her until she screams my name again. As she comes, I grip her hair and yank it hard.

There's nothing left but white-hot desire. I've never felt it like this before. Not for this long. Not with this kind of intensity. I pump into her, gripping her hips, until it's my turn.

I groan as an orgasm barrels down my spine, speeds through my body, and seizes me. It takes over, and it's a thousand times better than the solo one against the door. Hell, it's a million times better than I imagined.

Then it's more, when I collapse on her and she turns her face to mine and dusts my cheek with a soft, tender kiss. I'm still groaning in pleasure, but I manage a smile, too.

I gently flip her over, pull her up against my bare chest, and give her a soft kiss on her lovely, swollen lips.

"Mmm."

Then I whisper in her ear, "Knew I could make you come more than twice."

"That's because your dick is eight and a half inches."

I laugh and shake my head. "It's not the size that does it."

"Then what is it?"

I'm about to tell her it's how much I want her, it's chemistry, it's this sizzling connection between us. But a bell dings.

Shit.

We both scramble, and Henley yanks up her panties and jean leg. I pull off the condom and ball it up in the wrapper and stuff it in my pocket. I'll throw it out later. The soles of heavy shoes pound through the entryway office. I grab my shirt and tug it on. As Henley adjusts her shirt and stuffs her foot into her boot, she shoots me a *who the hell is here* look.

"Probably one of the guys," I say, my heart beating faster.

"Hey, boss."

It's Sam. A curious look spreads on his face as he takes in the scene—the tangled mess of her hair, the bee-stung lips, the wet spot on my shirt.

Pride surges in me, yet so does another feeling.

Hypocrisy.

I told Sam to watch what he said to the mechanic at John Smith. And here I am, fucking the lead builder on the hood of a car Sam's working on after hours.

"We're just working on the . . ." I point to the Lambo.

"I need to go. I have a . . . I have a thing," Henley says, and then nods at my guy. "Hey, Sam. Good luck with the Challenger."

She grabs her purse from the chair and hightails it out of here.

As I catch the parting glimpse of her with that big bag on her shoulder, I remember the change of clothes in it. And as I help Sam with the engine on the Challenger, all I can think about is what her *thing* could be.

Chapter 27

"I can take it from here," Sam says, a few hours later. "But thanks for staying late to help me."

"No problem." I grab a rag and wipe my dirty hands.

Sam needed a little help on this beast, and that's my job—to show him how to make an engine sing, not fuck a girl on the hood of the car he's restoring. Perhaps staying late is my penance for my hypocrisy.

"So." Sam clears his throat as he works on degreeing the cam. "You and Henley—"

I jerk my head, nerves prickling the back of my neck as I cut him off. "What do you mean?"

He didn't breathe a word about the two of us all evening, and it's not his place to either. Even so, I can't help but feel I crossed lines tonight when I decided to sleep with the rival.

Sam cranes his neck to look up from the engine at me. "Whoa. I was just going to say I didn't realize you and Henley used to work together."

I release a tight breath as I set down the rag. Momentary relief floods me. The question he's asked is simple. "Yeah, she was my apprentice five years ago."

"Karen mentioned it when we went out a second time."

"Karen the mechanic at John Smith? I met her briefly the other week when I stopped by."

Sam nods as he takes a reading from the dial indicator. "She likes Henley. She says she's a great builder. Karen loves having another chick there, and she said that all the guys over there have a lot of respect for her. They think she's doing a great job at the shop. I just hadn't realized you two had some history, and now you're working together on the show car. That's how tight this business is." He laughs. "Small world, huh?"

I force out a chuckle that sounds as if it's strangling me. "Yeah, it sure is."

I feel like an ass for telling Sam to watch his back on his date. Meanwhile, I torched my own advice to ashes a few hours ago. I'm not sure what to say next, but I decide to start with being less of an asshole boss about his personal life. "So, you and Karen are getting along?" I ask, and it feels like eating chalk. I do not enjoy talking about extracurriculars with my employees. Their private lives should be private. But, I started the discussion, so I need to finish it with a proper reset, not another warning on who to date.

"We're going to keep seeing each other. It's not like we're going to pool our resources and get one of those ten-thousand-dollar Snap-on Mammoth tool sets and open a shop together. But she's cool."

I laugh and gesture to the five-foot-high tool set I've got that contains everything under the sun that a professional builder needs. "A 10K Snap-on tool set is absolutely the sign of true love."

Sam taps his temple with his free hand. "I'll keep that tidbit up here in case someone ever gives me one."

"I'm glad to hear it's going well with her." I walk closer to the engine, and it's then that I see he's about to make an error.

"Hold on." I shift gears from after-hours affairs to the engine as I explain what he's doing wrong.

His face is crestfallen. "Oh shit."

I clap his back. "No worries, man. That's what I'm here for. Let's get this right."

I'm patient as I walk him through the next steps in degreeing the cam. It's painstaking work, and calls for incredible precision, but Sam listens and takes direction well. Soon enough, we've got the issue tackled.

He holds up a fist for knocking. "Man, am I glad you didn't leave right away."

I knock back. "You know you should never hesitate to ask me anything, right? Whatever you need help with. That's my job," I say, and this is way easier than who's dating who at the competition. I take some solace that I'm still good at teaching my guys.

He nods, an earnest look in his blue eyes. "I do. I appreciate it." Then he winks. "By the way, you do know this car is a dude, right?"

I laugh. "And does he have a name?"

"Of course. I'm going to call him Kyle the Sex Machine."

"That's an awful name for a car."

He laughs. "I know. But I named it that because I want to hear Mike say it."

"Now that you mention it, so do I."

* * *

When I return to my apartment, I pour a Scotch and work my way around the table for a solo round of pool. As I sink the balls, I think back on this evening. I managed Sam like a pro, segueing from work to his personal life. I should be able to manage a one-night stand with the same sort of ease and insight.

Nothing ruffles me. Nothing throws me off. Not work. Not cars. Not women.

But as I roll my neck from side to side, I'm not feeling so unruffled. I'm not experiencing the cool, blasé attitude I'd like to possess after an evening of delivering multiple Os to a woman I've wanted.

Instead, I'm wired and wound up. I pull on basketball shorts and a T-shirt and head downstairs to the gym in my building, where I run on the treadmill for five miles, trying to shed this antsy, unsettled sensation in my gut.

The exercise wears me out, and after a hot shower, I get into bed. Stupidly, I check my phone.

That's when it clicks— why I'm out of sorts. I drag a hand through my hair. "Dipshit," I mutter. I'm waiting to hear from her. Like a fucking teenager. A moony, mopey teenager.

For better or worse, I'm not the kind of man to sit around and wait for a chick. I'm a man of action. I open my contacts, find her number, and send her a text.

Max: Since you still don't like coffee, what do you like to drink?

The tension in me unwinds somewhat. I draw in a long breath, feeling it spread through my tight muscles, willing it to relax me. I close my eyes, ready to drift off, when my phone blips. I grab it from the covers in world-record time. I'll need to let Guinness know later what I've accomplished in the Over Eager Dude category.

Henley: Hot chocolate is my style.

In the dark of my bedroom, with the moonlight slicing soft rays over the covers, a smile spreads on my face. A flash of images pops before my eyes. Her unicorn and rainbow shirt. Her pink sparkly sunglasses. Her affection for bubble-gum music. The take-no-prisoners, keep-up-with-the-guys, do-a-man's-work woman has such a girlie side.

It's fucking adorable.

Max: Yeah, that sounds just like you.

But that's not quite enough to say to a woman you devoured on a car hours earlier.

Max: Also, your drink preferences are duly noted. And I hope your thing went well.

Henley: My thing went great. Glad to hear you've made the proper beverage notations. Ideally, gourmet hot chocolate.

My fingers hover over the phone, and I contemplate typing out one more text. Something witty. Something flirty. Something to let her know she's not just on my mind; she's the epicenter of it.

But the only thing I want to say right now is the hard truth.

I'm dying to know what your thing is. I want you to tell me what you do after work. I want to know your thing isn't the thing we did on the car. I toss the phone to the other side of the bed. If I say that, it'll be patently obvious I want more than one night with her.

And that would be very bad for business.

CHAPTER 28

Henley's To-Do List

—Sign off on the paperwork! Yay, this is going to happen.

—Finish install of crankshaft with Max.

—Resist urge to make dirty crankshaft joke.

—Double resist urge.

—Refrain from jumping Max on the hood of the Miura, even though, oh my God, how hot would car sex with him be on that gorgeous car? Only to be topped by Maclaren sex. Or maybe DeLorean sex. Or wait . . . Aston Martin sex.

—Fan self at image of Aston Martin sex.

CHAPTER 29

My lunch meeting with a new client runs late. The banker with the Hermes tie and tailored suit wants to discuss upgrades to his Bugatti. He already has a top-of-the-line model. I'm not sure what else he could want on it but a diamond-encrusted wheel. Nor do I find out with any sort of speed, since he takes a call after his steak arrives and barks orders at someone on the phone for fifteen minutes. I'm about ready to walk on account of the guy acting like a douchebag, but I decide to give him the benefit of the doubt. He could be having a shitty day.

During the fifteenth minute, I text Henley. I tell her I'm running late and to start without me on the final crankshaft work. When the guy stabs a meaty finger on the end button, his cuff rides up, revealing a Casio watch rather than a Rolex. For a guy who likes to show off his bling, the wrist adornment choice surprises me. But I bet he managed some sort of transaction involving that company. He's probably meeting them next. He signals the waiter and orders another porterhouse. His has gone cold.

When the waiter leaves, he returns his focus to the car conversation. "Where were we?" he asks as I take a drink of my iced tea.

"You wanted diamonds on the steering wheel?" I joke.

He laughs and runs a hand down his pink silk tie. "No, but tell me what else we can do to make it even better."

Nothing. Fucking nothing. You already have the best.

Some people have a bottomless appetite though, so I try to come up with some options he might enjoy when he takes the car for a spin outside Manhattan. He tells me he'll think about it. When the check comes, I pay, and when the lunch ends, he doesn't say thank you. As he stalks off into the afternoon crowds, braying into his phone once again, I mouth, "*You're welcome, dickhead. Feel free to never call me again.*"

What a waste of two hours. I pick up the pace as I make my way back to my shop, hoping to catch Henley for a few minutes. I find a message from her.

Henley: I already finished. Do I get a gold star for punctuality?

Max: Sounds like you earned one for speed.

Henley: Yes, I can be quite fast. You may have noticed.

The memory of her coming hard in less than two minutes flashes before me. Not like it's ever far away, but now it's front and center, and I'm fucking aroused as I walk to the shop. My mind is an old film reel, snapping over the same frame again.

Henley on the yellow Challenger, her legs spread, crying out my name.

As surreptitiously as I can, I adjust my jeans. The movie camera operator toys with me, switching to the scene with her bent over the hood, one lovely cheek exposed.

She was so willing, so ready, so damn turned on, too.

That's exactly what I am right now, and it's going to be a problem to work like this.

I need the antidote, so I stop at Duane Reade on the corner and head to the cold, cough, and flu section of the store. No, I'm not sick—and if I were, I'd make my brother prescribe some good shit since I hate being sick with a passion. But a quick survey of all the potential afflictions, from a twenty-four-hour stomach bug to a phlegmy cough, are enough to make me the opposite of horny. Ah, this is the true Deflategate, thank you very much, cold meds.

My eyes wander to the nearby Dramamine. They're the orange tabs, the ones she likes.

Ah hell. It can't hurt for the woman to have some on hand the next time she's on a boat.

Not with me, obviously, since I have no plans to take her anywhere. It'll just be wise for her to be prepared.

As I head to the checkout, my shoes seem to stop reflexively at the gourmet aisle. I scrub a hand across my jaw, considering a shelf of treats.

Maybe just one more item.

When I return to the shop, Henley's gone, but her handiwork has been left behind, and it's fucking fantastic.

* * *

Max: Nice work. I'm giving it a platinum star.

Henley: Lucky me. I had no idea your reward system went so high.

Max: I'm quite generous at times.

Henley: Generous. That's a good way to describe certain . . .

Max: Certain . . . what?

Henley: Parts of you.

Max: Glad those parts could be of service.

Henley: I'm giving your shop high marks.

Max: Anything to improve on?

Henley: Not sure. I might need another fuel injection before I can answer that question.

I run my thumb over her last text, stopping on the two words that tell me all I need to know. *Might* and *another*. As I read them, something inside my chest that has held me back rattles loose. I know with bone-deep certainty that I want another night with her. I needed to know she wanted it, too.

Knowing it changes everything, but it changes nothing. She's still the competition. She's still the lead builder at my biggest rival. She's still dangerous.

I'm well aware working with the competition on a project is one thing, while screwing her is entirely another. Sex is like liquor; it numbs the judgment center of your brain. It breaks down your guard. It makes you stupid.

But I tell myself I'll be careful. A two-night stand won't hurt anything. I'll be cautious. I'll keep a seat belt on at all times with her.

And really, don't seat belts protect you from any damage?

I don't let myself answer that question. Instead, I answer her.

Max: Had a feeling you'd want to take the car for another test drive.

Henley: I do enjoy seeing what sort of maximum speeds we can achieve.

Max: I'd enjoy seeing a hot ride stripped down to nothing.

Henley: I'd be amenable to that. And soon.

Max: I'd be amenable to that, say, tonight.

Henley: Tonight could be a hard one.

Max: Now is hard. Tonight is hard. It's always hard.

Henley: Ha. Yes. I've noticed that, too.

Max: Seems you have wandering eyes.

Henley: Perhaps I do. They wander to hard rides.

Max: Wander over tonight then . . .

Henley: Might be tough.

I groan in frustration with that response. She could have a million reasons, but all I want right now is her *yes*, so I fire off the next text without thinking.

Max: Wait. Let me guess. You have a thing.

Henley: I do. I have this thing a lot. I have to go.

Max: Does this thing have a name?

Max: Should I call the thing *it*? Or does it prefer to go by *the thing*?

Max: Hmmm. You might want to check your phone. Seems it has stopped working. Maybe all that thinking about my hard ride did it in.

She doesn't respond.

That's my cue to forget about her. No more flirting. No more texting. No more dirty innuendos. I can't keep playing with fire. A sense of relief rushes over me that it's over and done with. I haven't crossed the line again. She's still simply a one-night stand guilty pleasure. And that's all she'll be.

Project Forget Henley starts with a long bike ride with Chase after work, which helps narrow my focus to the sole task of beating my speed demon brother. I do so by about ten seconds.

"Killed it," I say, panting hard after our twenty miles on the Hudson River Greenway.

"You must be juicing."

I scowl. "Yeah, I'm on 'roids. You figured me out."

Chase gives me a studious stare. "You're still grouchy today. I guess that means you didn't sort out your little issue?" He grabs my shoulder. "I've told you, man. The best doctor's advice I can give you is that regular intercourse is good for your serotonin levels. Live a little and take the old dog out for a walk. It'll make you smile again."

I give him a nice brotherly smack upside the head as we walk our bikes toward my building, the headlights of passing cars illuminating the twilit street. "That is not a problem."

"Does that mean Miss Monkey Bread succumbed to your charms? Wait. Sorry. You don't have any."

"I'll have you know I'm the motherfucking definition of charming," I say, but the problem is I don't know if Henley thinks so. I've made the woman scream my name, but I don't have a clue what she thinks of me other than I'm a cruel bastard and an idiot who can't locate zippers on combat boots.

But honestly, the answer is she probably doesn't think of me at all. She never replied.

"Hey," Chase says as we near my building, "did you ever think of the fact that *succumb* is a very dirty word hiding in the midst of everyday language? It's basically *suck* . . ." He leaves a deliberate pause.

I hold up a hand. "And *come*."

He narrows his brows, an inquisitive look in his eyes. "When you said that just now, did you spell it 'c-o-m-e' or 'c-u-m'?"

"Dude. Are we really discussing the spelling of fucking semen when we speak? Either way, let me assure you, Scrabble King, 'c-u-m' is not a word."

Chase shakes his head adamantly. "It so is. It's the Latin word for *with*. As in summa cum laude."

"Says the summa cum laude graduate." I clap his back. "Never a dull moment with you, genius."

As he straps his helmet back on so he can ride to Chelsea, he gives me a quick salute. "If the problem isn't horizontal, maybe you're grouchy because there's another issue you need to sort out."

I arch an eyebrow curiously. "What issue would that be?"

"Tell the girl you like her. Isn't that what you told me?"

"I don't recall giving you that precise advice."

"But you meant to, I'm sure," he says, then flashes me a winning smile. I flip him the bird as he rides off into the night.

As I lock up my bike in the building, I'm not so sure what I *mean* to do with Henley. My intentions are a malleable thing these days. They seem to be at war with my actions, as well as my best interests.

After I cook myself dinner and catch up with Mia on the phone—she tells me she's won the new deal for her company, and that she went with the coconut face wash—I decide to have a soak. It's been a while since I indulged in that pastime. I find my favorite new playlist, turn up the volume, and set the phone on the plush white bath mat on the tiled floor.

I haven't used the tub since the night Henley was in it, and as I slide under the hot water I do my damnedest not to think about how the white marble touched her soft skin. I close my eyes and sink down into the steamy heat, the water sloshing precariously near the edge.

I do nothing for a few minutes, and it's what I need most right now.

Silent contemplation. A blank mind.

As I try to sort out the haze in my head, my phone rings. I blink open my eyes and peer over the edge of the tub. The name flashing on the screen is a gift from the gods. I consider diving out of the tub and onto the floor so I won't miss the call. But I'm a quick draw, even in water, so I grab a towel, dry my hand, and answer.

CHAPTER 30

"Broken Cell Phone Repair Shop," I say.

Her soft laugh greets me. "It drives you crazy, doesn't it?"

"Many things do. Be more specific."

"Not knowing what my *thing* is."

"Nope."

"I had a ton of meetings and stuff tonight. Just getting back to messages now."

That sounds reasonable enough. I lean back, resting my head against the marble. Water splashes.

"Are you in *my* tub?" she asks.

"No. I'm in *mine*."

"Are you naked?"

"No, I'm wearing flannel pajamas."

"Did you get me hot chocolate?"

Damn. She's like Babe Ruth calling his shot. I'm fucking impressed. "Depends on whether you deserve it."

My phone buzzes again. Glancing at the screen, I see it's the doorman. "One second," I say, then click over.

"Hello, Mr. Summers. There's someone here to see you. She says her name is Tiger."

My grin is too wide to contain. "Send her up."

Two minutes later, I answer the door, a towel wrapped around my waist, drops of water sliding down my chest, my hair slicked back.

The breath rushes from my lungs as I drink her in. She wears dark jeans so tight they look painted on, black sling-back heels, and a clingy red top. From her finger dangles a black leather jacket. She leans against the doorframe. "I'm here for my hot chocolate," Henley says.

"How do you know I really bought you some?"

"You wanted to lure me here. You set a hot chocolate trap because you're dying to know what I'm up to."

I snort. "Wow. What an elaborate snare I've devised." I open the door wider and indicate with my eyes that she should come in. She does and I close the door. "And this is all because it drives me crazy not to know what you do in the evenings?"

"It drives you batty, right?"

I shake my head as I pad across the floor to the kitchen. "Can I get you something? Scotch? Wine? Soda? Water? Arsenic? Hot chocolate?"

She winks. "Hot chocolate. Hold the arsenic."

The click of her shoes echoes as she follows me into the kitchen. I grab some milk from the fridge, pour it into a small saucepan, and heat it up, stirring it with a whisk. She eyes my work approvingly.

When the milk is warm, I pour it into a mug, then I snag the gourmet hot chocolate I picked up for her. It's Godiva. I scoop some into the mug, stir in the mix, and hand her the cup.

She takes a drink.

"Mmm," she murmurs as she closes her eyes. "Now this," she says, tapping the ceramic, "this I like."

I raise an eyebrow. "Good to know."

She sets it down. "You don't want to know what my thing is?"

"I think you want to tell me," I say. If she came all the way downtown to taunt me about my jealousy, then I'm going to make her work for it tonight.

"You think I'm involved with someone. You think I see him after work. You think I go somewhere and see a guy."

I grit my teeth at the images she paints but shake my head in my best denial.

"Do you?" she presses.

I shrug so damn nonchalantly they're going to photograph and frame this moment and hang it in a museum. Title: *Unruffled*. "I honestly forgot you even had a thing tonight."

"Liar," she whispers with a sly smile.

"Truth teller," I say, tapping my chest. I leave the kitchen and head to my living room.

"Max!" she calls out, stomping after me. Her fingers brush my right arm and I turn. She grabs my towel instead of the hand that she was presumably going for.

Presumably.

Either way I'm unfazed as the towel falls to the floor.

I can't say the same for her.

Her eyes pop.

They widen more as they drift down. She nibbles on the corner of her lip. She's so fucking transparent, and I couldn't be happier that she likes the view.

"Want me to stay like this? Or is it going to be too distracting for you?"

She huffs, grabs my towel from the floor, and chucks it at me. "Yes, Max. Your gigantic dick is super distracting."

I catch the towel easily. "Good," I say, deliberately taking my sweet time hooking it back on, making sure the gigantic dick in question remains in her line of sight.

I park my hands on my hips. "Now, what were we discussing?" I stare at the ceiling as if I'm trying to remember. I snap my fingers. "Right. You came over at nearly midnight to taunt me about whether I'm jealous about what you do after hours. Did I get that right, tiger?"

She marches back into my kitchen, snags the cup, and parks herself in the doorway to the living room. She downs a big gulp of the hot chocolate as she stares at me. "No. I came over for the hot chocolate, and it's so much better than coffee."

I'm not sure if that's a compliment. I don't know if it's her way of saying I'm hot chocolate now, instead of coffee. As if I've moved up on her list of drinks. She's here, so maybe I am cocoa to her. "Fine. You want me to say it, don't you?"

She wiggles her eyebrows, standing her ground in the kitchen doorway. "Yes."

I'm guessing she won't join me until I give in, so I might as well. "I'm jealous. You win."

I sink down on the couch, and she struts over, plops down next to me, and runs one fingernail down my bare arm, over my bicep, along my forearm to my wrist. Inside, I shiver. Outside, I reveal nothing.

She brings her face to my neck and licks me. The tip of her tongue traces a path to my ear, and it sets my blood on fire. I breathe out hard, saying her name like a warning. "*Henley.*"

She says mine, too, in that sexy purr. "*Max.* I take dance classes at the Hudson."

I smirk. "You do?"

She nods, a shy little smile on her lips. "I do."

"Really?"

"Is that so hard to believe? Is it easier to believe that I'm screwing someone or seeing someone?" she asks, affronted.

"I don't want you screwing or seeing someone else."

She scoffs. "You're insane if you think I'd let you do what you did to me on the car if I were screwing someone else."

My heart squeezes, and it feels like happiness and relief all at once. I'm so damn glad I was wrong. "I'm either insane or insanely jealous. Tell me about this class."

I reach for her calves and slide off her black shoes, letting the heels fall to the floor. She tucks her feet under her as she answers. "It's salsa, and it's sexy, and I'm terrible at dancing. But I love it. My friend Olivia tried it and told me to give it a shot."

"I doubt you're terrible."

She shakes her head. "I'm the worst student in the class."

Somehow, this makes me laugh. "There's no way you're the worst. And even if you are, it's awesome that you love it anyway."

"Taking apart an engine is so easy compared to dancing," she says as she takes another sip of her hot chocolate then wraps both hands around the mug. It's so cute the way she clutches it. I want to take a picture of how she holds that cup. It's yet another side of Henley—the girlie side.

"Why do you say it's hard for you?"

"You have to get your feet right. You have to remember the steps. You have to move in time to the music. And you have to have a good partner. I had one, but he dropped out."

"He?"

"Did you think I danced with a woman?"

"I didn't think about you dancing at all till two minutes ago."

"And what do you think now that you know?" she asks as she sets the cup on the coffee table.

"That the thought of you dancing salsa with some guy the night after I made you come hard on the hood of a car makes me crazy."

"A lot of things make you crazy. You should get that head of yours checked out. Maybe you're going mad."

"So who'd you dance with tonight, Miss Salsa Girl?"

"The instructor." She arches an eyebrow. "He's this tall, gorgeous, Latin-lover type, and he can dance like you've never seen."

I narrow my eyes and breathe fire. "When's your next class?"

"Friday."

"At the Hudson?"

"Yes."

"I'll be there."

"What?"

"I'm going with you," I tell her as I rope my hand in her hair, tugging it back. She gasps, that sexy, needy sound she makes when I get rough with her. "You're going with me?" She knits her brow in question.

"You need a partner. I need to not have anyone else's hands on you while I'm fucking you."

She shoves her palms against my chest, and I let go of her locks. "What makes you think you're screwing me?"

"The fact that you like making me jealous. The fact that you're here at this hour. The fact that I'm wearing nothing but a towel, and I'm rock-hard, and you haven't left. That's why."

"That's presumptuous."

I shrug. "This is presumptuous." I lift my hips, take off the towel, and toss it on the floor.

Her breath hitches. "That's not fair. I mean, seriously." She flings her arm in the general direction of my lap. "How did *that* happen?"

I chuckle. "How did *what* happen?"

She pushes my chest again, her eyes straying to my crotch. "How do you get to be six foot three, with these arms, and have a gigantic dick, too? It's ridiculous." She crosses her arms. "It's a completely unfair distribution of male assets. It's like you got the portion reserved for three other guys. It all went to you."

I smirk. "I was good in a past life?"

She stares at me and shakes her head. "And those eyes," she says softly as she gazes at me. Then, her voice is even more faint. "Those eyes."

My skin warms. I press my forehead to hers, slowing down. "I could say the same about your eyes."

The moment speeds up again. She darts out a hand, surprising me as she wraps it around my dick. I hiss in pleasure. I do like this kind of surprise. *A lot.*

"I can't help it," she says with a shrug. "It's like a stick shift calling out to me."

"A joystick."

She laughs and strokes my hard-on, and then I stop laughing. I sink back into the couch, spreading my arms over the cushions behind me, stretching my right arm around her. I grip her shoulder, drawing her near, as she busies herself with fondling me. I shudder on an upstroke. "Fuck, that's good."

"It was so good last night," she murmurs.

"So fucking good."

She licks me again, sliding her tongue along my neck, flicking it against my earlobe. Her hand glides down my shaft, and she cups my balls. I open my legs wider, giving her access to the goods. "Sleeping with you again would be a terrible idea," she says as she explores my erection.

Her actions say it would be anything but terrible.

"It's the worst thing we could do," I say, holding back a groan.

"Sleeping with the competition is foolish," she adds. "We might be working together now, but you're still my rival."

"You're still mine, too."

"It's too risky. I'd be"—she nibbles on my earlobe—"distracted." She drops her face between my legs and licks the head of my cock.

My whole body jerks in pleasure. "Jesus. That's fucking distracting for sure."

"Is this, too?" She paints a line down to the base with her tongue.

"Yeah," I grunt.

"Then we should just get this out of our system."

I nod. I'd agree to anything right now. "Yeah, we definitely need to get this out of our system."

"One more time," she suggests, then licks her way back up. I've become her ice-cream cone.

"That's all we need," I say on a broken breath.

"Then we're done."

"Completely done."

"So done." She moans as her mouth travels, and that sound sends a dark thrill through me. I brush her lush hair away from her gorgeous face and watch her play with my dick. This is the side of Henley that messes with me. That teases. That flirts.

Right now, she's flirting with my dick.

Her hair spills across my lap, and as she licks, she lets the strands trail over the hair on my legs. The ends tickle my thighs. She flicks her tongue in a long, lingering line going up, up, up.

She stops at the head then draws a luscious circle with her tongue.

My throat makes a deep, rumbly sound, signaling my lust. But I don't push her head down. I don't ask for more. I let her set the pace and just play with me. The next thing I know she's kissing my cock. She's leaving lipstick marks on my dick. Smooches and pecks, and then deeper, throatier kisses. My skin sizzles and pleasure tightens incomparably inside me.

She brings her lips to the tip and gently, so fucking gently, draws me in. I shudder, and clasp my hands around her head, holding her in place as she kisses my dick.

God help me. I'm not sure I can withstand this slow-burn blow job.

"Henley," I rasp out.

She looks up, the tip of my dick still in her mouth. Those brown eyes shine with gold specks. They twinkle with mischief as she slowly puts my entire dick in her mouth, hitting the back of her throat.

Holy fuck. I will come in seconds if she does that again.

I tug her up. I gather her close, pulling her onto my lap. I run my hands through her hair, marveling at how soft it is, how pretty she is, and how many times I've thought this about her. *Countless.* And countless times I've locked those thoughts up tight. Awareness bursts in me. I've never told her. I'm nearly ashamed that I haven't said this, so I say it now. "You're so fucking beautiful."

Her smile is radiant. It lights up her entire face. She glows. "Really?"

My voice is hoarse, and I've no idea why. "So. Incredibly. Beautiful."

She drops her face to my neck and nuzzles me. "So are you," she whispers.

Warmth rushes over me, and something else, too. Something unnamed. But then there's a familiar sensation—a deep and powerful desire, jostling every other emotion out of the way as she kisses my neck, and I run my nose across her hair.

I need her.

I untangle her from me, setting my hands on her slim shoulders. "I need you to take all your clothes off."

"Why?"

"Last night I didn't get to admire you. I want to see all of you. I need you naked. I need it so fucking much."

"Then you can have it." She stands and strips for me, and when she's down to nothing, I can't take my eyes off her, nor can I decide where to stare—the swell of her breasts, the softness of her belly, or the curves of her hips. I stare for a long time at the thatch of dark hair between her legs, then I drag my rough hands along those lovely, strong legs.

But her face is where I land. I stand and cup her cheeks. "Every inch of you is beautiful. Now, I'm thinking I'd like you to head over to the window, so I can watch your gorgeous face and admire your perfect ass while I'm fucking you."

"I like the way you think," she says, with a wink. She walks to the window and presses her palms against it. As she breathes out, the glass steams up.

So does my blood.

The edge of Manhattan twinkles in the windows, a collection of fireflies in buildings that reach for the sky. Just beyond, the East River seeps its inky dark waters across the night. Someone working late in the skyscraper mere blocks away could grab a pair of binoculars and zoom in on a man brushing a woman's hair off her shoulder then sliding his lips across her neck. The show would be impossible to turn off.

It's my peep show. My fucking perfect night.

Henley's back arches. She shudders. I press my chest to her, caging her in with an arm across her breasts. I map the soft flesh of her stomach, playing with the curls of her hair between her legs.

My fingers travel to the slick heat between her legs.

Her lips part, her eyelids flutter, her hips grind down on my fingers.

I growl against her neck as I slide my fingers deeper inside her. She grips me as she rocks back, her hips swaying and swiveling.

It's obscene.

It's wanton.

It's exactly how a woman should feel when a man touches her. A man she wants. A man who wants her.

"One last time," I whisper, then I break contact to grab a condom from my wallet on the coffee table.

She whimpers while I'm gone. "Max, get back here now."

I expect her to stomp a foot. "I'm not exactly lollygagging," I say, laughing.

"I know, but I'm dying for you."

I rip open the foil, slide the condom down my erection, and then grab her delicious ass. My palms cover her, my thumbs digging into the crease where her butt meets her thigh. She rises on her tippy-toes. I spread her open, raise her rear higher, and notch the head of my cock against her slick entrance.

"Ready?" I growl.

She sways back against me. "So ready."

"You sure?" I rub the tip against all that lush wetness.

"Max . . ." It's a needy, wild whimper.

"Tell me you—"

"I want you," she shouts. "I want you inside me. I want you jealous. I want you to have me one more time."

I part her lips so I can ease in, but once I'm there, I don't go gently. I shove inside, and we both groan in unison as I sink deep into her. Electricity crackles over my skin, and Henley melts into me. I band my arm around her stomach, gripping her tight as I rock into her.

I watch her in the reflection. She's never been hotter than she is right now. I'm fucking her in front of the floor-to-ceiling glass window, Manhattan is at our feet, and the sexiest woman I've ever known is giving herself to me.

"I'm just getting this out of my system," I say roughly.

"Please, please, please get me out of your system."

Heat rushes through my veins. It's addictive. I crave more of it. I want to feel this pleasure everywhere. And as much as I fuck her, she fucks me back. She grinds her sweet little ass against my cock, taking me deeper, her arms braced against the glass.

"Someone could see us," she murmurs, like that would be the height of scandal.

"I don't care."

"You don't care who can see me naked?" She's taunting in her playful way, riling me up.

I cup her tits, squeezing them as I fuck her fast and hard to make my point. She cries out a nearly ear-splitting *oh God.*

"It's my hands that are on your tits," I say roughly. "It's my cock that's buried so far in your sweet pussy. You think I care who sees?"

I slam my lips down on her neck. I suck the delicate flesh between my teeth. She shivers, and a wave seems to roll through her.

"My mouth is on your delicious neck. Ask me again if I care who sees me fucking you," I say, seizing her jaw as I thrust.

"Do you care?" she says in a feathery voice as I bury myself deep inside her, locking my gaze with hers in the steamed-up glass. She's lost—dazed, glossy eyes, heady expression, features twisted in pleasure.

"I don't care. Want to know why?" I jerk her closer.

"Why?" she asks, as if she's begging.

I run my index finger over her bottom lip. "Because it's my name on your lips when you come." I thrust. "Say it."

She trembles, a full-body shudder. A quake rumbles through her. I wrap a hand tighter around her hip, and then she shakes. It's almost violent. It's certainly erotic. And it's soundless at first, as her lips open in the most sensual O I've ever seen.

Then the noise comes. A long, sexy howl of ecstasy.

Of falling apart.

"*Max*," she moans, and my name is the sound of her bliss.

That trips the switch in me, and my own orgasm rattles loose, tearing through me as if it's redefining the very notion of momentum itself.

And when we're nothing but sated, tired, drugged-out sex hounds, I toss away the condom then scoop her up and carry her to the couch. I grab a warm, wet hand towel from the bathroom and clean her, then settle in with this naked beauty in my arms.

She's smiling, all limbs and soft hair.

Like a lovely foal.

Like a happy little clam.

She closes her eyes and wiggles against me. "I should go."

"Yeah," I say, bringing her closer. "You should go."

CHAPTER 31

Henley's To-Do List

—Leave.

CHAPTER 32

She snuggles closer as if she's trying to press every inch of her warm skin to mine.

I feel like I'm living in some alternate state. There's nothing else in New York City but us and the twinkling lights beyond the glass. She reaches for the blanket, the same one I covered her with after the ferry trip. She tugs it up to her breasts, then under her arms, making sure I'm beneath it with her.

I spoon her, kissing her neck as she burrows into my sofa like a little animal, making a couch-nest for the night.

"I really should go," she murmurs as she brushes her fingertips along my forearm, outlining the veins.

"You absolutely should leave," I say as I rope my arm tighter around her.

"Staying would be bad."

"It would be awful."

Heat from her body radiates into mine. I pull her closer. I want to press every inch of my skin against hers.

"If I stayed we'd probably talk," she says softly.

"About all sorts of things. Like how much you love girlie stuff."

"I do," she says, her laugh a soft jingle.

"You like sparkles and unicorns," I say, tracing lazy lines along her belly.

"You've caught me. It's true."

"Why?"

"They're the antidote to my grease-monkey days."

"Ah. I had a feeling."

"I spend all day long in this hyper-masculine field. I'm surrounded by guys and testosterone, and when I leave the cars behind, I want to be a woman again."

"So that's why you turn to dancing at night?"

"Dancing, and hot chocolate, and Belinda Carlisle blasting in my ears, and wishing upon shooting stars."

"It's hard, isn't it?"

"Wishing on a star?"

I shake my head, as I draw a line down her back. "Being a woman in our field."

She nods vigorously. "Um, yeah. You know *exactly* how I feel about that."

I draw a sharp breath, recalling the words she flung at me before she left five years ago. "I do."

"You didn't move me up because I was a woman," she says, like this is part of the public record of our work breakup.

I sigh. "No, Henley. That's not it."

She swivels around in my arms, spreading her palms over my chest. "It kind of was."

I don't want to go down the path of ancient history. The present has been hard enough. This is the first occasion since the ferry ride that we've managed time together without breaking out our ninja stars and nunchucks. "I swear, tiger. I was a cruel bastard, but not a sexist one. And if it makes you feel any better, I'm amazed at what you've done. You'll open your own shop in no time."

She clears her throat like that surprises her. "You think so?"

"Hell yeah. You're fantastic. You're fast, creative, and focused. You're sharp and clever. I can see you running your business. Can't you?"

She stares at my hair. "I hope so."

I press a kiss to the hollow of her throat. "Bet on it. Next year at this time."

"Ha."

"You'll kick my ass."

Her hand darts around my waist and squeezes my butt. "Damn straight."

"With that attitude, you'll be hanging up your shingle sooner. Maybe even sooner than a year."

She smiles faintly but looks away. Her breath hitches. She's silent, and it seems as if she's alternating between fiery and melancholy.

"Hey," I say, turning her shoulder so she faces me fully. "Are you sad about something?"

She drops her face into her hands and grumbles. "Ugh."

Worry jolts through me. "What's wrong, Henley?"

She talks into her hands. "I want to be taken seriously, but look what I did. I slept with you. *Twice.*"

I pry her hands from her face and raise her chin. "Newsflash. We're not blasting this across the trade mags. I'm not putting it on Snapchat. I'm not even on Snapchat."

She huffs. "Someone will know. I'll look like a harlot going into work. Someone will look at me and whisper . . ." She deepens her voice. "Hey, isn't that the chick who bangs Summers?"

"That's not how you'll be known in this business."

"Easy for you to say. You'll get pats on the back for nailing the chick builder on top of the Dodge Challenger," she says, and I wince.

When she puts it like that, she's right to some degree. Unfortunately. I wish she weren't, but there's still a boys' club mentality when it comes to getting laid. For better or worse, banging the hottest woman under the sun on top of a muscle car is brag worthy. But I'm not that guy. My private life is just that—private. "We're not broadcasting this. What's between you and me is between you and me."

"Thank you. And look, I'm not saying we should sneak around and be all cloak and dagger. We're not doing anything wrong."

I nod. "Nothing wrong at all, but we'll be cautious and careful."

"And we won't lie," she adds, and I'm grinning because clearly we're not out of each other's system. But I'm also impressed that she's so level-headed, especially since I know how hotheaded she can be. "I can live with your terms."

"Ha. Glad you approve. I've been working on my negotiation skills." Then her tone shifts. She sighs heavily. "I've tried hard to not get involved with anyone in the business. *Ever.* The only time . . ."

My ears prick. "The only time what?"

She swallows as if she's chewed something hard and painful. "The only time . . . is now."

Her statement sounds off, as if she's hiding something. But considering how long it took for her to fess up and tell me she danced at night, I'm not keen to push her on whether she once was involved with someone else in this business.

She presses her hand against my chest, her fingertips outlining my ink. "I appreciate you keeping this quiet. And I probably sound ridiculous since we screwed in your shop. How can I say I want respect and then do that with you? But . . ."

"But what?"

She flashes a naughty little grin. "You were impossible to resist."

My chest is a sunburst. "Good. And clearly, I could say the same for you."

"But the point is still this. I want respect. I want to set an example, too, for the other women in this field, like Karen. I've worked hard to make it as a woman in a male-centric field. Getting my engineering degree was key. Getting a job with you when I graduated was another. You were the best, and I wanted to learn from the best. That's why I pursued work with you. Remember when I tracked you down at the car show years ago?"

I nod, recalling the day I met her. I was showing off some new rides, and she marched up to me, told me about her college degree, flipped open the portfolio of cars she'd worked on during school, and the Camaro she restored for herself when she was a teenager. Then she said, "The next thing on my to-do list is landing a job as the apprentice to the top builder in the country. I'm a fast learner, and I'm not afraid to tackle any problem."

I hired her on the spot. "You were insistent."

"You asked me how I learned the trade, and you were one of the few people who didn't assume I must have been raised by mechanics."

"I was impressed you learned on your own. You had fire in your belly. You had drive."

"And that's why I work my butt off at everything. Even small things, like not swearing. I do that because I don't want to pretend I'm one of the guys. I want to talk to my colleagues and coworkers like a professional."

I run my finger over her top lip. "I admire that, even though I do want to hear you say *fuck* someday."

"But Max, do you see what I mean?" She shoves my shoulder. "Being around you makes me stupid. I flirt with you, and I get naked in your bathroom, and then I come over and jump you."

"You do flirt. And you did get naked. But I definitely jumped you," I say, correcting her.

"How will anyone respect me in this business if I'm just the booth bitch who screws the hottest builder around?"

I snort, for many reasons. "First, thank you for the compliment. Second, I presume you're not going around and sleeping with every dude in the business."

She rolls her eyes. "Ha. Ha."

"Don't judge yourself because we slept together. The fact that I've been dying to get you naked since I saw you again has nothing to do with my respect for your work. And third, you're not a booth bitch. You make the damn cars. You're the chick who makes a Corvette cool again. You're the one who souped up a Camaro at age sixteen. And you're the kickass gearhead who customized the beautiful red beast for Brick Wilson." I tap her temple. "That's where the respect comes from. What you do *under* the hood, not on the hood. And you've got that, Henley."

"Thank you," she says, and I can hear the gratitude in her tone. I can tell it matters to her that I respect her talent and her abilities. She taps my chest. "But I didn't build the red beast. We built the car together. I know that must have been hard for you.

To give up control to someone who's not at your level in the business."

"It was fine," I say, because anything more would be a lie. I didn't want to share the credit on the Lambo, but it is what it is, and I've had a good time working with her. "We've been a good team."

"What if I was at your level?" She brings her hands under her chin, and she looks vulnerable, innocent.

I blink. "Aren't you?"

"I don't own my own shop yet. I'm still not at your level."

I clear my throat. "What would be different if you owned your own shop?"

"Well, you say I'm your rival, but I'm still Aaron Rodgers to your Tom Brady."

I crack up, a deep laugh that takes root inside my chest and spreads across my body because she made a football joke of all things. I flop to my back and pull her into the crook of my arm. "Aaron, you are one fine-looking quarterback."

"And you have so many inches . . . I mean, rings."

I laugh. "I don't think we're Aaron and Tom, though."

"Who are we, then?"

I flash back to Creswell's comments at the first meeting. "Cybill and Bruce. Wait. You've probably never heard of them. They did this show called *Moonlighting*."

She smacks my chest. "I'm not that much younger than you."

"Six years," I mutter.

"I was twenty-one when you knew me before," she muses.

That's a big part of the issue. Not the age difference. But that I knew her before. That I was wildly attracted to her then. I've wanted her since the day I hired her. I've been attracted to her ever since she entered my line of sight. It was instant and electric, and I tried desperately to snuff it out. I refused to be the boss who wanted to bang his apprentice, even though I was. The strategy? *Resist.* I did, white-knuckling it through every day of longing for her. I didn't make a move because she was my employee, my apprentice, and my job was to teach her, not touch her.

Now, I have touched her, and it's astonishing the way we fit, the way she feels. I don't know how that changes things in business, on the project, or in my life. I'd like to think we won't lose focus.

But that may be wishful thinking.

I didn't pick up on the seat measurement. She's the one who went the extra mile and researched Brick's actual height. Did wanting her cause me to miss that detail? Or would I have missed it no matter what? I don't honestly know. All I know is when you mix business and pleasure, it's pretty tough to say you're all-business anymore.

She worries about respect, and I worry about distraction. She's moving up in her career, and I'm trying to maintain the pole position I've been lucky enough to achieve. This woman is her own brand of diversion because she's the competition. Though we're working on a car together, most of the time we will vie for jobs, like we did with Livvy. I compete fiercely with John Smith for business, and Henley's his lead builder. That, right there, is a conflict of interest, one I don't know how to resolve.

I glance away from her briefly, spotting the Dramamine pack on the table. I lean over the edge of the couch for it, and she pretends to cling to me, like she can't bear to let me go. "Don't leave the cocoon of the blanket," she teases.

"Just getting something." I hand her the packet. "It's for you."

She clutches them to her chest and flutters her lashes. "You are so romantic. Don't ever, ever let anyone tell you otherwise, Max Summers."

"I got you hot chocolate and motion-sickness pills. That's the height of romance."

She laughs then bumps her hip against me. I groan because it feels really fucking good. She sets the pills on the table, and I tug her back under the blanket.

As I bring her close to me, she murmurs, "Hey, Max?"

"Yeah?"

"You're totally out of my system." Her voice is sleepy sexy.

"You're so out of my system, too."

"I should go, then."

"You should absolutely leave."

But as I drag her closer, I inhale that spring apple scent that's now mixed with sweat, and sex, and me, and I can't for the life of me want to let her go.

She makes the decision for me.

She's gone when I wake up.

CHAPTER 33

She left a note behind. I discover it on the edge of my bathtub. It's a Post-It, and reading it does funny things to my chest. Things that feel both foreign and incredibly good at the same time. I carry it around all day.

To-Do List:

—Don't daydream about that guy you have a thing for.

—Don't stare at his fine butt when you work with him on the car.

—Don't let on you're thinking of last night by the window.

—Don't make stupid sex eyes at him.

—Do wear something so subtly sexy that he has to fight off dirty thoughts all day long.

As I head to work, I decide the first one is my favorite, and I'm pretty damn sure it's because it mirrors my own sentiments for her. But the other four items earn strong second-place showings. At the shop, I take her dos and don'ts to heart. When I work with her on the Lambo, I successfully fend off the filthy images. It's not easy, since she wears tight jeans and a black V-neck T-shirt. When she bends over the hood, I cop a peek at the swell of her breasts. They're heavenly. But so is that smile she wears. I'm seeing more and more of it these days. It stretches to her eyes, and the gold flecks in them sparkle when she shoots me a tiny grin.

"You're doing it," I say under my breath, since the guys are working on the Challenger several feet away.

"Doing what?"

I raise my eyebrows and mouth "sex eyes."

She shakes her head and whispers, "Stupid sex eyes." She raises her voice. "To be precise." Then she holds up the wrench and taps the engine to indicate the part she's working on. "Precise with the head gasket."

"And if you're not, you could blow a head gasket," I say, punctuating it with a sitcom soundtrack drumroll.

Henley pretends to guffaw as if this is the height of humor.

"We don't like his blown head gasket jokes, either," Mike barks as he walks behind me.

"Solidarity. Preach it," Henley says, thrusting her arm in the air, in a *rock-on* gesture. Then she calls out to Mike. "By the way, that's one badass set of wheels."

Mike flashes a grin. "Thanks. They're pretty sick. Want to see what we did under the hood?"

"Absolutely," she says, and she joins the guys for a few minutes as they show off their fine-tuning on the car. She nods, asks questions, and compliments them on their work. They don't leer at her; they don't stare at her tits. They talk to her, and she talks to them. It's everything she wants—respect.

Guess I'm the only one who's guilty of staring at her tits. *Shit.*

Lords knows, I salivated for this woman back in the day, too. I remember that during the last few weeks she worked for me, my attraction to her had magnified, like a drumbeat growing louder. The day I gave her the assignment for the Mustang paint job, I could barely take my eyes off her. She wore a blue button-down work shirt and dark jeans. Basic, standard clothes. But even with the top button undone, she looked like candy.

Quickly, I gave her the details on the Mustang, and then I took off for a trip to Boston. On the train to Massachusetts, I blasted music in my ears, pissed but grateful to be out of the orbit of my unrequited and wildly inappropriate attraction.

I vowed to do better when I returned. To just fucking smother it with a pillow till it choked its last dying breath.

Instead, I fought with her, and I fired her.

Maybe I'm the kind of guy she's worried about in this business. The kind who objectifies her. I scrub a hand over my jaw and try to make sense of this memory. It feels like a long-forgotten dream that you suddenly recall with perfect clarity. Then it sticks to you and repeats and repeats in your mind. Only, I don't know what to do about it or what it means, so I focus on the work.

As we finish up most of the customization and a few more promos that day and into the next, I find myself noticing how well she fits in this business. She's come into her own as a builder, exactly how I believed she would.

After the guys leave the next day, John stops by in the afternoon to survey the work. The clients are coming over this evening, and he wants to check the car out before they do. John whistles his approval as he surveys the vehicle. "Damn, you two make a helluva team," he says, then drops his hand on Henley's shoulder. The sight of him touching her pisses me off. It's like he wants to remind me she's his. She works for him. "Bet you wish she was still yours," he says, with a wink.

Under my breath I mutter, "She is." I do my best to bite back more words like "she's mine" and "get your damn hands off her." Instead, I look at Henley and say, "Yeah, we do make a great team."

John claps me on the back next. "I'm only busting your chops, Max. I'm just glad I'm the lucky son-of-a-bitch who convinced this woman to come work with me. She's the best," he says, then he gives the woman of the hour a big, bright smile.

I want to punch him.

And I'm not a violent man.

So I play at his game instead. "She's absolutely tops," I add, then give her my own grin.

He takes off, and I couldn't be happier.

Once he's gone, Henley gives me a curious stare. "Would you like some swords next time to go with your swordfight?"

I roll my eyes. "He's a little possessive of you."

"You're his chief competitor, and I'm his lead builder. Of course he's possessive."

"And no, I don't need a sword. Mine works just fine."

She wiggles her eyebrows. "Yes, it certainly does." She heads to the shelves to grab some tools, calling out as she goes, "But next time, leave me out of the whole talon-lock-over-territory thing," she says, brandishing her hands like claws.

I give her a salute. "Ten-four, tiger."

Still, I'm not about to let John win this game of one-upmanship. Besides, Henley is fucking awesome, and I want her to know that. Before David and Creswell stop by to check out the car, I tell her. Because she deserves to know, and because maybe I need to course correct. I want to make up for the overdose of attraction I felt for her in the past. "You've got it, Henley. Respect. You really don't have to worry. And you have it because you've earned it."

She tucks a strand of hair behind her ear. "Thank you. I hope so. I need it for—"

But she doesn't finish because the bell rings.

I wipe my hands and head to the door, opening it for our sharp-dressed clients. Creswell wears a bow tie and his skull shines like he buffed it, while David is decked out in a suit and his ever-present smile.

"She's almost done. All we need is the specialty emblem now for the hood," Henley declares, gesturing grandly to the Lambo. Her excitement is infectious. Creswell flings a meaty hand over his eyes and pretends to be blinded.

"It's like staring at the sun. She's gorgeous."

David strides over to the car, crosses his arms, and simply shakes his head in admiration. "I want to eat her up with a spoon."

I laugh. "Be sure to add whipped cream with a cherry on top."

We spend the next fifteen minutes walking them through the customization and showing off the work we did, recording it all on video as we go. To say they're pleased is an understatement. I couldn't be happier that the client is satisfied with my work. Correction: *our work*. Even though I shared credit on this one, Henley's role made the car better.

I flash back to five years ago. To the paint job mix-up. The fights. The insults. I should have been complimenting her work then to the Mustang client. Instead, I was cleaning up the mess we'd made.

Or was it the mess I made?

Maybe I didn't do enough then to right the wrong. But now, I can make sure she gets the credit she deserves.

I clear my throat. "Guys. I just want you to know that you chose wisely by having Henley on this project. I would have made you a fantastic car myself, but with her involved, it's even better."

"We couldn't be happier that you did it as a team. The two of you have a great spark," David says as he mimes making an explosion with his hands.

When Henley smiles, her eyes stay on me the whole time. The brown in them is the warmest shade I've ever seen, and it does that thing to my chest again. That flopping, flipping thing. I look away.

Creswell gives me a side nod, the universal sign for *I want to talk to you in private*. I lead him to my small office and shut the door.

"Everything good?" I ask.

"Everything's great," he says, then looks at his watch. "I'm heading to Miami for a day trip, but when I return I want to talk to you about a few other projects. We have customization jobs for some other shows in the pipeline, and we want you to do the work."

That familiar burst of pride and excitement takes root, but it's tempered by caution because the last time he did this, the network pulled a bait and switch. "Would these be solo projects or joint projects?"

Creswell chuckles. "The joint project was good for the cameras and the publicity. You and Marlowe have a great chemistry, and that helps us to promote the show. But for the other work, I think we'll take your expertise." His compliment makes me feel shittier than it should. "We'll set up a meeting for when I return."

We leave my office to find Henley and David laughing and chatting by the car. For a split-second, I remember how I felt when I saw them talking at the show. Jesus Christ, I've got to get a handle on my jealousy. It's like a fucking goblin on my shoulder, clawing and clutching at me.

"We just need to get the emblem from the supplier in Milford, Connecticut," Henley says to David. "He said he'd have it in by Saturday, then we'll install it, and we should be good to go with this beauty."

"I can head out there and pick it up," I offer.

"I'll join you," she says, and my heart skips a beat. More time with her.

"Then join me after," Creswell adds. "Come to my home for dinner. I live in Fairfield. Pick up the part and swing by, and we'll have something to eat. Roger will be there, too."

Ah, Roger must be his partner.

"Good old Roger," David says with a chuckle.

"Count us in," Henley says, and once they leave, she looks at me expectantly then spreads her arms wide. She squeals and punches her fists in the air. "They loved it. They absolutely loved it."

This is a moment that calls for celebration, so I stride over to her, pick her up so her feet are above the ground, and hug the fuck out of her. "We did it, tiger."

"I'm so happy they like it," she says, her smile as wide as the sky as she ropes her hands around my neck. "Is that what he was talking to you about in your office? How much they like it?"

I set her down and try not to meet her eyes, when I lie with a yes. It's close to the truth. "Yeah, he was telling me he liked how well we worked on it together."

She narrows her eyes at me, as if she doubts me, and the guilt inside me deepens. Then she shrugs happily. "That's great. I'm sure he figured since he asked you first that it only made sense to assure you how pleased he is."

"Yeah. Exactly," I say, each word like glass cutting my tongue.

If I tell her the truth, I could risk my business by revealing opportunities—ones she could try to pounce on. My business isn't just me—it's me and the guys I look out for, the bills I pay for them. Besides, a potential deal with Creswell isn't real yet. Potential work is a minefield of risks and opportunities, and this is precisely why being with her is dangerous. If I tell her the truth, then John Smith Rides would know there's work out there on the table. They could put forward a wildly appealing offer that convinces the network to pull this deal from me. After all, the Lambo was originally supposed to be a solo gig. Nothing is set in stone, so I need to remain a vault.

She checks the time on her phone. "See you at the Hudson later? I have some meetings, and then some guy called and wants to talk about customizing his Bugatti that already has everything," she says, rolling her eyes at the request.

"Banker dude?"

"Yup."

"I met with him the other day. He's kind of a douche. Watch out."

We're fishing in the same pond. It's not a big body of water at all, but it's full of some big fish. And we're going to keep bumping into each other with our reels and our hooks.

As I head downtown to shower and change then catch an Uber uptown to the Hudson, I imagine the street is littered with signs.

Slippery road.

Danger ahead.

Proceed with caution.

Then, when I see her in the class, I ignore them all.

CHAPTER 34

"You look so fine in a fancy shirt," Henley says, running a red fingernail down the buttons of my navy blue shirt. "And this is perfect for class."

Shockingly, I've never taken a dance class, so I asked Google what to wear, and this is the result. Nice jeans and a dress shirt.

More importantly, Henley is impressed both with my clothes and that somehow I don't suck as a dance partner. She doesn't, either.

"You're not terrible at all."

She shrugs. "I'm a fast learner."

It's a beginner's class, and I'm eminently grateful for that. I'm even more grateful that Henley wears a skirt, a little flouncy purple one that spins when I spin her, showing off her fishnet stockings. Her arms are bare, on display in a silky tank top.

"Break forward with the left foot. Rock back on the right," the instructor tells us, and with intense concentration etched in her eyes, Henley moves in time to the music.

I do something that possibly could be called that, if one was generous.

"You're doing great," she says.

"You lie."

She giggles as she threads her fingers tighter in mine. So far, I've learned that salsa isn't one of those dances where you can just hold her waist and she ropes her arms around your neck. Nope. My right hand rests on her back, and my left hand is raised between us.

"Fine," she says, sarcastically. "You're doing great for a big, brutish, bearish guy who's covered in motor oil all day."

"Hey. Watch that mouth," I say, staring at the red of her lips. "I'm completely adept at washing off all the grease that makes me dirty." When I dip her, her hair waterfalls along her back. "And you like me dirty."

When I pull her back up, she curls her fingers over my shoulder. "Dirty and clean."

"And you wonder why I'm addicted to the tub and shower," I say, as we move around in the midst of other couples. About a dozen pairs of dancers fill the room, and since none are Fred and Ginger, I don't feel too bad about my lack of skills. Besides, I'm holding my own at the most important job—being her partner so that no one else can be.

"Is that your deep, dark secret, Max?" she asks, narrowing her eyes. "An addiction to soap?"

"I have a whole array of them. Many flavors, many kinds."

She makes a purring sound. "You lure me with hot chocolate. Now you try to entice me with yummy-smelling soaps."

As the couples in the room execute spins, I follow suit. Her skirt twirls up as she turns, and I yank her back to me in time to the music. "Did I say I was luring you back?"

She gives me a pout. "Fine. I don't want to see your soaps. I don't want to smell them. I don't want to get in the shower with you and run my hands down your naked, wet chest," she says, punctuating those last few words so sexily that my dick has no choice but to betray me.

She knows it, too, because she presses her body against me, so my erection presses against her hip. I suck in a breath as she grins at me like the cat that has eaten the canary's whole damn family then finished them off with a dish of cream.

The instructor says something about a wave, and out of the corner of my eye, I see a woman near us sort of undulate her backside against her partner. Henley does the same, but with her front pressed to me.

"Good," I grit out, loving our game, loving that it doesn't seem to stop. "I don't want you under the hot shower, where these big, brutish, bearish hands would wash your gorgeous hair. Want to know why I don't want you there?"

She raises her chin, that defiant little gesture that is so her, and such a turn-on. "Why?"

"Because I'd lift you up, wrap your legs around my hips, and make you feel so fucking good you'd cry out my name again."

The smallest little hiss of breath escapes her ruby-red lips. I want to catch that sound in my cupped hands. Catch it, record it, play it back. It's the same sound she made the night I first kissed her. I want to kiss her so badly right now.

But the game continues. Her eyes turn to slits again, and she digs her fingers into my shoulders as we follow the music once more. "It's a good thing you won't do that, because then I won't get into your bed after, and let you wrap your big, brutish, bearish body around me."

"I'd hate that," I say with a sneer. I squeeze her fingers tighter. She squeezes back.

"I could tell." She moves her body even closer to me. "You'd detest every second of it."

"Every single second." I stare into her eyes as flames lick up my chest. I'm not sure if it's the heat from the room or the blaze between us. Maybe both. Maybe everything. "I don't want you back there tonight. Under the covers in my king-size bed."

She shakes her head as she licks her lips. "I'd hate feeling you against me all night long in that big comfy bed."

I try to stifle a groan. I want her so much. I want her in my shower. I want her in my bed. I want her to spend the night with me. And as she shimmies her hips, and we try mightily to salsa dance, it's so patently clear to me that I don't just want her with me so I can sleep with her. I want her with me so I can *be* with her.

I press my forehead to hers and say her name. "*Henley.*"

It's a relief to say it like this. No teasing. No agenda.

She raises her hand and brushes her fingers through my hair. I sigh because it feels so good. It feels even better when she brings her mouth to my ear and whispers my name. It sounds different now. This isn't how she says it when she's mad, when she teases, when she flirts, or when she comes.

It's new, and it's warm, and it feels like a shot of liquid gold in my heart. I need her to spend the night with me again. She has to know the "I don't want you in my bed" routine means "the only thing I want is for you to stay the night."

But I freeze when the instructor drops his hand on her shoulder.

"Very nice work," he says, and it's like he appeared out of nowhere. I pull back so I'm not so obscenely close to her.

"Thank you, Marco."

Marco is tall, trim, and toned. His hair is dark, and Henley was right—he has that Latin lover look about him. I clench my fists.

"You have a good partner," he says to her, then he turns to me. "Good work for a first class. It is not easy when a man has to both lead and show off a woman's skills. You did well."

"Thank you," I say, deciding I don't hate him.

"Will we see you again?"

I meet Henley's eyes, searching for the answer in them. She offers a small shrug then the most perfect answer when she says, "I hope so."

I hope so, too.

But as he walks away, something about what Marco said sticks with me for the rest of the class. *Show off a woman's skills.*

That's what I tried to do with Creswell and David earlier today. That's what I tried to do tonight. But it's something I failed at five years ago.

I failed because of what's happening here now. Because of what's been happening ever since I met this woman. I'm so attracted to her it's clouded my mind. It's messed with my judgment. I'd like to think I did the right thing by never saying a word, by choking down all these feelings when she worked for me.

But I might have done her a disservice.

When class ends, I take her hand and ask her to get a drink with me at the hotel bar. After we order, she tilts her head inquisitively. "Hey, you okay? You look serious."

I rub a hand across the back of my neck. "I was thinking about the Mustang Fastback."

She sighs. "The Mustang. The stupid Mustang. Can we move on? I messed up the color. You got pissed that I didn't listen. I got upset. You didn't promote me. I got mad and assumed it was because I was a woman. We fought. I lost my temper and called you names. You fired me. Here we are."

I nod, agreeing with the basic facts. "Yes, that's all true. But I don't think I was fair to you."

She blinks, as if I've just said I want to snowshoe naked in Central Park tonight. Maybe my comment is *that* unusual. "What do you mean?"

I swallow. My throat is dry. I grab the water glass the bartender brought to me. "This thing," I say, pointing from her to me.

"Yeah?" she asks cautiously.

"I felt it long before the Challenger. Long before the car show. I felt it the second I met you."

The look in her eyes tells me it is stranger than snowshoeing in the park. I've just said I want to cartwheel down Fifth Avenue.

"You did?" she asks, as if she's testing out speech for the first time.

"I was attracted to you literally in an instant. It never stopped. It never went away."

"You never let on when we worked together."

"Good," I say, somewhat relieved. "I wanted to do the right thing and be your mentor. I wanted to teach you everything I knew and help you become the best."

"You did teach me. You were incredible."

"And so were you. But what I'm trying to say is it became difficult near the end, and that's not fair to you. I wanted you so much, and I didn't realize this at the time, but when I gave you the assignment on the Mustang, I should have made sure I helped you more. I should have made sure it was done properly. I should have checked in with you and double-checked that you'd taken the codes down properly and that we were on the same page. Instead, I fucking left because it was so hard being near you. I didn't even call while I was out of town to check on the work."

"Max," she says softly, her hand wrapping around my arm, "I made a mistake. I thought you said one thing when you said another. Besides, I think lime gold is ugly. I couldn't imagine he wanted lime gold, so in my mind I figured it was champagne gold, and that's what I painted the car. And that's a big mistake because it takes a ton of work to strip it down and do it over."

I sigh. "I should have been more involved. I should have made sure it was all clear. Instead, I barked instructions, and I just left. All I could think about was escaping the way I felt for you."

She shakes her head. "I was hotheaded. I was stubborn. I was young. I was so damn sure that was what the client wanted. Don't blame yourself." Then she winks. "*Entirely.*"

I shake my head and grip her shoulders. "Don't you get it? I take my time with the guys. I'm patient. I teach them. I make sure they know what they're doing. I tried so fucking hard to do that with you, but the day I gave you the job I was looking at you in your jeans and your blue work shirt, and all I could think was how much I wanted you, and I had to get away from you."

She tries to rein in a laugh.

"Why are you laughing at me? I don't want to treat you any differently. You're supposed to hate me. You're supposed to hate me because you want to be respected. You don't want to be treated differently, and I did treat you differently that time. And then I came back to town, and I was pissed."

She laughs even more, and it's the same sound as the other night. That sound like bells. It fucking hooks into me. It's doing something to me. Everything about her is like a charm, from the way she dissects magic acts, to worshipping my tub, to needling me, to letting me into her warm blanket cocoon.

"I'm laughing because, fine, maybe you could have checked in and maybe you could have been a better teacher at times, but . . . C'mon. We're not talking sexual harassment here. You gave me an assignment, and I completely botched it. And it cost you time and money. And then I lost my cool. Do you not remember the drama queen I was?" she asks, tapping her chest. No, she's stabbing it. "I parked my hands on my hips and called you a cruel bastard. You want to talk about inappropriate behavior? I engaged in it, too."

The knot of tension in me loosens. "You were kind of hotheaded and stubborn," I say under my breath.

"And you were kind of a cruel bastard," she says, playfully.

"So we were both kind of jerks?"

She laughs. "Total jerks. I think it's safe to say, looking back, that we both could have handled our little work tiff differently. But it's behind us. Okay? Let's keep it there."

"Sounds like a fair deal."

She gives me a coy look. "But you were kind of a dick," she says playfully. "And now I know why." She leans closer and taps her fingers against my chest. "Because you wanted me." She says it like a taunt, a little song you sing to egg someone on.

"I did. I wanted you then. I wanted you when I saw you at the show. And I want you now."

"You wanted me then. You still want me now," she says, and she's singing again.

"Is this a new bubble-gum pop song?"

"Yes. I'm going to commission it to Belinda, and we'll make gobs of money off it." She shakes her hips and croons. "He wanted me then. He still wants me now."

I roll my eyes, but I let her give it to me. Because I deserve it, and because she's not mad. Because she's singing a forgiveness tune.

"So we can move past the Mustang?"

Her lips curve up. "We already have. We're past the Mustang. We're onto the Lambo. Why don't we talk about what car we're driving to Milford tomorrow? That's the car we should focus on."

I lean against the counter as the bartender brings our drinks. I toss a twenty on the black metal and thank him. "I've got a black sports car I built myself—"

She cuts me off. "I would hope you built it yourself. You're not impressing this car girl unless I know these hands made it from the ground up." She reaches for my hand and slides her fingers through mine.

"And I have a Triumph TR6. Don't tell the other cars, but the Triumph is my favorite, even though I didn't build it myself. I added safety features and rebuilt the important parts, though, as in new electrical."

"So it doesn't blow up?"

I laugh, loving that she knows her cars. "I thought that would be a good feature—blow-up resistant. Plus, it has a hot new paint job."

Her jaw drops, and she fans herself. "Color? What color?" She sounds as if she's hyperventilating.

I bring my mouth to her ear and whisper as if I'm telling her what I want to do to her when I take her home. "It's electric blue."

She moans. It's filthy and beautiful, and I want to hear that sound twenty more times tonight. Then tomorrow. Then the next night.

"Pick me up at two." She nibbles her lip, and adds, "And there's something I wanted to—"

I'm ready to tell her I don't need to pick her up tomorrow because she's staying with me tonight, but her phone beeps.

"Crap," she mutters, as she grabs it from her purse.

She points to it. "John."

I wave, letting her know to take the call.

"Hey there!" Her voice is bright and cheery. "How's everything going?"

She pauses, and I take a drink of my Scotch.

"Oh yeah? We can talk about all that. I'm totally up for it."

Another pause, and I arch an eyebrow.

"Absolutely." Then she laughs, and it's the same damn way she laughed with me. The goblin rears its head again. Stupid jealousy tornadoes through me.

I try to tell myself the woman is allowed to laugh with her fucking boss.

Boss.

Boss.

Boss.

That word reverberates.

That's what I was to her once upon a time.

"We can meet tonight. I'll be there shortly."

She hangs up, and my heart fucking falls out of my chest. It lands on the floor in a discarded, depressed heap. She grabs her mojito, takes a thirsty gulp, then gives me a guilty smile.

"I'm sorry. I can't stay. I have to take care of this."

"Sure," I say, keeping my chin up. "It's business. He's your boss."

She nods. "I've just got to finish—"

I wave a hand. "Go. Take care of it. I'll pick you up at two."

She stands up from the barstool. "Sorry." Then she leans closer and dusts her lips to my cheek. "Thank you for dancing with me tonight."

When she leaves, I'm the sucker alone at the bar, watching the most beautiful girl walk away.

In some other story, I'd chase her. But I already told her how I felt, and whatever she was about to tell me was cut off when John called.

That name echoes in my head. John Smith. The other night she said she didn't get involved with anyone in the business except for one time.

I've tried hard to not get involved with anyone in the business. Ever. The only time . . .

I didn't push her to find out who he was. But could it be him? The guy she's rushing off to meet at nine p.m. after we practically promised on the dance floor to spend the night together? After I told her I've always been attracted to her?

I grip the glass tighter, and when I look down, my knuckles are nearly white.

I set the glass on the bar and leave.

Chapter 35

Henley's To-Do List

—Don't bite nails.

—Stop stressing.

—Charge phone so you don't miss a call.

—Remind self it will happen, it will happen, it will happen.

— Don't check phone incessantly.

—Put deal out of mind and enjoy the day.

—Tell Max what you wanted to say last night.

—Shop with Olivia!

—Do bring a change of you-know-what on the road trip. Duh.

—Pat self on back for that awesome work this morning. Girl, you kick ass sometimes.

—Keep being awesome!

—Shave your legs. Just in case.

—Whatever you do, don't ask him for advice. Even though you want to. Don't. Do. It.

—He'd know what to do.

CHAPTER 36

As I grab my phone to leave the next morning, someone knocks on my door.

I yank it open to find Patrick. He hands me the screwdriver that he borrowed last night. We shot a round of pool then after he returned from an outdoor adventure trip. As he valiantly worked his way around the table trying to best me, he regaled me with tales of ropes and hikes and trails and wild late-night antics. I mostly listened. It was better than stewing alone over Henley's quick departure, though somehow Patrick pried a few minor details from me about my night. They were mainly along the lines of *I told her I was attracted to her, she went to a late-night meeting with her boss. End of story.*

He thanks me for the screwdriver, and I set it on the nearest shelf. I'll put it away later when I return from Connecticut.

I leave and lock the door behind me. "Gotta keep the riffraff like you away from my pool table," I say, a bottle of wine in hand for the host.

He claps me on my back. "Glad to see you're not still in a funk."

"I was not in a funk last night."

"Right. Sure. Whatever you say."

"I'm in a jolly mood," I say, slapping on a counterfeit smile as I head down the hall and stab the elevator button. "I beat you both times."

"Yeah. You're radiating happiness." Patrick pretends to waft the air toward him. "Mmmm. I can smell it coming off you in waves."

"Scent of Charming and Joyful, right? I'm going to bottle it and make millions," I say as the elevator arrives and we step inside.

Patrick wraps his hands around the brass bar and leans back against it, clucking his tongue. "You know, you could just tell her you're into her."

I snap my gaze at him. "What?"

"Oh sorry. Let me try that in simpler language. TELL HENLEY YOU DIG HER FOR MORE THAN SEX."

I roll my eyes. "That's not the issue."

When the elevator reaches his floor and the doors open, he casts me a parting glance. "But what if it is? Sometimes a lady likes a man who's direct and doesn't play games."

That's insane. I have absolutely not played games with Henley. And I don't know how she could think I just want her for sex. Hell, I was the only one who even breathed a word last night about feelings.

I shove his comments out of my mind as I head around the block to the parking garage where I keep my Triumph. This is the car I'd always wanted as a kid. It was the car I dreamed of. The one I longed for. There's nothing I don't love about this baby.

I haven't taken her out in a few weeks, so I pause for a moment to pet the hood and ask her how she's doing.

I cup my hand over my ear. "What's that? You missed me? Aw. I missed you, too, Blue Betty," I say as I run my fingers along the pristine windshield. I place the wine on the sliver of a backseat—it's basically big enough for a small gift for your rich friend—then slide into the beige leather driver's seat, lower the top, and back up. Nothing says a perfect fall day like a drive to Connecticut in your restored electric-blue roadster.

When I arrive at Henley's block in her SoHo neighborhood, I scan for the nearby garage to park for a few minutes. I could call her and have her come down, but even though this is Manhattan, a man should make an effort when he picks up a woman. Calling her is like honking a horn at a chick before a date.

Except this isn't a date.

It's an I-don't-know-what-the-fuck-it-is.

But there's no need to find the garage, since Henley's standing at the curb, looking like she just stepped out of *The Great Gatsby*. Big sunglasses cover her eyes, and a red silk scarf is tossed elegantly over her hair. A purple dress shows off her legs. She holds a bottle of champagne and a little jacket.

Lord have mercy.

I forget I'm annoyed. I forget what time it is. I nearly forget my name. I pull over, double-park, and call out, "Have I gone back in time, Daisy Buchanan?"

She laughs as she pats the scarf. "Perhaps you have, old sport. I fancy a drive to the country."

As she walks over to Blue Betty, I hop out, head around the back, and open the passenger door for her. But she doesn't get in. Instead, she hands me the bottle, then says as if she's in church, "I just need a moment."

She hops on the hood, and falls back in slow-mo, as if she's making a snow angel on my car. A look of exquisite bliss spreads across her face as she murmurs, "I understand love at first sight. I fall in love with every Triumph TR6 I see."

Nothing, not a damn thing, has ever looked finer than Henley in her purple dress as she luxuriates on the hood of my ride. I would snap a photo if I were a cell-phone-picture kind of guy. But I'm not, since I know it'll last forever in my mind's eye.

"Glad to hear you like Blue Betty."

She rolls to her side and strokes the hood. "And you gave her a name," she says, utterly delighted.

"Of course I gave her a name."

"She is beautiful," Henley says, planting a quick kiss on the metal then hopping off the hood.

I set the champagne in the back, then Henley slips into her seat and smooths her dress as I shut her door. I return to the driver's seat and cast her one more admiring glance. As I drink her in, from the scarf to the royal purple of the dress, I picture her getting ready a few minutes earlier. I wonder what her place looks like. If she's neat or messy. If her apartment would share secrets about Henley she has yet to reveal. I've never seen where she lives. I don't entirely *get* what she's up to. Most of all, I have no clue what she wants from me, or how to even broach the topic again, so I sidestep to safer ground. "So this is the girlie Henley?"

"It seemed appropriate for our expedition."

I tip my head toward her building. "I bet your place is full of pink and rhinestones."

She swats my arm. "Shame on you. I'm a diamonds kind of girl. Now, let's be on our way." She shoos me along, and I steer away from the curb and navigate through SoHo toward the

FDR Drive. As we head out of the city, we're quiet. I'm focused on driving, but I'm also honestly not sure what to say next. Last night felt like the start of something. The door opened on the dance floor, then widened when we cleared the air about our split, but it swung shut abruptly as soon as she hung up her phone. I'd been so sure where the evening was headed, then it unraveled into the mystery of her once more.

She reaches into her purse and fishes around. As I stop at a light, she shows me a crinkly clear plastic bag with a blue bow on it. Inside are two bath bombs.

"For you," she says, with a shy smile. Is Henley shy about something? About anything? If she is, she wears shyness well, because that smile is endearing. "To say I'm sorry I had to leave early last night."

Her apology intrigues me. The light changes, so I hit the gas, say thank you for the gift, and let her continue. She taps the outline of the white and tan bath bomb. "This is Cedar Grove. So it's super manly. And the other is Peach Dreams."

"So, super manly, too?"

She laughs and shakes her head. "Peach Dreams just smells pretty." She smiles and brushes some loose strands of hair from her face.

"Want me to put the top up?"

"Not until hail is shrieking from the sky. Besides, that's what this is for," she says, running a hand down the scarf. She relaxes into the seat as I turn onto the FDR Drive. She sets the gift in the console.

I glance at it briefly then return my eyes to the road. I can't help but wonder if the gift means something. Two bath bombs. One masculine. One feminine. But as soon as those ridiculous thoughts land in my brain, I'm fucking embarrassed. This girl does not want romance from me, or mushy thoughts of cou-pledom. I don't know what she wants. I push them into a far corner in my head then kick some dirt over them. She's simply saying she's sorry for cutting out early, not for dashing my hopes for a sleepover, with homemade pancakes for breakfast as a bonus—and I make kickass blueberry pancakes. Besides, I ought to know better. I need to stick to my own guideline—don't sleep with the enemy.

Though, I've already crossed that line a few times. Better amend the rule to—don't fall for the enemy.

I try my best to keep her at a distance. "Thank you for the gift, but you don't have to say you're sorry for anything."

"I do."

"No, you don't. You had business to take care of. Did you get everything squared away?"

Out of the corner of my eye, I notice a pained look on her face. "I think so," she says, but it doesn't sound like she believes it. She brings her fingers to her mouth, as if she's about to bite her nail. She stops herself, placing her hands in her lap.

Out of instinct, I set a hand on her thigh. "Hey, are you okay?"

She nods, and it's the tough kind. The *I'll be fine* style. "I will be."

"Anything . . . you want to talk about? Even though it would be weird for us to discuss business, I guess."

"Isn't that what we're supposed to avoid?"

"That probably means I shouldn't ask you about the Bugatti guy, either."

She thrusts her arms in the air, her mood shifting instantly. "Bulletproof glass. I'm survivalizing his car."

I crack up from her enthusiasm. "For real?"

She nods as we cruise along the FDR, the wind from the open top whipping past us, a lone gray cloud hanging low in the sky. "Can you believe it? I signed the deal yesterday, and he brought the car in this morning. I was at the shop early to meet him, and I'm starting the work on Monday. He's a total zombie freak."

That surprises the hell out of me. "Never would have pegged him for a zombie guy. He seemed pure Wall Street all the way."

"I thought so, too, but then I noticed this," she says, tapping her wrist. It's bare and slender and pretty. And holy fuck, did I just actually think a woman's wrist was sexy?

"What about his wrist?"

"His watch. It's the kind zombie survivalists wear. It's a Casio model that's popular among that crowd."

"No fucking kidding? I remember that watch. I figured he repped the company or something. Never occurred to me it meant he was a *Walking Dead* believer."

"As soon as I saw it, I knew what would get him fired up. I told him his Bugatti was already fast enough to get out of a horde of brain-eaters in less than three seconds, but had his Veyron been outfitted to withstand the walking dead in the apocalypse? Hook. Line. Sinker," she says, then mimes reeling him in.

For a moment, I wait for the goblin on my shoulder to reappear in a new form. To rage with work jealousy over her winning a potential deal that I not only didn't get—I didn't know how to win. But the green-eyed monster never rears his head. And that's not only because I didn't want to work with the guy. It's because she deserves this deal. She spotted the way in that I didn't see.

I've got to give her credit for sealing the deal. "Good for you, Henley. I'm impressed. And I'm proud of you."

"Thank you. I'm proud of me, too," she says, and there's a lovely happiness in her tone that warms my heart. She looks at me, and her eyes go wide.

"What's wrong?" I say, flicking my gaze back to the concrete ribbon in front of us as we head onto I-95. On the horizon, the sky darkens.

"We just discussed business, and you didn't flip out and I didn't flip out."

"Does that mean we're not enemies anymore?"

When she kicks off one heel and sets her foot on the dashboard, she says, "You weren't my enemy last night."

"On the dance floor?"

She shakes her head. "When I got home," she says, and her voice takes on a softer edge. "That's why I'm sorry I had to leave early."

And color me even more intrigued. "What did you do when you were back at your place?"

CHAPTER 37

She doesn't say a word. Instead, as we cruise along the highway, she tugs at the hem of her dress. My fingers grip the wheel tighter as I watch both the road and her.

Her right hand dances along her calf, gently stroking her skin. I breathe harder. That hand. Those legs. She travels up to her knees, revealing more of her flesh. A noise echoes from my throat. The purple fabric rises higher, over her knees, up her thighs, each second making the temperature in me tick up. The heat shoots one thousand degrees as her skirt reaches her waist.

She wears pink panties. So simple. So sexy. "Once I was in my apartment, I did . . . this," she says as she drags her finger across the panel between her legs.

I groan as she tugs the skirt back down. I will my focus to the critical task at hand—driving. "So those busy little fingers kept you entertained?"

"Very entertained."

"Bed, couch, or shower?"

"Bed. I have a flowered bedspread, in case you were wondering what my place looks like. It's a deep rose with vines and petals along the edges, and I have more pillows than the sky has stars," she says, as she fills in the missing paint by numbers. I can see her place so clearly now.

"I bet you look like a goddess on it. A dirty goddess with your fingers in your panties."

"My hand was between my legs in seconds. I thought of what I was missing last night."

"What were you missing?"

"Your mouth on me. Everywhere on me," she says, her voice breathy. "All over my body."

"That can be arranged."

She drags her fingers along her neck. "My neck." Then over her chest. "My breasts." She slows at her belly. "My stomach."

I grip the wheel so damn hard I'm surprised I don't rip it out of the dashboard. "We can conduct a reenactment of this anytime you want. Just say the word."

She slides her hand down her thigh, over her skirt. "Between my legs."

"I can pull over right now."

She seems lost in the memory. "That's where I wanted to be last night. That's where I wished I was. I wanted my fantasy to be real so badly."

And if I had any questions, she's answered most of them.

"It can be real," I say, and my voice is hoarse, rough with need.

As we cruise along the highway, I want nothing more than to watch the woman come. I want to hear her breath hitch, and I want to watch her fingers fly faster along the wet panel of her panties. I'm dying to see her get herself off, right here in my car. Legs spread. Feet on the dash. Head thrown back. I want to witness her orgasm wracking her body, see how she shudders, then I want to stop the car, climb over her, and fuck her through her afterglow to another, and another. I want to do everything with her and to her.

The first drop of rain splatters against the windshield, breaking my filthy fantasies.

I signal, slow, and pull onto the shoulder to raise the top. Once it's up, I turn to her. Her eyes are a pure chocolate brown. Vulnerable.

"Hey," I say. "You forgot one place where my mouth would be."

"I did?"

I grab her face in one hand and crush her lips, kissing her like I would have if we'd stumbled out of the bar together last night, drunk on each other, high on the flirting, ready to go to her place or mine. To tear off clothes, map each other's skin, drive each other wild.

I kiss her like I would have if I'd undressed her, worshipped her body with my tongue and lips, then moved her beneath me and lowered the full weight of my body onto hers. I haven't had her like that. Under me on a bed. I want her on her back, her hair fanned out on a pillow, her beautiful body revealed to me. She trembles as I kiss her, and the uncertainty I felt this morning melts away. She ropes her arms around my neck and pulls me closer.

Goddamn, I want her now. I want her deeper and closer. But as the rain lashes the windshield, I'm acutely aware we have a deadline to meet. The supplier closes shop soon.

Not to mention the other little issue. As I separate, I flash her a lopsided grin. "I'm all for car sex, but side of the road on I-95 feels like the textbook definition of a bad idea."

She laughs warmly. "I'm with you on that one." She runs the back of her fingers along my cheek. Softly, she says, "Max."

"Yeah?"

"The same."

I furrow a brow. "What's the same?"

"Everything you said last night. It's the same for me. I've been attracted to you since I met you. I feel it everywhere."

The world shifts on its axis. It's like my entire body is plugged in. I'm crackling and electric and so turned on. But there's more to it than that. Something stirs inside me again—something that feels foreign and strange but is completely welcome, too. "Is that so?"

She nods. "When I said I've tried hard not to get involved with anyone in the business, and the only time I've been involved is now," she says, reminding me of her words from the night on my couch, "I also meant the only time was with you before. Even though we weren't a thing. But I was so into you, it pretty much felt like we were involved."

"Same here." I press a final kiss to her lips, partly so I won't ask the next thing on my mind—*how involved are we now?*

I don't want to ruin the moment, and I don't want to miss our deadline. And I'm glad I'm saying sayonara to the goblin and the insidious thoughts he planted in my head of her and John Smith.

When I merge back onto the highway, I ask her if she wants to listen to music. She tells me she has a playlist, and I say I do, too.

"You have a playlist?" she asks, surprised.

As she shoots me a challenging stare, I pick up where she left off last night. "She wanted me then. She still wants me now," I say, singing for her.

She laughs, then takes my hand and threads her fingers through mine. Like that, we drive through the rain. The tension in me unwinds. The worry about what's happening between us fades away. I don't entirely know what we are, but I know something is happening and it's not stopping, and somehow we'll figure it out.

Until I realize near Milford that her fingers are sliding out of mine. They're slipping into her purse, and she's checking her phone.

My chest tightens. I don't know why this bothers me so much.

But it does.

It really fucking does, especially since she can't stop checking her phone. The goblin rears its head again, roaring back to life. Only this time I'm jealous of something else.

I'm jealous of whoever it is that knows this woman better than I do. I want to know her. I want to understand her. I want to be the one she tells why she's nervous, why she nearly nibbled on her nail, and what she's waiting for.

But I'm not that guy.

* * *

We are mostly business as we stop at the supplier and pick up the emblem for the Lambo. The rain splashes in thick streams from the sky, and Henley pops open a white umbrella with lavender polka dots as we head into the supplier's shop.

Small talk about the car and the show occupies us for several minutes. Then we say good-bye and return to my Triumph with the special-order emblem. As I back out of the lot, silence fills the small space between us again. It's thick, like smoke you can barely see through.

As I shift the car in first, I glance at her, and she locks eyes with me. I swallow past the dryness in my throat. Someone needs to speak. Someone needs to fucking figure out what's happening between us.

For a moment, as I plug Creswell's address into the GPS on my phone, Patrick's comment rings in my ears.

Tell Henley you want more than just sex.

With my hand on the knob of the shifter, that reality forces its way front and center. That's the issue. That's the rub. I want to be that guy for her. I want to know what's going on in her life. I want to be more than her one-night, two-night, three-night stand. I want to be the guy she gets off to *and* the guy she goes out with.

I've got it bad for this girl.

As I signal onto the road to our client's house, slowing my speed on the rain-slicked concrete, I noodle on what to say, and how the fuck to navigate being something more with her when she's the competition. How I can make heads or tails of all the reasons why I shouldn't spend one more night with her. We'd have to confront the prospect of trade secrets, shared clients, and more every day. We'd constantly be pursuing the same deals. We'd bump elbows and heads, and knock into each other all the time. Those phone calls and stolen moments away would only intensify. It's a small world, maybe too small to be involved with my rival. To top it off, she distracts me to no end.

She makes me lose focus.

She makes me want to be with her.

She makes me fucking *feel.*

And that's the problem. I feel something for her.

But I want her more than I don't want all the fucking complications.

I curse out loud as I turn the corner.

"Are you okay?" she asks.

Shit.

That was supposed to be said in my head.

And she reminds me of me now. She reminds me of when I asked earlier on the ride if she was okay. Her comment makes me wonder if she feels the same pull. The same intensity. The same whatever this is.

The same.

I try to shake off the tempest of questions rattling my brain and dragging down my heart. The GPS lady tells us Creswell's house is one mile away. Dusk is falling.

"Yeah. I'm fine," I mutter, then the words tied up inside me unknot. "What's going on in your life?" I ask at the same time as she blurts out, "What's happening here?"

I keep going. "It drives me crazy not knowing. It drives me fucking insane."

"Between us. Because there's something happening."

But the next thing that happens is my phone. It buzzes loudly in the holder. Creswell's name flashes on the screen. I swipe and answer him on speaker.

"Hey! We're almost there."

"Thank God I caught you," he says, his voice heavy with relief.

Henley's eyes meet mine, and hers are full of concern.

"What's going on?"

Creswell breathes out hard, as if he's been running for miles. "I'm here with Cynthia, and she's hurt, and I need to get her something."

Henley makes a T with her hands. "Hey, Creswell," she says. "Who's Cynthia?"

"Cynthia is my girlfriend. I'm at her house. We just returned from the ER."

"Oh my God," Henley says, straightening her spine. "Is she okay?"

"She'll be fine," he says, and I can hear his shoes clicking against the floor. He must be pacing. "She was at her house earlier, making a salad to bring tonight, when she sliced off her finger."

My eyes nearly pop from my head. "She sliced off her finger?"

"Yes, the tip. It was a bit bloody. The surgeon sewed it back on, but she's quite shaken, as you can imagine."

"Of course. What can we do to help?"

"Let us know if we can get you anything. We'll help however we can."

"You're near my house?" He asks it as if that's the answer to his prayers.

A quick check of the GPS tells me we're five hundred feet away. "Almost there. What do you need?"

"My spare key is under a rock on the side porch," he says, detailing exactly how to find it as I scan the mailboxes for his number. "Once you get it, plug in the code to the security system."

He gives us the number, and Henley grabs a Sharpie from her purse and writes down the number on a pad of paper.

"I would go myself, but I can't leave her."

"Of course not," Henley says, her voice all calm and concerned. "What does she need? A pillow? A change of clothes? Her eyeglasses?" she asks, rattling off the usual suspects.

"No. She needs Roger. He always calms her down."

I pull into his driveway and cut the engine. "Who's Roger?"

I had thought Roger was his partner. Hell, maybe Roger is his other partner, and they have some unusual threesome thing going on.

But the next words from Creswell clear up the Roger confusion completely.

"He's my monkey."

CHAPTER 38

Henley's To-Do List

—Duck if he throws something.

—Find nearest banana.

—Look away if his paw is between his legs.

—Get him.

—Scratch that.

—Make Max get him.

CHAPTER 39

Roger is naked.

"I thought he'd be wearing a diaper."

"Creswell said he was well trained. I guess he's house trained, too," Henley says, her tone one of awe as we approach the wild animal who lives with our client in a pristine two-story Connecticut colonial.

Roger swings from the top of the enclosure in Creswell's living room. We take careful, measured steps toward the huge wire cage that runs from the floor to the ceiling and looks like it would fit in a zoo. Inside is a miniature forest, and Roger seems to enjoy it —he jumps from the wire to a branch on a little replica of a tree. Then he leaps to the front of the cage and sticks a small hand through the holes.

Henley points at him and covers her mouth. A dart of worry shoots through me, since she looks scared. But instead, she bounces on her heels and suppresses a childlike shriek. She spins around, doubles over, and says, "Oh my God, he's so fucking cute!"

It's the first time I've ever heard her swear.

She spins back and grabs my arm, clutching me in excitement. "Look at him! Just. Look. At. Him."

Roger is, by any definition of the word, a pipsqueak. He's a Callimico monkey, Creswell told me as I'd parked the car and looked for the key. He's a rescue from Bolivia, and his right arm is permanently injured. That's why he lives here.

He's all black and no bigger than a squirrel. His tail is a yard long. His hand is the tiniest thing I've ever seen, and his fingers are long. His fur gleams so brightly he could be a monkey shampoo model.

"Is he going to throw anything at us?" Henley asks as we near the cage.

A quick scan of Creswell's clean living room, from the immaculate hardwood floors to the shimmering glass coffee table and unmarked, unscratched beige leather couch, tells me that the man wasn't lying when he said Roger was well trained. There's not a trace of monkey projectile or monkey mark anywhere.

"He doesn't seem to be taking aim at you with any missiles," I say as we reach the cage.

Roger's small brown eyes widen and he shoots out his hand, clasping as much of Henley's shoulder as he can grasp. "Oh my God," she shrieks.

"Is he still the cutest thing you've ever seen?"

Her smile is huge as she nods. "He's adorable. I'm in love with him."

I raise my eyebrows as Roger makes a chattering noise, like a little lovebird in a tree. "I think he's in love with you, too."

Following Creswell's instructions, I unlock the door to the enclosure, opening it slowly. Roger yanks his paw back into the cage. I'll be honest—I'm expecting the primate to just take off. To race across the living room, scamper up the stairs, and swing from the chandeliers. And I'm ready with my arms wide open to try to catch the guy if he gives me a run for my money.

Memo to bookies: Bet on the monkey, not the man.

The second the door creaks open, Roger leaps—but not across the living room. He flings himself at Henley with a happy shriek. A look of terror flicks across Henley's eyes, but it morphs quickly to a wild thrill as she welcomes him in her arms. His tail seems to have a mind of its own, and he wraps it around her waist. She cuddles him in the crook of her arm, snuggling the tiniest creature I've ever laid eyes on.

Henley coos at him. It is the sound of a woman falling for a child. "Hey there, sweet thing," she says to him in a soft, doting tone.

Roger bares his teeth in a smile then makes his lovebird chatter once more.

"Told you so. The dude is smitten," I say, as Henley strokes his chin. Roger lifts it higher, giving her full access for a petting session.

"Gah! I'm smitten, too. I thought he was going to throw poo at me or jerk off."

I crack up. "And instead, he's putting out for you."

Henley shoots me a stern stare. "He is not putting out. He's a sweet boy." She looks at the monkey in her arms. "Are you a sweet boy, Roger? Yes, you are. You're such a sweet boy. Do you want a banana?"

On that note, Henley strides out of the living room in her purple dress, a black primate snug up against her, me behind her. She heads to the state-of-the-art kitchen with its marble island counter and Sub-Zero fridge. A back door with a small dog entry cut into it leads to the yard. Perhaps Creswell has a dog, too. Or maybe Roger uses the dog door. Henley grabs a banana from a fruit bowl. Roger shakes his head and leans away from her, snagging a slice of a Macintosh apple that's been left on a plate. Maybe it's the remains of his lunch. He bites into it and then finishes the wedge a minute later.

"He even eats apple chunks adorably," Henley says, so completely head-over-heels for Roger.

I look at my watch as a bird squawks from the yard. "We should get the calming monkey to Creswell."

Henley wraps an arm tighter around him. "Unless I steal him first," she says then adopts an evil tone. "Muahaha. Roger is mine. He's coming home with me."

I tip my forehead to the front door. "First the monkey bread. Now the monkey love. What'll be next?"

"Monkey business," Henley says as we leave. She snags her umbrella from the front porch, pops it open, and covers Roger with it, like a doting mama.

I shake my head, amused.

She nudges my side with her elbow. "Aww. Don't tell me you're jealous of a monkey, Max."

"Not unless he can have monkey sex with you."

She covers one of his ears with her hand. "Don't talk that way in front of Roger. He's young and impressionable."

"And you're far gone," I say as I open the car door. Gently, Henley sets Roger in the back, next to the wine and champagne. He grabs the buckle that I'm pretty sure was designed to strap in golf clubs, and slings it over the world's smallest waist. Clearly, this isn't Roger's first rodeo. He's a regular passenger.

As I hit the gas, with the woman I'm crazy for in the front seat and a miniature monkey in the backseat of my prized Blue Betty, I'm right where I was a few minutes ago, and that means it's time to finally deal with the elephant in the room.

Or really, to get the monkey off my back.

CHAPTER 40

Henley's To-Do List

—Finish the conversation.

CHAPTER 41

She speaks first. "It's a business deal I'm working on."

Henley makes this announcement as she twists her body in the front seat so she can pet Roger in the back.

"You and Roger have a business deal?" I ask, since two-plus-two isn't equaling four.

"No. The thing that's going on with me. The thing that distracts me," she says as we return to the conversation we had before the Monkey Mayday Call. "The reason I kept checking my phone. The reason I left you last night to meet with John. I have to keep it totally quiet or it could fall apart. I'm sorry if I'm distracted. I'm not supposed to be saying a word, but I can tell it drives you crazy. So I wanted you to know."

She must be working the biz dev angle hard, wheeling and dealing and lining up new clients. She's got the skills under the hood, but I bet she's damn fine at luring new clients, too, and I do understand the need to keep that close to the vest.

"I get it," I say, as a long stretch of rain-slicked quiet country road spills before us. The GPS voice instructs us to stay on this road for a mile. "It does drive me crazy, but that's not fair. The truth is, I'm a jealous ass when it comes to you, and I don't know how to stop feeling this way."

She adopts a shocked expression. "You're jealous? I hadn't noticed at all."

"It can be pretty hard to spot at times. You might need a magnifying glass," I say drily, as the windshield wipers flick against the glass. "Listen, Henley, I'm sorry I've been so worked up. I just want to know what's going on in your life, because I want to know you. You asked what was happening here between us, and that's what's happening," I say, drawing a deep breath. Then I decide it's time. It's just fucking time. I can't keep stewing in my own frustration. "I know I've said that us being involved would be a terrible idea, but after the last few days, all I can think is that us not being involved would be much more terrible. I want to know you even more. Because everything I know already I like so much. So much that lately you're all I think about."

She leans across the console and brushes her lips against my cheek. "The same," she whispers. "It's the same for me. I think about you all the time."

All that crazy stuff that was happening in my chest? Those funny feelings like pancakes flipping and the world spinning in circles? I get it now. I understand it fully. Because my heart soars as if it's rising in a hot air balloon. As she pulls back from my cheek, I want to tell her everything I feel for her. "Everything that drives me crazy is just because I'm crazy for you."

Her voice is rich with happiness. "I'm so crazy for you I want to tattoo my name on your arm so everyone knows you're taken."

I laugh then reach for the Sharpie she left in the console. "Do it."

"For real?"

"Why the hell not?"

She uncaps her black pen. I've got one hand on the wheel, one on the shift stick. She writes on my forearm. Ten seconds later, she declares, "Done!"

I glance down, and her tattoo couldn't be more perfect. It says *Tiger.*

I'm about to tell her more, to say how we'll find a way to manage work and us, and that there's nothing we can't figure out, when the robotic voice of the GPS interrupts us.

"You are nearing your destination. Turn right in two hundred feet."

I flip on my turn signal as a pair of big brown eyes shine from twenty feet away. My heart gallops. A deer stands before me in the middle of the road; it must have just run onto the street and stopped.

"Shit," I mutter, as I lay my hand on the horn, but he doesn't move, and there are no more choices to be made.

My pulse jackhammers as my choices crystallize to only one. I jerk the wheel to the right, slamming on the brake as I skid into the shoulder, out of the way of the animal.

An ear-shattering, bone-crunching din rips through the air. My head snaps back as a white airbag inflates instantaneously, jamming into my chest. The sound of crunching metal fills my ears and Henley's head slams back against the headrest.

Roger yelps, Henley moans, and the engine sputters to a stop.

The deer scampers across the street and into the woods. He's gone.

* * *

"Henley!" I shout her name as cold, black fear floods my veins.

Roger shrieks from the backseat.

I ignore him as the world narrows to this second. To this single solitary moment as Henley's head lolls against the headrest, her eyes closed, the airbag wedged against her chest.

I shake her shoulder. "Are you okay?"

Terror races through me, as if I've been pumped full of it. I've gone from fine to horrified in less than three seconds, faster than a sports car can hit sixty. My heart pounds in my ears, and blood roars in my skull. I fumble around her, reaching for her seat belt and unsnapping it.

"Are you okay?"

No response. But she's breathing. And I can't fucking believe that's the hope I'm holding on to—that she's breathing. I need more than breathing. I need everything.

"Henley, open your eyes," I say, desperation and fear ripping through me as I try to shove the airbag out of the way.

A hard, black thing swipes across her shoulder then her face, and I startle. Henley's lips part. A small chuckle escapes. Her eyes flutter open. Roger is swiping his tail across her cheek. Roger is petting her face with the tip of his tail.

Roger. Good old Roger.

No wonder Cynthia needed him. Henley turns her face to me and smiles. "I'm okay."

I press my forehead to hers and breathe again. It's not even a sigh of relief. It's absolute gratitude.

* * *

The front end of Blue Betty is wrapped around a tree.

"Guess that's what we call a tree hugger," I say as I inspect my prized possession, now crumpled into the trunk of an oak. Thank Christ I took the time and spent the money to install these airbags. Complete pain in the ass and completely worth it.

"I'm so sorry this happened to your baby," Henley says, running her hand down my arm. The car's the only one damaged. I'm fine, Henley's fine, and so is the monkey. Come to think of it, the deer is probably enjoying a nice serving of grass somewhere not far from here. We stand in the bank on the side of the road, while Roger clings to Henley's side again.

I pat the battered hood. "It's okay. She took one for the team."

"But Max," Henley says, sadness coloring her tone. "This is Blue Betty. She's a—"

"She's a wreck."

But I'm not. And as I assess the devastation to the car I've wanted since I was a kid, the one I painstakingly restored with my own hands, I don't feel that crushing fear, that rush of nerves.

Blue Betty is just a car, and I've got Triple A, as well as the wherewithal to fix it. "Let me call a tow. Why don't you take your new boyfriend to Cynthia and Creswell," I say, nodding at the monkey. Cynthia's house is a few hundred feet away.

Henley gives me a knowing look, her brown eyes clear as day as she gazes straight at me. "*He's* not my boyfriend."

"I know someone else then who'll apply for the job."

"Tell him he already has it," she says, stroking the primate's head.

I grin like a man who just bought a beautiful vintage Triumph, not a man who's standing by the wreckage of one. I retrieve the emblem, the champagne, and the wine from the floor of the car as Henley walks along the driveway in her purple dress, with Roger in her arms. My prized car has been butchered, and all I can think is how outrageously happy I am.

I guess this is what it feels like to fall in love.

CHAPTER 42

Henley's To-Do List

—Max.

CHAPTER 43

Despite her bandaged finger, Cynthia insists we stay and eat. The Vicodin the ER doc gave her may have something to do with her mood. Or maybe the monkey does. Over the next three hours, I learn that Cynthia runs a network of wild animal rescues around the northeast. She and Creswell met at a charity function and immediately bonded over their shared passion for saving wild creatures.

"I fell in love with him when he told me how he adopted Roger," Cynthia says over the wine, while we dine on a gourmet pizza they ordered from a nearby brick-oven pizzeria.

Turns out the little dude was injured in the wilds of Bolivia. While he was en route to a zoo in the U.S. to make a new home in captivity, the rescue group escorting him noticed he was quite sociable with people, and recommended he live with humans rather than in a zoo.

Creswell also cares for an injured fox named Susanne, who uses the dog door to let herself in and out of the house, as well as a hawk named Fred whose damaged wing prevents him from flying well. I yank up my sleeve and show them my hawk tattoo.

"Very cool," Cynthia says. "Any special meaning to it?"

"Besides hawks being badass, powerful, and wildly intelligent?"

Henley laughs, along with our hosts. "And that right there is your meaning," she says.

When dinner is over, the couple walks us to the door. Creswell pulls me aside for a moment. "We'll connect this week. Call me and we'll set up a time," he says.

"Absolutely."

As we head down the steps to our waiting Uber, Henley asks me what the conversation was about. "He was just—" I stop. We're about to get in a car with a stranger. Now's not the time to dive into a conversation about business deals and why I'm getting more from a client and she's not. "He was thanking us for getting Roger," I say, and then I do my best to forget I just lied to her.

I'll have time to sort out how to manage business and her. We splintered in the past because I failed badly at managing business and emotions. I need time to figure out how to do it right. This is a whole new road to travel down, and I don't want to crash and burn again. Tonight, though, I want to focus on whatever is happening between Henley and me, and nothing more.

Preferably, I want to focus on what'll happen at the B&B a few miles away, where we're spending the night. Creswell booked us a room after Triple A towed my car. I guess the cat's out of the bag about the two of us, but judging from the way Henley held my hand at Cynthia's house, she doesn't care, and neither do I.

When we reach the quiet inn, a kindly woman with gray streaks in her blond hair hands us an old-fashioned room key and tells us room eight is at the top of the stairs and down the hall.

The second the door to our room creaks closed, I push Henley against the wall. My hands are on her face, in her hair, yanking down the straps of her dress. My mouth seals to hers, and I kiss her like it's the only thing I've been thinking about for the last three hours.

Because it is.

The kiss is as rough and hungry as our kisses have ever been, but it's different, too. It's layered with a new urgency. Wet and deep, it's punctuated by moans and groans. Our kiss sparks with hot, fevered tension.

I don't think either one of us has held back physically since we hurtled down this path, yet it's as if a dam has burst tonight. Whatever need we had for each other has ratcheted up a hundredfold. Her hands tug at my shirt, grab at my jeans, push at my clothes.

Soon, her fast and eager fingers have stripped me to nothing, and I've got her down to my favorite clothing style. *Bare.*

I stop for a second to stare at her. "Look at you," I say, as I run my hands down her sides, clasping her trim waist in my grip. "You're so fucking stunning. And you're mine."

She grabs at my hair and yanks me closer. It's a reminder of how hard she pulled my hair the first night I fucked her. It's a reminder of how we fit together. "And you're mine," she says, dragging her nails down my chest, over the planes of my abs, and straight to my cock.

Dear Lord. This woman is my perfect match. She's fire. She's heat. She's rough and tumble. She takes my dick in her hand and strokes, but I'm not letting her pleasure me first.

I swat her hand away. "Get on the bed. Now. Spread your legs for me."

She heads over to the quaint four-poster canopy. I wrap a hand around the post and give it a shake. The bed squeaks. "Good thing I'm prepared to pay whatever it costs to replace this if we break it," I say, as she lies back on the mattress.

A groan rips from my throat as I stare at her, spread out on the inn's Holly Hobbie quilt. Her brown hair is like a fan around her face.

"*Goddess.* Yes. I was right. That's exactly how you look," I say roughly, as I get on the bed, set my hands on her legs, and spread them apart.

She lets out a needy gasp.

But before I can spend some much-needed time worshipping her pussy, she sits up, clasps my face, and looks me in the eyes. "Say it again. How much you want me."

My lips quirk in a grin as she reminds me of me. Of how I talk to her in these moments. Without letting go of my grip on her, I push her knees up to her chest, as I bring my face closer to hers. "You want to know how much I want you? You sure?" I ask in a taunting tone, since I've got her pinned. Literally.

She narrows her eyes at me. "Fine. Don't tell me. Lick me instead."

"Oh, I intend to. But first," I drop my face to her neck, lick a path to her ear, and whisper, "so much more than I've ever wanted anyone." Then I meet her eyes and I go serious for a moment. No teasing. No playing. "It's more than just physical. You know that. I want you because I'm so fucking crazy for you."

"I could listen to you say that all night. Preferably after I think about how often you used to say I drove you crazy with my attitude."

"And for that, I'm going to take my sweet time."

"No." Her voice turns desperate. "Please, Max. Don't tease me. Please just make me come."

I let go of her knees, drop a kiss to her nose, and return to the sweet paradise between her thighs.

I moan as I taste her. She moans, too. And I do as she asked. I don't tease her. I kiss her pussy the way I kiss her lips. With hunger. With need. With a bone-deep desire to consume this woman.

She writhes and moves beneath my mouth as I open her legs wider. She wraps them around my head, rocking into my face, grabbing at my hair. "God, it's so good. So much better than last night," she cries out as she bucks up into me.

The image of her getting off alone in her bed twenty-four hours ago flashes before my eyes. I picture her fucking herself with her fingers to thoughts of me. That image makes me harder, makes me go faster, makes me even greedier to bring her all the pleasure in the world.

And I'm pretty sure I do, because she curls her fingers around my head and cries out in ecstasy. She pants and moans and jams her hands in my hair as she comes so damn hard on my lips.

Then I crawl up her body and lower myself to her. *Fuck.* This feels so fucking good.

She wraps her arms around me as she breathes hard, coming down from her orgasm. "I'm on the pill. Are you safe?"

I nod. "Completely."

"Then get your gigantic dick inside me. I want to know what it feels like when you f—" But she stops herself. She's not a girl who swears. The monkey curse was borne of that moment. Her expression turns softer. Her eyes more vulnerable. "Make love to me, Max."

My heart squeezes. It feels like it can barely fit inside my chest. This woman who once seemed to hate me is now letting me in. She's letting me have her—heart, mind, and body. I want to take care of her, and treat her like the gift that she is.

"I will, baby," I say, as I nudge her legs wider and wedge myself between them. I rub the head of my dick against her, and she stretches her neck, moaning my name. Her back bows, and I'm not even inside her.

I burn with lust.

I push forward, sinking into her. When I'm all the way in, a shudder wracks my body. Our eyes meet. It's intense and almost too much—this connection I feel with her. The way she gazes at me. How her eyes blaze with more than heat, more than desire. It's like looking into a mirror because everything I see in her eyes, I feel as well. This woman I've wanted for years and fought with for weeks is finally beneath me in bed, her arms wrapped around my neck, her legs hooked around my waist. And she's fucking crazy for me, too.

"I must have been really good in a past life to have you now," I say as I start to move inside her.

"Maybe you were a monkey," she says in a purr that's somehow still sexy despite what she's saying. But maybe that's part of why I'm crazy for her. Because she says things like that in the heat of the moment, because she calls me an idiot before I screw her on a car, because she sings to me when I tell her I'm into her.

"Lucky monkey. Lucky guy," I say, as I swivel my hips and thrust. Her lips fall open. Her back arches.

And I fuck her. And I make love to her. And I have her.

For the first time, it doesn't feel like we're hiding truths from each other. For the first time, I know we're both all in, and that it won't stop at tonight. I hope it won't stop for a long, long time.

"Feels so fucking good," I rasp out as I reach a hand to her hip, hiking one leg up higher.

"So good," she moans, pressing her hands against my back, bringing me closer, even closer, so the full weight of my body settles onto her. I move to my elbows, but then she takes my right hand and slides her fingers through mine. And hell, if I wasn't already falling in deep, that does it for me.

I'm barely aware of where we are, except that we're all tangled together—arms, legs, limbs, sweat, and heat. And like that, I fuck her while holding her hand, our fingers tightening together as she nears the edge. She flies first, crying out my name as she comes. I follow her there with a long, low groan that doesn't seem to stop.

At last, I move off her, but I don't let go. I pull her close to me, spooning her the way she likes it. "For the record, that wasn't monkey sex. Next time it will be, though."

"Funny thing, Max. I like all kinds with you. Non-monkey sex and monkey sex."

"Good. Because you're going to get a lot of both."

Tomorrow we can figure out the details. Tomorrow we can hash out how this whole thing works with business and secrets and deals.

Tonight, I just want to be at peace with the woman who tattooed her name on my arm, and deep in my heart.

CHAPTER 44

On the train back to Manhattan, Henley invites me over for dinner.

At last, I'll get to see her place.

"I make the most incredible mac and cheese from scratch. You'll pretty much never want another woman ever again once you have my mac and cheese," she says, tapping her fingers against my chest.

"So mac and cheese is your closing sales pitch, basically?"

"Absolutely," she says with a confident nod. "I told you—I'm an excellent girlfriend. Mac and cheese is one part of an awesome whole." She gestures to her purple dress and red scarf, same outfit as yesterday. "But obviously, I'm going to change before you come over tonight."

We both showered this morning at the B&B, and by shower, I mean a spectacular blow job that stopped short of the finish line so it could turn into a screw against the tiled wall as water streamed down her sexy back. And then, there was soap and shampoo and all that jazz.

But neither one of us was prepared for last night's sleepover, so we're both in the same clothes as yesterday, though Henley told me she brought along a change of panties, figuring she would need it. Obviously, she needed it. As the train chugs into New York, heading for Grand Central, I check the time. We'll arrive in twenty-five minutes, and that makes me even more aware of another countdown clock.

The one that ticks to *the talk*. Sooner or later, we need to discuss how this is going to work. I need to tell her about Creswell's interest in having me do more work for his network shows. It only feels fair to tell her, even though it might upset her. But that's part of what we'll have to sort through. As I think on what to say, she peers at her phone for the first time in a while, and it occurs to me that she's cut back in that department during the last several hours, and I couldn't be happier.

She's been happier. She's been less tense. Though, let's be honest, multiple orgasms probably do that to her, too. But as she scans her messages, a harsh sigh sounds. She purses her lips and stares out the window.

"Hey. Is that your business deal?" I ask, rubbing her knee.

She nods and bites her lip. "It's my attorney. He says he's going to call me in thirty minutes."

"I hope it's good news."

She turns to me as the city rumbles by. Her eyes are big and earnest. She takes a breath and squares her shoulders. "Max, I'm trying to buy into John Smith Rides. To become a fifty-fifty partner with him."

My jaw comes unhinged. I rub my finger against my ear. "What did you just say?"

She clasps her hands together as if in prayer. "Please don't be mad at me. I couldn't tell you because I signed an NDA. My lawyer made it clear this had to be completely confidential or it would fall through, but I hate keeping this from you now that we're . . ." She trails off as if she's afraid to say what we are.

Maybe I am, too, because I open my mouth to supply the answer—*together*—but nothing comes out. I'm too shocked. I never expected her business deal was this big, this competitive, this direct. When she mentioned she was working on one, I figured she was reeling in a huge new contract with a high-roller client. Never did I think she'd be getting into bed with my biggest rival.

I try to say the word once more—*together*—but it sticks in my throat.

"I'm sorry," she says, and something like guilt passes over her eyes, as if she's done something wrong. "I know this comes as a shock, and you probably think I'm sneaky and underhanded, but you have to know I was forbidden from telling anyone. And I didn't think it would matter anyway. Besides, when we worked on the car for the show, we never traded secrets or discussed business, and John checked out the work. The only deal that ever came up between you and me was the Bugatti zombie guy," she says, rattling off the facts, and I can tell by the speed of her words that she feels horrible. "But you mentioned him in an offhand way, and I already had a meeting with him, and it was just one of those things. You need to know I'm not trying to go after your business, but now that you and I made it official, I couldn't keep this from you, Max."

She reaches for my hand and takes it in hers, then locks her gaze with mine. At this moment, she looks so young and innocent, but earnest, too. Gone is that hard edge. Absent is the chip on her shoulder. All that's left is honesty, a wish to do the right thing.

Tension tightens my body from the force of habit. If I was concerned before about how we'd navigate our relationship and business, I should be a hell of a lot more concerned now. And yet, is there anything wrong with her not telling me? I've kept business details to myself, and all things being equal, if I were buying into another shop I wouldn't tell a soul either. Especially if I'd signed an NDA. What kind of man would be pissed at his woman for wanting to buy a business? She couldn't tell me because she couldn't tell me.

And yet, here she is, *telling me*. Because she didn't want to keep it from me.

I barely deserve this woman.

I squeeze her hand, and all the tension subsides. "Don't feel bad, tiger. Am I thrilled you're buying into my rival? No way. But I respect you and I respect this choice. You were already working for him, so I suppose this is no different. We were going to face this issue. Now we're just going to face it when you've got more skin in the game. Fact is, I'm fucking proud of you. For going after what you want. For pursuing it. And then for telling me."

She clasps her hand to her chest. "Oh my God, I'm so relieved. I felt awful. I didn't want to keep carrying this around, and I wasn't supposed to say anything, but I reasoned that you'd learn soon enough. But we'll figure this out. I mean, Venus and Serena Williams have played tennis against each other, and certainly there have been other competitors who find a way. Prosecutors and defense attorneys, actors vying for roles..."

She looks so hopeful that we'll pass our first test.

That's what this is. The chance to see if we can make it all work.

Even though I'm shocked, I have to believe that we'll be fine. "Whatever happens, we'll be good. And I hope it's a good deal for you, Henley."

"I hope it goes through. Smith and Marlowe," she says proudly, like she enjoys the sound of it. "It'll be my chance to grow and expand in New York. I've been working so hard on it."

As the train slows near Grand Central, I figure her honesty is reason enough for mine. If she has the guts to serve up something this big, the least I can do is let her know the truth about Creswell. The truth I should have told her last night.

"Listen," I say, squeezing her hand. "When you asked me what Creswell wanted to talk about, I wasn't entirely truthful."

She cocks her head to the side. "You weren't?"

I shake my head. "He told me last week he wants to talk to me about doing more work, and last night when he pulled me aside, he was following up on it."

"Oh." Her voice sounds empty.

Briefly, part of me wonders why I'm telling her. We can't just serve up every possible business deal to each other on a platter, can we? And I don't plan to share every business deal with her in advance. But since I kept the truth from her, this seems to be one I *should* share. "I'm telling you because this is part of what we need to figure out—how we're going to deal with the fact that we're going after the same business. Even though I suspect most of the time we'll need to keep things quiet."

"Right," she says, taking her time with that word. She points at me. "Except you weren't honest."

I wrench back. "What was I supposed to say?"

"I don't know. But maybe not a lie? Maybe not 'it's about a monkey.' You could have said you were discussing work possibilities down the road."

"Then you'd have known, and you might have gone after the work," I say matter-of-factly.

Her eyebrows shoot into her hairline and she recoils. "Excuse me? You think it takes me hearing about work to go after it? I've been talking to him, too, trying to win work. If he wants you, that's great. But my pursuit of his business has little to do with you telling me he *might* have work. My job is to go after potential work—not to sniff around and hope you'll drop a hint that there's business to be had."

"Fine. Then why are you upset?"

She narrows her eyes. "Duh."

"Duh, what?"

She taps her chest. "Because I was honest with you. I told you yesterday I was working on a business deal, and I had to keep it quiet. Then I told you the whole truth just now. But you flat out twisted your story and lied to me."

When she puts it like that . . .

My shoulders fall. "Shit. I messed up. I'm just trying to figure all this out, and I didn't know how to handle it. I didn't truly know what was happening between us either."

She shakes her head and crosses her arms. Then she stares out the window for a second. She snaps her gaze back to me, then finally, her expression softens. "Look, it's fine. I get that it will take time, and there will be stumbles."

I breathe more easily. I don't have the moral high ground on this one, and she's granted me a reprieve. That's all I can ask for. I take her hand. "Yes. Let's keep figuring it out together."

When we exit the train and walk past the big clock in the station, her phone rings. She zooms back into all-business-Henley mode. "My lawyer," she says, and then stops in place to talk to him.

I do my best to keep busy by checking my own phone and giving her some space, but I can still make out her words.

"That's it?"

She's quiet.

"Just like that?"

More silence as she listens.

"There's nothing we can do?"

Another pause.

Then her voice starts to break. "So, the deal is just off? Did he say why?"

The longest pause in the history of pauses comes next.

Her knees buckle, and she grabs at a sign.

CHAPTER 45

Henley's to-do list

—Don't cry.

—Don't cry.

—Don't cry.

—Go invest in tissues since you're crying.

CHAPTER 46

"What the hell just happened?"

I set my hands on her slim shoulders to steady her. She's shaking. Her right hand covers her mouth and her lip quivers. She blinks back tears. My poor girl. She's trying so hard to be tough.

She shakes her head.

"Tell me. Let me help you."

A sniffle is my answer.

"Henley," I say in a soft but firm voice, "was that the deal to partner with John?"

She nods and swipes a hand roughly across her cheek.

"And he nixed it?"

She nods and gulps.

"Because of?" I ask, though I think I know the answer already. I dread the answer. Because it's everything she's tried to avoid.

She closes her eyes, and jams a fist against one, rubbing away a rebel tear. She opens them. "He pulled the offer," she says, forcing out the words in between tears. "He said he's worried I won't look out for his best interests."

A new emotion digs into my bones. *Anger.* I grit my teeth, then ask carefully, "Because of us?"

She nods. "He thinks since I'm involved with you that means I won't put Smith and Marlowe first," she says, then she waves her hand like a fan across her face. "Who am I kidding? There's no Smith and Marlowe." A sob bubbles up.

"How does he even know about us? Did one of the guys say something?" For a second, I think of Sam and Karen. I never asked Sam to be quiet, but maybe something came up inadvertently? I'm sure it didn't take rocket science for Sam to put two and two together. Hell, if Creswell and David thought we had chemistry, maybe it's not that hard for anyone to tell.

"He asked Friday night, and I told him," she says, her chin up high. "He saw us at your garage. He watched all the web promos. You don't exactly look at me the way you look at Sam or Mike, and I don't exactly look at you like you're Mark from my shop or one of the guys. I didn't want to lie, and I also knew what was happening between you and me was real, and it was going to come out one way or another. So I told him."

I'm torn inside between the utter awesomeness of her faith in the two of us and my frustration for her and her deal falling to pieces. "I'm sorry this is happening to you." I feel like I'm failing, just fucking failing at saying the right thing to her. This is all new to me. Relationships. Managing a woman's emotions.

"I wanted this so badly. I've been working so hard to make this happen," she says, her voice wobbly as the Grand Central clock ticks toward one in the afternoon.

"I know, tiger. I know you have. But fuck him. He's a dick."

"That's easy for you to say. This was my job. I came back to New York for this. We talked for months about me becoming his partner. The deal was I'd be his lead builder, and if it worked out, I'd buy in as a partner and he'd cut back his own hours and let me do more. Now that's gone," she says, slashing a hand through the air, as if she's swiping the dishes off a table. "It's just gone. And just like there's no Smith and Marlowe, I don't even know if there's a Marlowe. I don't even know if I still have a job."

That's when the waterworks unleash. Tears leak from her eyes and spill down her cheeks. As I tug her in close, shielding and protecting her, those tears dampen my shirt.

I stroke her hair, trying to comfort her. In the span of twenty-five minutes, I've gone from shock that she was partnering up with my biggest rival, to accepting that we'd work through it all, to reassuring her that somehow she's going to be okay even though the rug has been cruelly yanked from under her.

I've got to figure this out for her. "Henley, let me help you."

She pushes her hands against my chest and raises her face. Her eyes are nearly black. They're hard, like she's wearing armor. "And you," she hisses. "You don't even believe in me. You always underestimated me. You thought I couldn't even get the work with Creswell unless I fucking snooped on you."

I recoil, not so much from the accusation, but the swear. She's serious. Holy shit. She's serious.

"That's not true," I say, but I sound as if I'm backpedaling.

"It is." Her voice splinters again, and another round of tears fall. "And you lied to me."

"Henley, stop. I'm trying to help."

"I was under NDA," she says, stabbing her chest. "And I *still* told you because I wanted to be honest with you. And you— you were just trying to protect a deal. You could have said 'Just discussing some business with him' and left it at that the two times I asked about what Creswell was talking to you about. But both times, you said your conversations were about something else. How does that make me feel?"

I heave a sigh and try to right this ship that I've sunk through my own jealousy. "Terrible?" I offer.

"It makes me feel like you don't trust me. But I trusted you, Max. I wanted to come to you. I wanted to ask your advice on this deal because I knew on Friday night it was starting to unravel. When I met with him after the dance class, I could tell John was getting cold feet." Her pitch rises, and her eyes are like pistols, aimed at me. "I had to fight a battle with myself to honor my commitment to confidentiality, but all I wanted was to come to you. I've always admired you, always wanted your insight, and you—you couldn't even give me the truth. And now what do I have?"

"Henley," I say, imploring. "Let's work this out."

"I have to go."

"Wait," I say, grabbing her wrist. "Don't go. Let's talk."

She shakes her head. "I need to try to figure out what I'm doing with my life at this point. But before I can do that, I'm literally going to spend the afternoon crying, and I'd rather you not see it." She raises her chin, that defiant, proud chin, and then she turns on her heel and leaves the train station.

CHAPTER 47

As I pace around my garage, talking on the phone to a guy named Leon who runs the best auto repair shop in the tri-state area, I know Blue Betty is in good hands.

"It'll take me some time, but I can absolutely fix this baby for you," Leon says in his gruff, no-nonsense tone as he details the bodywork that needs to be done. "That must have been a hell of a tree."

"Stubborn motherfucker, that's for sure."

"Well, if you'd hit the deer, the car would be worse, probably."

"The deer probably would be, too," I say, deadpan.

Leon laughs lightly. "True, that."

I hang up the phone, check my messages, and then I kick the wall.

Slamming the toe of my work boot against the concrete of my shop doesn't magically deliver a message from Henley to my phone. Nor does it get her to pick up when I call. Every time I try her, it goes straight to voicemail. I'm not sure if she's ignoring me or if her phone is off.

I'm not sure of anything, especially what to do or say to help her.

This isn't the engine in a Challenger. This isn't a set of spanking new features on a Lamborghini. And this sure isn't Livvy's old Rolls restored to tip-top condition.

Hell, this is more like my Triumph, bent so far out of shape that even I had to send it to an expert. I know how to fix cars, but that sort of repair job is for someone who specializes in mangled beasts. I build and refine. I don't pull snarled cars off the side of the road and untangle their broken parts from their whole ones.

I pace around the garage as night falls, wishing I had another vehicle to work on, something to shape from the ground up. Something I know how to do. I don't know how to make things right with Henley.

I putter around the shelves with my tools for another hour, cleaning and polishing and generally making sure everything is spit-shined. But when I'm done, and she's still not answering, it's time for me to get serious.

I lean on the hood of a car and dial my sister's number.

"Hey, you," she says on the first ring as the honking of a horn sounds close to the phone. "I'm almost late to a business dinner. I need to be there in one minute."

I curse under my breath.

"What's wrong?"

I square my shoulders. "Nothing. I'm fine. I'll catch you later."

"Max," she says, chiding. "Is it Henley? Did you tell her how you felt?"

"That's not entirely the problem."

"Then what is entirely the problem? Give it to me in twenty seconds."

"She lost a huge business deal because of me. Because of us. She's not talking to me right now."

"But she's in love with you, too?"

"What? I didn't tell her I was in love with her."

Mia sighs then laughs. "Seriously. It's like you never learn. Now listen, I need to go, but I'm going to tell you what to do, and if you don't follow my instructions, I will beat you up with my furious fists and powerful muscles, like I did when were kids."

"I don't remember it working out that way."

"Then you're remembering wrong," she says, and then she gives me her recipe to fix my broken relationship. And *recipe*, I suppose, is fitting, since she sends me to a baker.

CHAPTER 48

Chase wears a stethoscope when he answers the door. He sets the disc on my chest. I swat it off. He places the back of his hand on my forehead.

"Mild fever," he declares, then pats my throat. "Tender glands." He taps on my skull. "Oh, wait. I found the cause." He turns to Josie, who's wiping flour off her hands on a cherry-patterned apron. "Nurse, it seems our patient has a case of man-itis."

She shoots him a doubtful look. "Are you sure, Doctor? I thought he had acute man-itis brought on by complications of lovesickness as well as failure-to-tell-the-woman-he-loves-that-he-loves-her."

I point my thumb at the stairwell. "What do you know—there's an opening for me at urgent care right now, and it comes without any hazing. See you all later."

I turn to go, and Chase clamps a hand down on my shoulder. I could shrug it off. I'm bigger and stronger than he is. But his words keep me here. "C'mon, jackass. What did you expect? You gave me a hard time about Josie, and look where I am." He gestures to the woman of his dreams making cinnamon rolls in his kitchen on a Sunday evening. The bastard is ridiculously happy, something I was twenty-four hours ago. Now, I feel ridiculously clueless.

I sigh and head into his apartment. "Mia made me come over," I mutter.

"Sisters are so smart," Josie says.

"Take it from her," Chase says. "The woman has two older brothers of her own. She knows her stuff."

"That I do. Also, Mia texted me a nine-one-one." Josie pats a chair at the kitchen table and tells me to sit. She sets her chin in her hands. "I understand you need a little help from a lady to sort things out with *your* lady."

I hold out my hands, showing there's nothing in them. I've come up empty. "This isn't an engine in a Dodge. I don't entirely know what to do. But Mia said I'd need a woman to walk me step-by-step through how to properly apologize, and she was heading into a dinner. So here I am."

Josie smiles and pats my hand. "Well, first, you're going to take some of my cinnamon rolls when you go see her, and you're going to tell her they're an invitation to come over for dinner when you sort this out. But before you do that, tell me what's going on."

Chase joins us, parking his butt on a chair, too. They listen as I tell them the basics. "And honestly, I feel like it's all my fault," I say, when I'm done.

Josie gives me a sympathetic smile. "Some of it is."

"But that doesn't mean you can't fix it," Chase adds, this time without teasing or giving me a hard time.

I scrub a hand across my jaw. "What do I fix? Does she even want to see me again? Is what I did so awful?"

"Let's break this down," Josie says. "You held something

back, and you covered it up. I get that you had your reasons, but you need to apologize. You also need to let her into your whole heart. She's going through something tremendously shitty. Having a huge deal pulled out from under her is awful."

"I can't even imagine," I say, because the reality is I've been both good *and* lucky in business. I learned my trade, put in my time, and then moved up. Each year I became better, and each year my business grew.

Henley has been dealt some bad breaks. In some cases, she bore a decent part of the responsibility, like in our split. But this one? This one is Grade A, top choice, absolutely unfair, and not her fault.

"Let me help you imagine how she feels, then," Josie says, meeting my gaze. "She probably feels like a failure. She probably feels like she's been judged. And she probably also feels like she put herself on the line for you."

Chase chimes in, "You just need to let her know you're there for her."

I flash back on one of the last things she said to me at the train station. She wasn't even sure if she had a job anymore, and she wished she could have come to me for advice.

That's when I know what to do. I know exactly how to restore this old junker of mine.

I push back on the chair and stand up. "I've got it." I clap my brother on the back. "Thanks, man." I give Josie a hug and then head to the door.

"Why do I feel like he's about to make things worse?" Chase asks Josie nervously.

I glance back, and Josie shrugs. But the look in her green eyes is a hopeful one. "I bet he knows what he's doing."

She hands me a bag of cinnamon rolls, and I go.

CHAPTER 49

Henley's to-do list

—Get your act together.

—Straighten out this mess.

—Turn on your phone. You can't hide forever in the couch, the chocolate potato chip ice cream, the tropical island Pinterest boards, and the Go-Go's.

—But "Vacation's All I ever Wanted" and the pictures of Bora Bora are calming me down.

—Buy cheese.

—Face the music.

—Fight for things with Max. He's the one thing good you've got, and you will not lose him, too.

CHAPTER 50

The great thing about being the so-called king of the Manhattan custom car business—sorry, John, it's not you—is that your suppliers will take calls on a Sunday evening. They'll open their warehouses in New Jersey and meet you after hours. They'll do deals after hours.

And since I've got my black sports car, it doesn't take me long to drive out to Jersey, grab what I need, and lug it back into the city. After a few pit stops and a sweaty run up the service elevator in my building, I snag a smaller version of my gift and order an Uber. The driver takes me to Henley's block and I call her another time. It rings and rings and rings.

No answer. Seems she's turned on her phone, but now she's ignoring me. That doesn't bode well, especially considering I'm dragging fifty extra pounds for her right now.

But I won't back down easily.

And maybe I won't have to back down at all, since my phone buzzes with a text.

Henley: Missed the call! My arms were full of cheese! Dinner will be late tonight. But I promise it'll be delicious. Does 9 p.m. work?

I glance at the time. It's eight. Little does she know I'd wait all night for her.

Max: I'll be here.

I park myself on her stoop.

Five minutes later, a beautiful brunette walks toward me, a grocery bag on her shoulder, jeans on her legs, combat boots on her feet. My heart speeds up, and it's such a strange sensation, but one I'm going to have to get used to. I stand, swallow, and wait.

Nighttime casts shadows on her, but even though she freshened up, I can tell she wasn't lying when she said she'd spend the day in tears. As she passes under a streetlamp, her face is illuminated. Her eyes are red. I walk down the street, and when her gaze meets mine, she flinches as if she's surprised to see me. A well of nerves rises inside me. But screw that. I'm not nervous. I know this is right. I'm 100 percent confident I can help. My job is solving problems, and I know how to fix this one.

Then her expression shifts to something else. It's hard to tell in the dark, but maybe it's relief. Her lips part softly, like she's simply glad I'm here.

I stop when I reach her. I cup her cheek. I press a soft kiss on one eyelid then the other. Her breath flutters as I touch her, and I'm grateful that I can make her start to feel better.

I step back and take the bag off her shoulder. She lets me.

"Did you spend the whole afternoon crying?"

She nods.

"Do you need to cry some more?"

She shakes her head, and then she fixes on a smile. "I'm tough."

I run my knuckles over her cheek. "Truer words were never spoken." I gesture to the bag of food. "Let me help you make the mac and cheese."

Her stomach rumbles. "I'm pretty hungry. Might need to order in. I don't know if I can wait for mac and cheese, which is kind of shocking, considering I tunneled my way through a whole pint of ice cream today."

"I have a solution for you."

She arches an eyebrow and regards me skeptically. "To the ingestion of too much ice cream?"

"To the job situation."

She drags a hand through her hair and shakes her head as we walk toward her building. "Max, you can't solve this for me."

"You're right," I say when we reach her steps.

She points to the shiny red metal box on the landing. "Did you put that there?"

I set down her groceries and meet her gaze. "First, I'm sorry I wasn't honest about Creswell. That was shitty. I shouldn't go around thinking you're trying to steal business from me. That's not who you are, and that's not how I want to be. I don't have an excuse, but I want a chance to do better. This kind of thing"—I point from her to me and back—"it's all new to me. And I'm probably going to fuck up a few basic things. But I hope you'll forgive me."

She lifts her chin. "This *thing* you mention. What is this thing of which you speak?"

"Does that mean I'm forgiven for lying about the conversations with Creswell?"

She shoves my chest. "Yes, idiot. Just don't do it again."

"I won't."

"So this *thing*. Does it have a name?"

I quirk the corner of my lips. "It does have a name." I tap my chin, like I'm trying to remember. Then I hold up my finger as if I've finally got it. "Yes. It does. This thing—I'm pretty damn sure it's called love."

Her brown eyes are a fireworks show. They twinkle. They spark. They're so fucking gorgeous.

I grab her waist and pull her close to me. "I'm not just crazy for you. I'm in love with you, tiger. I'm madly in love with you."

I don't even give her a chance to answer. I dip my mouth to hers and kiss her, and I find her answer in the way she kisses me back, in how she melts into my arms.

But even so, I don't mind it at all when we separate and she breathes out the sweetest words. "The same. It's the same for me. I'm stupid in love with you, Max Summers," she says, and nothing in the world has ever been better than those words. My heart does some seriously crazy cartwheels in my chest. She grabs the collar of my shirt then tugs me closer. "I'm so in love with you that I don't care about that dumb deal."

She crushes her lips to mine. She kisses me this time, and she's as fierce and as fiery as she's ever been. She's my tiger, and that's how I want her to be. We pull apart, and her lips are bruised and swollen. I hope mine are, too.

"Speaking of that dumb deal, I've got something for you," I say.

"That shiny red toolbox on top of the stairs might have made my heart beat faster."

"I thought it was me that got your blood flowing," I tease.

"Yes, but Snap-on tools have been known to do wonders for this girl." She bounces on her toes. "Did you get me a new set of wrenches?"

I nod. "I did. But that's just a starter kit," I say, gesturing to the fifty-pound basic tool set.

She tilts her head and gives me a quizzical look. "But those are incredible."

"They are. But what would be even more incredible is a whole new complete set of Snap-on tools, wrenches and everything else under the sun. I figure you'll need it for your new job."

She takes a step back and gives me the dirtiest stare in the history of the universe. "No."

"No what?"

"No. I am not taking a job with you," she says crisply.

I laugh.

"I mean it," she says, crossing her arms. "You can't waltz over here and solve everything by offering me a job. That's not what I want. You can't just fix it for me like that." She snaps her fingers.

I laugh harder. "Woman, let me tell you – I've *learned*. I'm not trying to solve it for you. And I'm not offering you a job with me."

She blinks, confused. "You're not?"

I make a flubbing sound with my lips, then I point to the night sky. "Tiger, you're well beyond working with me. You're not an apprentice. You're not a mechanic. You're not even a lead car builder."

"I'm not?"

I shake my head and set my hands on her shoulders. "Five years ago when you were my apprentice, you were the most talented person I'd ever worked with. Now, you're still the most talented person I've ever worked with. You told me this afternoon that you might not have a job and that you also wished you could have come to me for advice, right?"

She nods, waiting expectantly.

"And in the past, I didn't get to give you that advice, because I let my attraction for you get in the way of clear thinking. I didn't teach you as best I could. I didn't guide you at the end. But I'm going out on a limb, and I'm going to do it now."

"Do it then."

I stroke my chin, collecting my thoughts. "The way I see it, you were ready to do a deal with John. You were going to buy into his business, right?"

She nods. "I was."

"I'm presuming that's because you wanted, understandably, to have access to his network and contacts in this city."

"Yes."

"But what have you accomplished in the mere few weeks you've been with him? You've landed Livvy as a client, and you got the Bugatti guy all on your own. Am I correct?"

A smile tugs at her lips. "That's correct."

"Plus," I say, raising a finger to make my next point, "I'm pretty sure the network guys wanted *you* to help build the Lambo for the show. Not him. Am I right?"

"Yes, but that was partly because they wanted *us*," she says, motioning from her to me.

"Partly, but it was also because you and me—we're the top two builders in this city. Not John and me. You. And. Me." I don't care if that sounds cocky. It's fucking true.

She stomps her foot. "Max, I appreciate it. I truly do. But I need to make it on my own, not because my boyfriend is the king of New York."

"And you will be the queen." I place my index finger on her lips to shush her. "It's time, Henley."

"Time for what?"

"It's time for you to open your own shop. You don't need John. You don't need his contacts. And you don't need me to succeed. If you were going to buy into his business, you've obviously got the money to start a shop. And you already have a few key clients. What you don't have is someone to tell you that you can do it. So, I'm going to be that person. And I want to show you how much I believe in you."

She knits her brows together. She parts her lips, but she can barely speak. Something like "what?" comes out of her lips.

"I believe in you. I know you can do it," I say.

"But what about us? We'd be competing even more directly than we are now. I thought you found it distracting?"

I scratch my chin. "Funny thing. I realized the most distracting thing was not having you. I'm not distracted from work now that you're mine."

She laughs in disbelief. "You're not distracted anymore?"

"I was distracted because I didn't know how you felt. I was distracted, wondering if you liked me."

"You idiot. I was crazy about you."

"You hated me."

"Because I wanted you. Loathing you was the only way to deal with it."

"And then loathing turned to love. But my question for you is this—are you going to be okay being the chick car builder who's banging Max Summers on a regular basis?" I ask with a laugh, repeating her one-time words.

She wags her finger at me. "No. I'm going to be okay being his girlfriend. I told you, I make an excellent girlfriend."

"You do. And you make excellent cars. So I also bought you what any self-respecting, professional car builder needs to run her own shop. It's the big-ass Snap-on Mammoth tool set, and it's waiting for you."

And she shrieks.

Roger has nothing on her.

Her own orgasms have nothing on this scream.

I'm surprised someone doesn't call the cops.

Quickly, she covers her mouth. "Are you serious?" she asks through her fingers, her eyes wider than moons.

"This tool set," I say, waving at the one on her steps, "that's just to whet your appetite. At my place you'll find the five-foot high, ten-thousand-dollar kit that has every tool you'd ever want."

"Hammers?" she squeals, and I nod. "Wrenches?" Another nod. "Screwdrivers? Gear pullers? Pliers? Hand sockets?"

"Everything."

She leaps on me. I nearly tumble into the railing. But I steady myself, and I hold on to the woman in my arms. She's wrapped around me like a monkey, and she's planting kisses all over my face.

"I did good, huh?"

"You did so good. I can't believe this," she says, and now she's crying again, but these tears are tears of happiness. "You really think I can run my own shop?"

"I know so."

"I love you."

"I love you, too."

"I love you so much I want to skip the mac and cheese and go see the tool set at your place."

I arch one brow. "That sounds more like you just want to pet the tools."

"Oh, I do. That's what I meant. I just wanted it to sound like it was about you," she says, laughing.

"You can make me mac and cheese another time."

"Tomorrow?"

"Or the next night."

"Or the next."

But tonight, I take her back to my place, and after we eat some sandwiches and a cinnamon roll, and she paws the tool set with the same kind of excitement she showered on my tub, I get her in the bath.

She insists we use the Peach Dreams bath bomb, and that works just fine for me. I don't care if I smell girly when I've got this woman in my arms, lavishing me with kisses and so much love.

But we don't get it on in the tub.

C'mon. That shit is hard. That's a recipe for banged elbows and bonked heads. Not to mention, it's really hard to go down on a woman when she's underwater. The same applies for blow jobs.

So I dry her off, carry her to my bed, and I make love to her all night long.

In the morning, we go to work.

EPILOGUE

Several months later

Henley's pad was decorated in ruby red, fuchsia pink, and dove gray. Her fridge was slathered in magnets with stylish images of women in vintage dresses holding martinis and kittens with captions like "I don't know how to tell you this, but you don't have a hamster anymore."

Her coffee table was covered in framed pictures of her friends, her sister, her brother, and the rest of her family. We visited them in California recently, and they grilled me, making sure that I was the right fit for her. I'm pleased to report that I passed. Her couch was a comfy cranberry-red one, and it's been donated to Goodwill, along with some of her other furniture. She said good-bye to her bed, but she's keeping the comforter and all the pillows. They've found a new home on my bed, which is now our bed.

My home is now ours.

As I stand here with her, the last bag packed up, she waves good-bye to her pad in SoHo. She blows it a kiss, then shuts the door, locks it, and leaves the key with the super.

"Good-bye, Girlie Home," she says, as we head down the steps to the curb. Blue Betty awaits, and she's even prettier than before. Leon repaired the hell out of her, and Henley fine-tuned the damaged engine. I hired her to give my prized possession a little extra oomph. I wanted the best for my sports car, and my girl is the best. Don't get me wrong—I kick unholy ass with the exotics and the high-end vehicles. But Henley has a magic touch with hot rods.

No pun intended.

Marlowe Custom Cars has landed several big clients in the three months it's been open, and I couldn't be more proud of this woman. She's beat me out on a few deals, and vice versa. The Lambo and *Midnight Steel* became huge hits, and sent even more business her way and mine. Sometimes we vie for clients, and it turns out the two of us thrive on the competition. It makes both of us better, tougher, more ferocious.

During the day and at night.

For now, I open the door and she slides into the passenger seat, then we head home, where we abuse our toothbrushes together.

As I pull into the lot where I keep my cars, a flurry of excitement rushes through me. I rein in a grin as my eyes land on a gift I got for her. She sees it, too, only she doesn't yet know it's hers.

She points and grabs at my arm as I turn the corner in the lot. "Look at that '69 Mustang."

"Damn," I say with a low whistle. "That is one fine car."

As we drive closer, her nose crinkles. "But it's white."

I shudder. "So boring."

"I would never paint a Mustang white."

"You'd paint it pink, wouldn't you?"

"You know it."

I pull into the spot next to it and cut the engine. We get out, but instead of heading toward our building, I open the door to the Mustang.

"It's yours. You can paint it pink, tiger. You can paint it black. Hell, you can paint it lime gold if you want."

Her jaw drops open. "Oh my God, are you serious?"

I nod, loving her excitement. "I'm completely serious. You can absolutely paint it lime gold."

She punches me lightly. "I meant, did you really get it for me?"

I cup her cheeks. "You're moving in with me. It only seemed fitting to give you a garage-warming gift."

"You're such a gearhead, and I love you."

"I love you, too. Want to take it for a spin?"

She waves a hand dismissively. "No. Of course not. I would never want to take the '69 Mustang that my big, brutish, bearish boyfriend got me out for a ride. Let's go play Monopoly instead." Then she jumps up and down. "I want to take it for a drive now!"

I head to the passenger door. When I get inside, I say in my best offhand tone, "The keys are in the glove box."

She pops it open, then freezes. When her eyes widen, the brown in them is the sweetest shade I've ever seen. "Max," she says in a reverent whisper as she points at the blue jewelry box. "Is that . . .?"

I grab the box and pop it open. A diamond as bright as the sun gleams.

"Oh my God." She clasps one hand to her mouth and tears streak down her cheeks. My tough-as-nails, take-no-prisoners girlfriend has the softest heart, the most emotional soul, and the sweetest smile.

"Will you marry me?" I ask, as I do my best to somehow drop to one knee in the front seat of a car. It's not easy, and by no means is this a perfect proposal position, but I hardly think that matters when she shrieks her yes, and I slide the ring on her finger. It's not a small ring by any stretch. It's what's known in certain circles as a big-ass diamond. It's four carats. She won't be able to wear it often since she works with her hands and gets them dirty, so when she puts it on, I want the whole damn world to know from miles away she's taken.

But more than that, I want her to enjoy it, and Henley likes her sparkles and her bling.

"It's the most beautiful thing I've ever seen," she says, and then she kisses me. "Besides you."

Once the happy tears stop, we go for a drive, and somewhere out in the country beyond Manhattan, we pull over, and we christen the passenger seat.

* * *

A few nights later, Henley plays hostess. The guests are my brother and his wife, Josie, since they're married now, my sister, Mia, since she's in town, Patrick, and Henley's best friend, Olivia.

After Henley serves her now-famous homemade mac and cheese, she asks in a mock-curious voice, "By the way, did anyone happen to see the serving spoon?"

Then she shows off her ring.

"I'm blind, I'm blind," Mia calls out, shielding her eyes.

When she pours more wine, she asks, "Did anyone happen to see the cork?"

She shows her ring yet again.

"It's like looking at the sun," Olivia declares.

When she sits down next to me, she admires it once more. "Seriously. Is this the most perfect ring ever?"

"I kind of like mine," Josie says, glancing at her band and engagement ring.

"The Summers men do have most excellent taste," Henley says.

Mia clears her throat. "Ahem. Where do you think they learned how to pick out rings?"

Patrick laughs and raises a glass. "To the happy couple, and the secret weapon of a sister who helped choose the most beautiful diamonds."

We all raise our glasses and drink to that. Patrick locks eyes with my sister, and something seems to pass between them. Maybe a knowing grin. Perhaps a wink.

I'm not entirely sure. But when the meal ends, and Henley and I are in the kitchen cleaning up, I whisper in her ear, "Did you see that look Patrick gave my sister?"

Henley giggles and grabs my forearm. "Honey, I think Patrick is giving your sister a lot more than looks."

I freeze. I'm not sure how to process this news. "Seriously?"

"Sometimes, you're adorably clueless," she says, then she shares her theory on what's up with Patrick and Mia. When she's done, she swats me with a towel. "But that's a story for another time. We need to get back to our guests."

We join them in the living room for a round of pool, and I lose interest in everything but beating them all quickly, so I can get my fiancée under the covers and under me.

ANOTHER EPILOGUE

A little later

Here's something I want to know. Why the hell is sleeping with the enemy such a bad idea?

It's the best thing that ever happened to me.

I used to think aged Scotch, expensive pool tables, and one-night stands were the height of pleasure. Then, my greatest guilty pleasure ever—screwing Henley—turned into the greatest bliss of my entire life.

She's what floats my boat. Life is short, so I do my best to savor every second of it with her. Sometimes that means doing it on the pool table, and sometimes that means lounging with her in the claw-foot tub. Other times, it means we engage in our favorite hobby. Our *other* favorite hobby. Tinkering on cars.

I helped her with the paint job on her new Mustang. Big surprise—she went with a bubble-gum pink, and she named the car Belinda. She loves that beast something fierce, but not as much as she loves me. I know this because she not only tells me —she shows me all the time. She treats me like a king, making sandwiches for the guys when my buddies come over, hanging up the towels in the bathroom, and never nagging, just like she promised on the ferry. But that's surface shit. What she does for me most is the simplest thing of all—she makes me happy.

Every day, she makes me realize there's more to life than work, work, work. Like magic shows. When Penn and Teller came to town the other week, I took her to the show, and we spent the rest of the evening developing a blueprint for how they pulled off the phone in the fish trick.

Newsflash—we still don't know.

We tried the ferry again, too, and thanks to the orange non-drowsy Dramamine, Henley made it on and off the vessel without conking out or turning dizzy.

We also like to go salsa dancing. I never thought I'd say that, but then again, I never thought a woman like Henley would become my wife.

I suppose she's all my guilty pleasures now, but I never feel an ounce of remorse for spending so much time with her.

Some nights, I can't believe we used to hate each other. But other nights, I think we both know it was another four-letter word that was brewing between us all along, and it just took time to turn from a glow to a blazing heat. It also took a pet monkey, a mangled roadster, and a Sharpie tattoo for me to realize that I felt the opposite of hate.

We like to remind each other of this as we play a little game. At night when I slide into bed, she'll often turn to me and say my name.

"Max?"

"Yes, Henley?"

"I don't want to kiss you."

"Good. I don't want to kiss you either."

"And then I don't want you to strip me naked."

"Thank God, because I'm not going to do that at all."

"And after that, I hope you don't make me feel like I'm seeing stars."

"Planets, tiger. Maybe even galaxies."

Then, when we're through, she'll snuggle up next to me, and tell me she loves me.

And I'll whisper in her ear. "Same. It's the same for me."

THE END

Sign up for my newsletter to receive an alert when sexy new books are available!

Curious about Mia and Patrick? Their love story will be told in HARD WOOD, coming in the fall! But first, be sure to meet the rest of the gang!

Women often say a good man is hard to find. And a hard man is even better.

That's why I'm quite a catch — good, hard, loaded, and wait for it...I'm ready to settle down, too. But the woman I want to pitch my tent with is precisely the one I need to stay far away from.

After that fantastic night with Mia Summers, I'm ready to give her many more. But there's a hitch in my plans — she just hired my company. If there's one thing I'm committed to, it's running a squeaky clean adventure tour business. One of the iron-clad rules?

Don't screw your customers.

I can follow my own guidelines. After all, it's only a week-long trip with Mia and her employees over the trails and down the hills I guide them on. I can obey the rules—even if it's hard in the woods.

I'm about to give myself a badge of honor when the storm of the century hits, sending everyone else running for cover, but us. It's my biggest temptation and me, alone for a long weekend. You don't screw the client, especially when you're already in love with her . . .

But what's a guy to do when she's so hard to resist?

HARD WOOD will release in November!

FULL PACKAGE

I've been told I have quite a gift.

Hey, I don't just mean in my pants. I've got a big brain too, and a huge heart of gold. And I like to use all my gifts to the fullest, the package included. Life is smooth sailing....

Until I find myself stuck between a rock and a sexy roommate, which makes for one very hard...place.

Because scoring an apartment in this city is harder than finding true love. So even if I have to shack up with my buddy's smoking hot and incredibly amazing little sister, a man's got to do what a man's got to do.

I can resist Josie. I'm disciplined, I'm focused, and I keep my hands to myself, even in the mere five-hundred square feet we share. Until the one night she insists on sliding under the covers with me. It'll help her sleep after what happened that day, she says.

Spoiler—neither one of us sleeps.

Did I mention she's also one of my best friends? That she's brilliant, beautiful and a total firecracker? Guess that makes her the full package too.

What's a man stuck in a hard place to do?

FULL PACKAGE is available everywhere!

BIG ROCK

It's not just the motion of the ocean, ladies. It's definitely the SIZE of the boat too.

And I've got both firing on all cylinders. In fact, I have ALL the right assets. Looks, brains, my own money, and a big c&$k.

You might think I'm an as%*$le. I sound like one, don't I? I'm hot as sin, rich as heaven, smart as hell and hung like a horse.

Guess what? You haven't heard my story before. Sure, I might be a playboy, like the NY gossip rags call me. But I'm the playboy who's actually a great guy. Which makes me one of a kind.

The only trouble is, my dad needs me to cool it for a bit. With conservative investors in town wanting to buy his flagship Fifth Avenue jewelry store, he needs me not only to zip it up, but to look the part of the committed guy. Fine. I can do this for Dad. After all, I've got him to thank for the family jewels. So I ask my best friend and business partner to be my fiancée for the next week. Charlotte's up for it. She has her own reasons for saying yes to wearing this big rock.

And pretty soon all this playing pretend in public leads to no pretending whatsoever in the bedroom, because she just can't fake the kind of toe-curling, window-shattering orgasmic cries she makes as I take her to new heights between the sheets.

But I can't seem to fake that I might be feeling something real for her.

What the hell have I gotten myself into with this…big rock?

BIG ROCK is available everywhere!

MISTER O

Just call me Mister O. Because YOUR pleasure is my super power.

Making a woman feel 'oh-god-that's-good' is the name of the game, and if a man can't get the job done, he should get the hell out of the bedroom. I'm talking toe-curling, mind-blowing, sheet-grabbing ecstasy. Like I provide every time.

I suppose that makes me a superhero of pleasure, and my mission is to always deliver.

But then I'm thrown for a loop when a certain woman asks me to teach her everything about how to win a man. The only problem? She's my best friend's sister, but she's far too tempting to resist--especially when I learn that sweet, sexy Harper has a dirty mind too and wants to put it to good use. What could possibly go wrong as I give the woman I've secretly wanted some no-strings-attached lessons in seduction?

No one will know, even if we send a few dirty sexts. Okay, a few hundred. Or if the zipper on her dress gets stuck. Not on that! Or if she gives me those f*&k-me-eyes on the train in front of her whole family.

The trouble is the more nights I spend with her in bed, the more days I want to spend with her out of bed. And for the first time ever, I'm not only thinking about how to make a woman cry out in pleasure --I'm thinking about how to keep her in my arms for a long time to come.

Looks like the real Adventures of Mister Orgasm have only just begun....

MISTER O is available everywhere.

WELL HUNG

Here's what you need to know about me -- I'm well-off, well-hung and quick with a joke. Women like a guy who makes them laugh. Even better if he's loyal and hard-working. That's me.

Enter Natalie. Hot, sexy, smart, and my new assistant. Which makes her totally off limits...

Hey, I'm a good guy. Really. I do my best to stay far away from the kind of temptation she brings to work. Until one night in Vegas...

Yeah, you've heard this one before. Bad news on the business front, drowning our sorrows in a few too many Harvey Wallbangers, and then I'm banging her. In my hotel room. In her hotel room. Behind the Titanic slot machine at the Flamingo (don't ask). And before I can make her say "Oh God right there YES!" one more time, we're both saying yes--the big yes--at a roadside chapel in front of a guy in press-on sideburns and a shiny gold leisure suit.

We'll just untie the knot in the morning, right?

The trouble is . . . I don't know how to keep my hands off my soon-to-be ex-wife.

WELL HUNG is available everywhere!

Acknowledgments

Thank you to Rob Kinnan for the tireless attention to auto details, including the insight into lime gold. Thank you to Susanne Gigler for the monkey knowledge and making sure the monkey scenes read authentically. Roger would not have existed without your insight.

I'm grateful to Lauren McKellar for all she sees. I owe so much to my early readers — Jen, Dena and Kim played such key roles in shaping this story and making Max and Henley's love story crackle and shine. Karen, Tiffany, Janice, Virginia and Marion provided eagle eyes, and I appreciate them immensely.

Huge thanks to Helen Williams for the amazing cover. This woman knows hot men and what to do with them. I am always grateful for KP Simmon for strategy, insight, guidance and friendship. Thank you to Kelley, Keyanna and Candi for everything every day.

I am grateful for the support of writer friends like Laurelin Paige, Kristy Bromberg, CD Reiss, Marie Force, and Lili Valente.

Thank you to my husband for believing in my books, making great sandwiches and telling jokes. My children are the loves of my life, and they make me happy every day. And so do my dogs.

Last, but never least, a big, huge thank you to all my readers. You make my dreams possible, and you've made them come true. I hope you've enjoyed Joy Ride as much as I enjoyed writing it for you.

CONTACT

I love hearing from readers! You can find me on Twitter at LaurenBlakely3, or Facebook at LaurenBlakelyBooks, or online at LaurenBlakely.com. You can also email me at laurenblakely books@gmail.com

Also by Lauren Blakely

FULL PACKAGE, the #1 New York Times
Bestselling romantic comedy!

BIG ROCK, the hit New York Times
Bestselling standalone romantic comedy!

MISTER O, also a New York Times
Bestselling standalone romantic comedy!

WELL HUNG, a New York Times
Bestselling standalone romantic comedy!

THE SEXY ONE, a swoony New York Times
Bestselling standalone romance!

THE HOT ONE, a sexy second chance
USA Today Bestselling standalone romance!

The New York Times and USA Today
Bestselling Seductive Nights series including
Night After Night, After This Night,
and *One More Night*

And the two standalone
romance novels, *Nights With Him* and
Forbidden Nights, both New York Times
and USA Today Bestsellers!

Sweet Sinful Nights, Sinful Desire,
Sinful Longing and *Sinful Love*, the complete
New York Times Bestselling high-heat romantic suspense
series that spins off from Seductive Nights!

Playing With Her Heart, a
USA Today bestseller, and a sexy
Seductive Nights spin-off standalone!
(Davis and Jill's romance)

21 Stolen Kisses, the USA Today
Bestselling forbidden new adult romance!

Caught Up In Us, a New York Times and
USA Today Bestseller! (Kat and Bryan's romance!)

Pretending He's Mine, a Barnes & Noble and
iBooks Bestseller! (Reeve & Sutton's romance)

Trophy Husband, a New York Times and
USA Today Bestseller! (Chris & McKenna's romance)

Far Too Tempting, the USA Today Bestselling standalone
romance! (Matthew and Jane's romance)

Stars in Their Eyes, an iBooks bestseller!
(William and Jess' romance)

My USA Today bestselling
No Regrets series that includes *The Thrill of It*
(Meet Harley and Trey)

and its sequel

Every Second With You

My New York Times and USA Today
Bestselling Fighting Fire series that includes
Burn For Me (Smith and Jamie's romance!)
Melt for Him (Megan and Becker's romance!)
and *Consumed by You* (Travis and Cara's romance!)

The Sapphire Affair series...
The Sapphire Affair
The Sapphire Heist

Out of Bounds
A New York Times Bestselling sexy sports romance

The Only One
A second chance love story!

Made in the USA
Lexington, KY
29 April 2017